Sanctuary for Seers

A Stranje House Novel

Other Novels by Kathleen Baldwin

—————————ೞೲ—————————

The Stranje House Novels:
Exciting Alternate History Spy series for Teens

A School for Unusual Girls
Exile for Dreamers
Refuge for Masterminds
Harbor for the Nightingale
Sanctuary for Seers

—————————ೞೲ—————————

The My Notorious Aunt series:
Humorous Regency Romps

Lady Fiasco
Mistaken Kiss
Cut from the Same Cloth
The Persuasion of Miss Kate

—————————ೞೲ—————————

A Regency Novella
The Highwayman Came Waltzing

SANCTUARY
FOR
SEERS

A Stranje House Novel

KATHLEEN BALDWIN

INK LION BOOKS

SANCTUARY FOR SEERS

COPYRIGHT © 2023 KATHLEEN BALDWIN

All rights reserved.

Published by Ink Lion Books

Copyedits by Chris Hall – TheEditingHall.com

First Edition June 2023

Printed in the United States of America

0 9 8 7 6 5 4 3 2 1

For Tracine and the lovely Readers of Cache
Valley for being the best cheerleaders ever!
And
Pat with gratitude for your brilliant true stories
and advice on the norms of the paranormal.
And
D'anah for inspiring me all the way from
Australia.

SANCTUARY
FOR
SEERS

A STRANJE HOUSE NOVEL

SERAPHINA WYNDHAM'S CLOAK
OF MANY SECRETS

August 1814
Stranje House on the Southern Coast of England

LADY DANESKA LIES ON THE BED in a feverish struggle. Infection stemming from a gunshot wound holds her in delirium, and she thrashes as if she's fighting her way through an overgrown maze. I sit beside her, watching discordant colors engulf her in a swirling cloud of turmoil—dark raging against dark. It is rare to see anyone as convoluted as Lady Daneska. It has been days now, and I'm not sure she'll survive. At times, the infection worsens and putrid green vapors snake around her, strangling her in their noxious coils.

That is not all that lingers around her. If anyone knew *all* that I see, they would lock me in an attic again.

And never let me out.

Telling the truth about such things upsets people, and it makes them exceedingly wary. Even one's own mother. It wasn't until much later, after being locked in the attic a number of times, that I learned to keep certain observations to myself. By then, it was too late.

The attic at our estate was not an altogether unpleasant place. It's true that mice snuck about in the shadows, the windows creaked at night, and the roof moaned in the wind. And after a week or so, the diet of bread and water did become a trifle monotonous. Even so, I found dozens of old books to read and numerous trunks to explore. Eventually, I even devised a way to sketch on the backs of old papers using pieces of moldy wood.

I admit it terrified me the day they came and thrust a sack over my head. Certain they intended to throw me in the river as they'd threatened, I clawed at the bag and screamed until I was breathless. One of the footmen flung me over his shoulder and tossed me into our carriage. "Hush," my mother ordered. Quaking, I quieted my muffled sobs and begged her not to drown me. "Not another word," she snapped. "Or I *will* stop at the bridge. Count yourself fortunate that I'm taking you to a reform school instead."

That was the day they bundled me off to Stranje House. Why they felt the need to cover my face, I cannot fathom. Were they afraid I'd memorize the route? Even with a flour sack over my head, did they think I would forget each turn and jog in the road, the rumble of wooden wheels over cobblestones as we passed through Worthing, or the clacking as we crossed the long wooden bridge at Shoreham? Were they afraid I would come running back across all those miles?

They didn't want me.

That is reason enough for me to never retrace that frightful journey.

More importantly, the day they brought me here to Stranje House proved to be the best day of my life. Even so, despite six wonderful years under Miss Stranje's kindhearted tutelage, I remain cautious. I have not dared to tell even her the extent of my...

What shall I call it—this troubling ability?

Observations?

No, that is not it by half.

Extraocular perceptions?

Perhaps.

I suppose it is conceivable that I was born with the ability to see beyond what others consider normal. After all, some people do see in the dark better than others. How many of them, I wonder, see the more ethereal beings who roam in the dark?

Or even those who walk in the light.

It is one thing to observe and remember too many details, to recall details that are inconsequential and seemingly trifling to you but quite upsetting to your family. Details such as your grandfather's face, even though he died when you were only two. It is even more upsetting to them if you notice things that ordinary people cannot see at all, even if they are looking straight at them. The difficulty arises in distinguishing which elements are perfectly normal, and which ones seem unusual or disturbing to other people.

I cannot always tell.

And I cannot risk being locked away in some cellar or attic for good, or worse, hauled off to Bedlam. That is what people do with those deemed insane. Thus, it requires a great deal of sorting out the solid facts from those that are not so solid.

For instance, now.

We absolutely *must* have Lady Daneska's help in our search for the kidnapped Prince. She is the only one who has even an inkling about where Napoleon and Ghost might have hidden England's Prince Regent. Britain will be plunged even deeper into this hopeless war if she does not wake up and help us find him. Yet, I dare not mention to anyone all the *things* I observe hanging about Lady Daneska, nor the inner battle she is fighting. I can only relate those aspects for which I can provide some sort of tangible proof.

There must be something I can do to yank her out of the muddy torment sucking her under. I reach for her hand atop the coverlet. As if she senses my touch, Lady Daneska stirs. The sickly green cloud around her ceases its frenzied roiling and dissipates somewhat.

Gradually, her breathing slows to a calm, steady pace. Almost peaceful. I scoot closer, watching, hoping. Her eyelashes flutter, blinking against the late morning sun as it slices through gaps in the curtain. She coughs, tugs her hand away, and squints at me. "Mouse?" Her voice, which is usually falsetto and treacly, grates out in a low, weak whisper.

"Yes, it's me, Seraphina. Here, try to drink some of this water." I raise her head and press a pewter mug to her lips.

She accepts a trickle of moisture, groans, and turns away. "*Souris Blanche,*" she says with a tone of weary irritation.

Souris Blanche. White mouse.

It is a good sign that she feels well enough to belittle me. "Yes, it is I, your beloved white mouse." I don't bother to repress the sharpness in my tone as I set the glass down and plant my hands on my hips, wondering if, given her current condition, she even hears me.

Aah! There it is, a familiar flash of hatred sparking around her. She heard, and even though she has been four days in a feverish stupor, she finds the strength to summon her hot dislike of me. *Good.* That is some improvement at least.

I wipe sweat from her brow and tuck the coverlet back up around her shoulders. She moans and struggles against the bedclothes. We ought not to have traveled from Brighton with her in this condition, but we had no choice. We could not risk remaining there. If Ghost decided to return for her not even the walls of the Brighton Pavilion would stop him.

Daneska bats at my hand as I smooth back sweat-tarnished strands of her normally golden hair. "Where's Tess?" she demands, showing more lucidity than she has displayed in days. "Why isn't she here?"

"She sat vigil at your bedside all night." I press my palm against Daneska's forehead. Her fever is down but only slightly. "She'll likely be back as soon as she's rested."

Her eyelids flutter open, long enough for her to glance irritably at me, not that her annoyance wasn't already evident, wafting around her like a poisonous fog. She has always hated me. She used to badger me relentlessly when she was a student here at Stranje House. *La petite souris,* she used to call me. *The little white mouse who wouldn't die.* She has always mistaken my quietness for fear.

Poor Daneska. She views everyone in the world as either predator or prey. She has no use for prey—other than to bend them to her will.

"Go away," she murmurs and sinks against the pillow as if falling back asleep. Except I know better. Her eyes may be closed, but her ire simmers with scalding heat—a kettle ready to boil over. Finally, she grits her teeth and croaks at me, "Send me someone else."

I intend to rile her, to provoke her out of this endless drowsiness. We need answers. "Very well. Would you prefer Miss Fitzwilliam's company?" I say this, knowing full well she detests Georgiana even more than she does me.

Lady Daneska responds with several unladylike syllables in her Prussian tongue.

"Hmm, I see. So, not Georgie." I pretend to be dismayed. "That must mean you would like Maya to come and sit with you."

In a burst of fiery rage, her eyelids blink open. She shifts her hand beneath the blankets. I'm certain she is instinctively reaching for the dagger that is usually strapped to her thigh, her favorite of the five blades we removed from her days ago.

Anger achieves what constant care could not. It awakens her to full consciousness.

Except Daneska buries her rage and turns sly. Her deceptiveness turns into a shadowy curtain, dimming what little light had shown within her. Her lips writhe as she hisses with a scratchy throat, "Yes, do send in dear sweet Miss Barrington. I would like to thank her for her betrayal." The air around her surges with wine-colored venom.

Weary of her malice and duplicity, I exhale my exasperation. "Your spite is pointless, Lady Daneska. It will not help you heal."

"Spite?!" she tosses the word at me. "I feel nothing so paltry as *spite*."

At least that much is the truth. Her hatred sends sticky strands spinning around her like a spider trapping a fly. Does she not see the suffocating nature of it? She flinches and groans as if its nauseating grip is squeezing the life out of her.

"Daneska! For pity's sake. Fight this fever, not us. *We* are not your enemies."

She mumbles something unintelligible.

I need to get her talking again. There's a chance she might inadvertently give us a clue about where they're hiding Prince George. "Drink." I offer her the mug of water again. "You must be thirsty." I raise her head and hold the mug to her lips. She takes a feeble sip and flops back down. I set the cup on the night table and rest my fingers on the pewter handle. "You know," I begin carefully. "You ought not be so angry with Maya. You asked the impossible of her. Surely you knew she would never betray those she holds dear?"

"Who did she love so dearly? You?" She asks this as if I am next to nothing. "The others?" She manages to smirk before closing her eyes.

"Yes, *me*. Tess. Georgie. Lady Jane. Miss Stranje. All of us." I lift my chin. "And Lord Kinsworth—don't forget him."

She says nothing.

"This is her father's homeland." Still, there is no rise from Daneska, so I press on. "And now it is hers, too."

I wait, with hope drifting away. Daneska's eyes remain shuttered, and she lies there motionless.

"Maya is loyal," I add, and then decide badgering her might be a better approach. "You knew that. Did you truly expect her to go against her own character?"

Lady Daneska moves her lips slowly. "We *had* an agreement." She grinds out each syllable. "She was to give us what *we* wanted in exchange for..." Daneska groans and shifts her head against the pillow as if it is uncomfortable. "Maya wanted to go home to India. Napoleon wants England. A trade. It should have worked." Her words murmur quieter and quieter, as if her strength is fading—spent on useless anger.

The clock on the night table ticks loudly, keeping time with her shallow breathing.

"It should have worked!" she blurts hoarsely. Her perfect brow pinches, and I notice her fingers curl into a fist.

"Except it didn't," I whisper.

Thank God.

There is a soft mew from her, much like the sound of a lost kitten. She is losing consciousness again. I shake her shoulders. "Wake up. Where have they taken Prince George? Tell me."

Nothing.

I gently unwind her curled fingers, knowing there will not be an answer. Not now. Perhaps not for days. I stroke her pale hand until it relaxes. I cannot help but pity Lady Daneska. It's true she is hateful and vicious. And I remember all too well the way she flaunted her success in London and in Brighton. There was a time when it seemed as if her cunning and cleverness had earned her everything she wanted—position, wealth, and power. She was Emperor Napoleon's darling, his pet spy, and paramour to Ghost who rules over the powerful Iron Crown, yet she also maintained an intimate friendship with the Prince of England. Sadly though, I have always sensed a twisted and profound restlessness within Daneska. Not one corner of her soul is at peace.

How can I *not* feel sorry for her?

Lady Jane glides quietly into the room. I feel her presence long before I hear her speak. Jane is completely unaware of the warmth and grace she radiates. "I thought I heard voices," she asks. "Is she awake?"

"She was, but she's drifted off again."

"Did she say anything of value?"

It is all I can do not to laugh. Jane evaluates all things in the context of their usefulness in life's stratagems. For her, life is a chess game to be played. I like Lady Jane. She's safe and reliable. Around her the air is clear and fresh, like a blue-sky day.

I shake my head. "Not unless you think it is of value to know she still wants to kill Maya. Or that she'd happily slit my throat at the slightest provocation."

Lady Jane chuckles lightly. "I see. So, nothing has

changed. I had foolishly hoped she might wake up feeling grateful that we saved her life, remorseful for her treachery, and eager to tell us all the Iron Crown's secrets."

"It's, Lady Daneska? You knew better."

"I suppose." Jane sighs. "Perhaps we can trick her into divulging something. She must have some idea where they're holding Prince George. *He* would've told her some of his plans."

He.

Ghost.

Master of the Iron Crown.

I cringe at the thought of Napoleon's cutthroat secret society. I cannot scrub away the memory of Ghost brutally cutting his own spy's throat. The man failed in his assignment to track Maya and me in Brighton. Instead, we followed him and stumbled upon Ghost's whereabouts. As punishment, Ghost slashed his spy's throat. He knew we were watching—he may have even killed him *because* we were watching. I shiver, unable to forget the whirling blackness around him that seems to suck away every morsel of light or hope.

"How can she love such a man?" I ask under my breath.

Lady Jane lowers her voice to barely a whisper. "Years ago, when he was Lord Ravencross, before we mistakenly thought he was dead. Ghost wasn't always so..." She hesitates. I wonder if she's remembering when he held her hostage and how he sliced open her leg—leaving her with a scar she will carry all her life. She shakes off the memory. "He wasn't always so vicious. He has gotten worse. The Napoleonic wars were traumatic for many soldiers."

"After what he did to you? How can you defend him?"

"He could've killed me, but he didn't." She shrugs. "I'm not. It's just that there's something very sad about him. Perhaps the war turned his heart. That's all."

I bristle. "Thousands upon thousands of men went through those wars. They didn't all come as back vengeful killers."

Though we are speaking in hushed voices, Lady Daneska mumbles as if joining our conversation, "His father..." Her voice trails off and her ordinarily smooth brow rumples up in what appears to be a grimace of consternation, or perhaps it is pain. "... vile."

His father.

We'd heard rumors about Gabriel and Ghost's father, how harsh and brutal the old Lord Ravencross had been to his two sons. I shake my head, banishing thoughts of my own parents. "Even if their father was cruel to them, why did Ghost have to choose this path? Look at Gabriel, he didn't grow up to be a vicious traitor."

Jane pursed her lips for a moment. "He struggles against a hard heart. Tess has told me as much. Some wounds are..." Jane takes an inordinate interest in straightening the coverlet on Daneska's bed. "Some wounds cut very deep." She sighs.

I look away, studying the shadows as they move

against the far wall like the ones in my old attic. "Soul deep."

Lady Jane and I fall silent. Both of us are acutely aware of how mothers can devastate us, and yet fathers seem to hold the power of heaven or hell in their hands. For good or evil, they alter our lives irrevocably.

I glance over and notice Daneska's cheeks have brightened into red blotches. Quickly pressing my palm against her forehead, I grimace. "Her fever is rising again."

"Blast!" Jane rushes to my side. "She better come out of it soon, or we're done for. It won't be long before Parliament will be screaming to escalate the war—a war we are already losing dismally. Lord Castlereagh sends a runner every day asking for an update on her condition." Lady Jane purses her lips. "We'll need to administer more of Madame Cho's fever tincture."

I retrieve the bottle, but Jane takes it from me. "I'll do this. Miss Stranje sent me to relieve you. She asks if you would stop by her study. Apparently, there is a matter of some importance she wishes to discuss with you."

"With me? You're the one who discusses strategy with her."

"We *all* discuss matters of strategy. You know that." Jane sniffs, and I see pride whistling up her neck like a pink wind, but she brushes it away and smiles serenely. "I don't know what she wishes to confer with you about. Although, I did see a man bringing her papers early this morning."

"Papers?" I cannot keep from frowning. "They can't have anything to do with me."

She shrugs. "I've no idea. He met with her in her office and left directly after."

Except Lady Jane is not telling the truth right now. Her countenance darkens, and she refuses to look in my direction, and I also note the telltale twitch at the corner of her left eye. "You have some idea. You just don't want to say."

She glares at me, a typical Lady Jane scolding glare. "You do realize there are times when it is better not to *always* know when a person is lying."

"And you know perfectly well that I can't help it. So, you may as well tell me."

"No." She crosses her arms. "I would just be speculating."

At least she's telling the truth now. "Speculating about what?"

"Nothing." She waves her hand, trying to dismiss me, but I stand and wait.

"Oh, very well." She huffs at me. "The messenger looked as if he'd come from a long way away, that's all. Not from London. The London runners have a look about them, and they tend to arrive at regular intervals. This fellow... looked different. More like one of her spies bringing her a report rather than a simple courier."

"What do you think it means?"

She shrugged. "Go and ask her. I'd only be guessing."

"Except you are ever so good at guessing."

And I do not like surprises.

"Truly, I do not know. No, Sera, don't look at me like that." She sniffs loudly. "Oh very well, since you are being obstinate about it, I wondered if it might possibly pertain to something about Mr. Chadwick."

At the thought of Quentin Chadwick, my insides tighten, and breath catches in my throat.

"Ha! You turned pink at the mere mention of his name." Lady Jane pokes my shoulder. "I've never seen anyone blush so quickly."

Lady Daneska moans.

"Go," Lady Jane orders. "I have to give Daneska this smelly medicine before the fever cooks whatever is left of her brain."

I pause at the door. "You needn't worry about that. Her brain is still intact and as warped as ever. Watch out that she doesn't grab the spoon and try to stab you with it."

CHAPTER 2

PLAGUE MASKS
AND PREDISPOSITIONS

LADY JANE LAUGHS as I make my way down the hall. I, on the other hand, fight a queasy feeling rising in my stomach. My steps slow as I near Miss Stranje's office, and I trace my fingers along the oak paneling as if cataloging each groove and imperfection.

Something feels wrong.

Her door stands slightly ajar. I push it open, and she stands to greet me. "Come in, Sera."

She stood.

That means bad news.

Also, she's doing her best to hide a worried expression.

I love our headmistress's features—they hide nothing. Not really. Oh, she tries. Like now, she is struggling to disguise some sort of worry. Miss Stranje can mask her features so that she looks as stern and forbidding as a black-hooded, metal-nosed, plague doctor. Despite her façade, the air around her usually glimmers as golden and bright as the morning sun.

Our first meeting, more than six years ago, is etched indelibly in my mind.

At first, I only heard her.

My mother and our footman dragged me into Stranje House that day and prodded me up the stairs with the sack still tied over my head. When we entered Miss Stranje's office, Mother pinched my arm and hissed a warning in my ear, "Keep quiet."

I smelled books. Musty ones, new ones, *many* books—I could tell because they dampened the sound in her office. Her skirts rustled when she approached us. I stood as still and straight as I could manage.

Miss Stranje issued a command, not loud, not harsh, not even scolding. Yet her low wintery tone froze me to the bone. No one could've ignored that icy directive. "Remove the hood from your daughter's head."

My mother gulped loud enough that I heard it despite my heart thundering and that wretched flour sack hindering my ears.

The next words Miss Stranje spoke sent my stomach plummeting to the floor. "Let us see what sort of trouble you are foisting upon me."

The footman yanked off my hood.

I stood in this very office, shaking so hard I was afraid I might wet myself until my vision cleared, and I saw her. One look, and I knew all that black bombazine she wore was a disguise. She smelled of rose-scented soap. I liked that it wasn't lavender. Lavender smells so elderly and musty. Beak nosed and hawkeyed, she stared at me for several minutes without saying a word.

I fancied she was actually giving me time to study her. The longer she stared, the more certain I became.

Meanwhile, my mother, uncomfortable in the heavy silence, hemmed and hawed. She promised more money if Miss Stranje would only agree to reform me and somehow change me into a marriageable young lady. "I've heard you have... uh... *methods*. Unconventional, perhaps, but you come highly recommended."

Still, Miss Stranje said nothing.

"It needn't be a peer who takes her," my mother blathered on. "A merchant will do. A farmer, perhaps. Or even a soldier. After all, she isn't a bad-looking child. Oh, I'll admit she's a trifle pale with all that white hair, and perhaps a bit thin, but she's only just turned eleven. She may yet fill out. One can hope."

In the face of Miss Stranje's wordless scrutiny, my mother resorted to pleading. Surely someone of Miss Stranje's reputation could make something of me, she argued. She suggested the headmistress might keep me under lock and key if need be—*take whatever measures are necessary.* She babbled on about how if the school's staff were instructed not to engage me in conversation and, as she so delicately stated, "to ignore anything I might say about, er, invisible beings, all would be well."

My mother's agitation finally drew a response from Miss Stranje. The headmistress held up one finger to shush her.

At that, Mamma's lips clamped together abruptly. A second later, she began blustering irritably under her breath and finally blurted, "Look here—you cannot shush me. I am a lady of standing. My uncle is a peer of the realm."

Miss Stranje ignored her and leaned closer to me until we were nearly nose to nose. Then, in a voice I'm quite certain not even my mother could hear, she asked, "Do you trust me, Seraphina Wyndham?"

She knew the answer long before I gave her a slight nod.

"Very well." She pulled back and whirled upon my mother. "I will show you to our discipline chamber now."

I thought Mamma might burst into tears of relief. "Th-this means you *will* take her?"

"Possibly." Miss Stranje heaved a weary sigh, as if my presence constituted an enormous burden that she was only reluctantly considering. "The last sum you mentioned might entice me to attempt it. Mind you, I make no guarantees. Additionally, as stipulated in my letters, you must approve of my methods first, and sign these documents relinquishing her care to me." She pointed to a thick stack of papers.

"Yes, yes, of course." My mother's face widened with relief. She took one mincing step forward. "Lead the way to your discipline chamber. Although, I must confess, a friend explained your methods to me prior to my writing to you about Seraphina's... um, her... uh... predisposition. I understand that in cases such as hers, drastic measures must be taken. You needn't show me to your, um, *discipline* room." She retracted her step. "I'm willing to sign any—"

"This way to the chamber." Miss Stranje opened the door. "If you are unwilling to comprehend the severity and risks of my '*methods*,' you may take your daughter and return home."

Mamma promptly scurried through the door. I am ashamed to admit she did not balk at the torture devices she witnessed in Miss Stranje's notorious discipline chamber. Instead, she pursed her lips at the banging and pitiful cries of "Have mercy!" emanating from what appeared to be an iron mummy case. That hoax on my mother was the first time I heard Tess's voice. I loved her Welsh lilt, and despite her ruse, the frankness escaping through the air holes in that iron sarcophagus.

Mamma turned to Miss Stranje and brusquely stated, "If this is what it takes to make her behave properly, then so be it."

And that was that.

To say I have never looked back would be a lie. Doesn't every child yearn for their mother, no matter how misplaced that affection may be? Even so, I will forever be grateful to Miss Stranje for taking me in. Instead of being afraid of my peculiarities, she taught me how to embrace and use them. At least, the *peculiarities* I allow her to know about. Some things are better kept to oneself. I cannot risk losing her, too.

"Come in." Miss Stranje waves me forward, breaking the spell of those memories. "How is our patient?"

"Lady Daneska's fever returned. Though, overall, she seems to be growing stronger. She had a brief period of wakefulness a few minutes ago. And..."

"You were able to speak with her?"

"Yes. A little." I fidget with my skirt. "Sadly, Lady Daneska appears as hateful and contrary as ever." I stand at attention in front of Miss Stranje's desk as she taps her forefinger thoughtfully against the edge of some papers.

I interrupt her tapping. "Lady Jane said you wished to speak with me."

"Yes, I do." She points to the chair. "Have a seat, please." Miss Stranje is being too solicitous. When she goes so far as to shut the door, my warning bells jangle even louder.

I take a deep breath. "Is something wrong?"

Instead of returning to her customary place behind the desk, she chooses to sit in the small Queen Anne chair beside me and clamps her lips into a thin line. I'm quite certain she is unaware of the radiance that surrounds her, but today something presses it down closer to earth.

"For some time now…" she begins but stops, staring at me with the same earnestness I saw on the first day we met. "Sera, I'm afraid I have some disturbing news."

"I can tell."

"Yes, I suppose you can." She glances away, as if the wall of books behind me has caught her attention.

"*Please*, just tell me who in my family died."

Her attention snaps back, brows lifted. "No one died." *How very curious.*

"No?" I cock my head to the side. "What is it then?"

"Well… you see, for some time now," she launches into what must surely be a prepared speech. "Your parents have not sent your quarterly tuition. And—"

"Wait." I interrupt. "They stopped paying you? Why?" I draw back. "When? For how long?"

"A year and a half," she says quietly. "The funds ceased without explanation. It had been so long, and my letters ignored, that fearing the worst, I sent one of my men to investigate." She reaches out as if she intends to take my hand but does not. Instead, she stands abruptly and paces on the worn rug beside her desk.

Her uncustomary agitation unsettles me so much that I retreat into my inner cave, safe from her spiking emotions. I cautiously word my next question. "You sent someone to see what had happened. And what did he learn?"

Her shoe catches on the rug, and her step falters. It is not in her nature to stumble.

I brace myself for the worst. "Someone must have died."

Her shoulders sink, and she shakes her head slowly. "No. That's not it."

"What then?"

Banishing whatever grieved her, she squares her shoulders, dons her stern plague mask, and looks directly at me. "There is no easy way to say this, Sera. Your family has sold their estate."

"Sold it?" I blink. That makes no sense. "Why?"

She raises her palm to stave off my questions. "My man talked with the farmers on neighboring estates. He traced your family to Dover. I am sorry to say, he learned that your family booked passage and set sail for The Americas several months ago. Apparently with no intention of returning."

Suddenly my world tips sideways.

"What?" I squint at her. "Surely, not. It can't be. They would have sent word—to you at least." I shake off my tilting world. "No. No, there must be some mistake. Your man went to the wrong estate. He must have."

Her lips tighten again. She sits and grasps both of my hands. "Their behavior is incomprehensible to me as well. The man I sent—Mr. Clayborn—is a reliable fellow. His investigative skills are first-rate. He checked with the harbormaster, and the ship's manifest listed your family as passengers bound for New Bedford, Massachusetts."

I stare at her fingers clasped around mine and pull away.

It must be true, then. They've left me.

To fend for myself.

Alone.

She continues explaining as if offering me more details might somehow soothe me. "Their ship, Gilead's Gull, left port at the end of March. The crossing was fairly smooth. Although they encountered a squall shortly before entering Buzzards Bay, they made it through with only a broken mizzen mast. Gilead's Gull left her passengers in Massachusetts and returned safely to Dover last month. Mr. Clayborn went so far as to locate the captain, who recollected that your entire family disembarked in sound health. Where they were bound after landing in New Bedford, he had no notion."

Where they went next doesn't matter.

Nothing matters.

Least of all, me.

My head throbs. Blood pulses in my temple, thumping and banging like the relentless turning of a carriage wheel. The room blurs at the edges, and it feels as if I might disappear altogether. Vanish, like an unwanted vapor.

She is talking.

Her lips are moving, but I cannot make sense of it. I strain to hear her over the pounding in my head.

"... despicable behavior. Beyond the pale." Her hands

clench into fists. "You have a phenomenal mind, Sera. Phenomenal! Do you hear me? You have a memory unlike any I've ever seen. And your uncanny perceptive abilities are nothing short of miraculous. I cannot fathom how your family failed to see that."

Does it matter?

They're rid of me now. Forever.

I learned the answer to her question long ago. Why did they send me away? It's simple. They were afraid. I force my lips to move. "Fear."

And if you knew the truth, you would be afraid, too.

I cannot bear to look at her.

How can I?

So, I fix my eyes on her hands, watching her fingers curl tight and then uncurl only to tighten again. Her office suddenly feels unbearably cold as if winter has come early and robbed the room of all warmth. I shiver and, through quivering lips, ask, "Are you going to throw me out?"

It is a perfectly reasonable question given the fact that there will be no more money coming to pay for my upkeep. Miss Stranje's mouth opens as if I've shocked her. Then she frowns, and her golden light flares to almost white. "Heavens no! Certainly not!"

Certainly?

I would not have thought my mother would throw me away, either.

Yet she did.

Nothing in life is certain.

Nothing.

What sort of freakish daughter am I that my own mother runs away from me without a word?

The room closes in on me. Weakness robs me of speech and leaves my lips quivering with shame. I fight a foolish urge to collapse against Miss Stranje's chest and cry. To sob like a baby—a lost unwanted orphan. Embarrassment burns my cheeks. This weakness, this horrible sense that I might fade away into nothing is undoing me.

Facts.

I must cling to the steadying world of facts and reason.

I grip the edge of the chair, dig my fingers into the cherrywood and take stock of reality. This is what I know. I am alone in the world now—a penniless waif. I cannot afford weakness.

I must not become the white mouse Lady Daneska thinks I am.

My chest heaves up and down, like the steam engine Georgie and Mr. Sinclair built. I stand abruptly and the chair nearly topples, but Miss Stranje catches it. I must get out of here.

"Sera?"

I cannot look at her. Pity will be in her eyes. It will break me.

Go.

Walk out.

Leave.

"Sera," she calls to my back. "Your family may yet send

a letter. You know that mail takes a very long time crossing the Atlantic. Do not give up hope."

There is no hope.

Summoning words nearly gags me. They bump out of my throat in broken pieces. "Th-they will not write."

I cross the threshold into the hall, one foot stumbling in front of the other. She is behind me. *Please don't follow me,* I pray silently. Her footsteps slow, letting me escape.

Good. I scurry down the staircase.

Going where?

Away.

Outside.

I must get out of the house. I cannot think with these walls closing in on me.

CHAPTER 3

FATALLY UNIMPORTANT

CLOUDS BILLOW AND TUMBLE across a faded blue sky, racing to join a gray storm rising in the west. I head toward the sea, striding along the edge of the towering cliffs. The salty wind chaffs my cheeks—a thousand invisible slaps awaken my numb mind.

What am I going to do?

I stop at the highest point of these cliffs, Queen's Cape, and stare out at the vast sea. I've no means by which to support myself. Nothing with which to pay my tuition. How will I earn my way in the world?

I might be able to serve as a governess. Or a nanny. Except who would trust a woman with no family connections? And what tales might the neighbors from my home parish tell a prospective employer? I have no idea how much my mother may have confided to our neighbors, or the people in our village? What if someone noticed me pacing in our attic window? No doubt, they would've guessed it was the Wyndham's mad daughter—the girl who, as a child, sketched portraits of dead people and supposedly spoke to otherworldly beings she saw walk among us.

The minuscule list of my employment options shrinks even further as I dismiss being a governess or nanny. Lost, I stare out at the ocean. From that great height, waves create a lulling rhythm as they roll in and wash out. Larger waves crash against the rocks hard enough that a fine mist rides up on the breeze and cools my face.

One last, although highly improbable, alternative taunts me.

Marriage.

A last resort, to be sure.

Last resort or not, it is as improbable as finding gold coins in my stocking. One must have a suitor first. I swallow against the salty air stinging my throat and forbid his name from entering my mind, yet it marches in uninvited.

Mr. Quentin Chadwick.

He's a friend, not a suitor.

Some obstinate part of me argues that the young

gentleman brought flowers more than once, and he was rather attentive in Brighton. He even made me laugh on several occasions—no small feat. Lady Jane is right. I do like him. How could I not? His innocence bounces happily about him like an adoring pup. Yet his mind is bright and quick while his manner is impossibly charming. And his eyes are—

Oh, bother!

None of this qualifies him as a suitor.

I mustn't indulge in nonsensical daydreams.

Flowers and pretty speeches notwithstanding, I clearly recall that in many of our conversations Quentin Chadwick seemed far more enamored with our school for spies than he did with me. So much so that he is now training with Captain Grey's band of diplomatic attachés who serve Lord Castlereagh in our fight against Napoleon. Which is simply another way of saying he is training to become a *spy*. And spies don't take wives. They can't.

I kick a rock over the edge. It pings, flips, and bounces until it finally strikes the shore below with a nearly imperceptible *plunk* against the heap of stones below.

More to the point, Mr. Chadwick hasn't visited me as a suitor, friend, or otherwise since we left Brighton. And now that my family has completely severed all ties with me, it's doubtful Quentin will want anything more to do with me. Why would he? I'm a prodigal daughter, castoff, with no dowry to offer him, no rank, no title—*nothing*. His doting parents would never approve of such an inequitable match for their son.

Wind whips against my dress and hair, nearly lifting me off my feet. *I am anchorless. Untethered to anyone on earth.*

I'm like those clouds twisting and turning in the sky above me—little more than air. And worth even less.

What will I do?

Where shall I go?

The ocean waves beckon. The tide is rising, and if I were to leap out far enough, it might carry me far, far away. And no one would ever—

"Are you planning to jump?"

Tess!

How did I not sense her approach?

I whirl around. "What are you doing here? I thought you were sleeping."

"I was." Her tone is sharp, almost a snarl.

"A dream woke you?"

"Something like that." She walks to the edge and stands beside me. "Well? Were you going to jump or not?"

I ought to lie, but I can't. "The thought passed through my mind."

I'm glad it's Tess asking. Any of the others would be maudlin and smother me with sympathy. She's not that way. Although, now that I think on it, Lady Jane would probably lecture me. Georgie would pelt me with fifty reasons why I ought not to even consider such a thing. And Maya... Maya would destroy me with one withering look of sad disappointment, and then she would tell me she thought I was stronger than that.

Except this has nothing to do with strength. This has to do with—with being insignificant. *Fatally unimportant.*

"The thought passed through your mind? Does that mean it's gone now?"

"Not entirely."

"Hmm." She sits on the ground and lets her feet hang over the precipice. She plucks up a stone and hurls it out into the sea far below. It flies out so far, the splash is imperceptible—it disappears into nothingness.

Which is what I'd considered doing.

Awkwardly, I manage to sit next to her, letting my legs dangle dangerously over the edge—like hers. Except she is wearing her running dress. I am clad in a prim and proper morning gown, and white stockings, both of which will no doubt be badly stained by the grass and dirt. I don't care. I pluck a small stone out of the grass and toss it at the beguiling waves. Mine falls short.

"There is an afterlife, you know," she says this as if it is a scold.

I almost laugh. "*This* is what you say to me? *Me*, who knows far too much about the world beyond this one. I'm quite aware, thank you."

"Then you know, you would not simply disappear."

I gape at her. "How did you know that's what I—?" I bite my lip, unwilling to divulge more.

The corner of her mouth turns up in a wry smirk. "It is not hard to guess."

I exhale and turn away, peeved that here at Stranje
House, even my most shameful private thoughts cannot be
kept secret. To be fair, though, Tess does more than guess;
she dreams of deaths to come, of others' deaths. I soften.
It must be dreadful to live with such horror night after
night. *Did she see me die?*

"You dreamed it?" I ask.

She shrugs.

"Did I jump?" I frown. "In the dream, I mean."

She shakes her head. "I have no idea. I saw you trapped
in some sort of miserable fog, and there was a ship. What
I did see, or rather, what I *felt*, was your family sailing away
and leaving you lost in a horrid choking cold fog." She
shivers as if still feeling the chill. "And you were so..." She
stops talking and takes a deep breath. "I'd never seen you
that miserable before. Ever. Not *you*."

I squeeze my eyes shut and clutch a fistful of grass. "I'm
sorry." It's my fault she suffered through that. "Truly, I am.
This morning Miss Stranje told me that my family sailed
to America. They left no word. Nothing. Not even a note.
And I... I..."

"You wanted to scream."

I nod. "Among other things."

"They abandoned you. Why wouldn't you scream? You
probably didn't, though, did you? I would have. I would've
howled with rage."

Of course, she would. She's part wolf. Not really, but
Tess is as wild and untamed as any wolf. It's why our pack

of wolf dogs love her so much. I glance at Phobos and Tromos sitting six feet behind us, patiently guarding her, while their three nearly-grown cubs frolic after voles and crickets they've startled from their hiding places.

"Left me without a penny." I toss the grass in my palm over the cliff. They catch the wind but inevitably spiral downward, ripped sprigs of life, cut short by my thoughtlessness. "My parents haven't paid any tuition for three quarters. I've no idea how I will repay Miss Stranje."

Thunder clouds rumble in the distance. Thankfully, Tess does not turn to me with pity. She does not offer empty platitudes or do any of the things that would make me feel even more lost and hopeless. Instead, she nudges me with her shoulder and scoots closer to me, as if in this war of life, we are *both* lost daughters.

I bite my lip, fighting the tears that threaten. Not heartbroken tears, tears of gratitude for her companionship. A little of the darkness in my soul lifts.

I lean my head on her shoulder. "I'm sorry to have caused you to have those awful feelings."

"It's your family who ought to be sorry. Not you." Tess knocks a chunk of dirt loose with the heel of her half boot. The clod falls straight down onto an outcropping of seagrass. It splatters apart and dislodges something. An object glints briefly in the sunlight, then clinks against stones as it tumbles down to the rocks at the base of the cliff.

Tess puts out her hand to stop me from leaning over. "Careful!"

"Yes, but did you see that?" I point.

"I saw you leaning too far out." She grabs hold of the back of my dress.

"That dirt clod knocked something off that ledge down there. It looked to be brass."

"What does it matter?" She yanks on my dress, tugging me back as I strain to get a better look. "Whatever it is, it isn't worth diving headfirst after it."

"If it's what I think it is, it just might." I scramble to my feet. "It might matter a great deal. I'm going down there to find out." I dash toward the west side of Queen's Cape, where there is a winding route down to the beach.

"Wait!" she shouts, and Phobos yips as if in agreement "I'm coming with you."

"No time! A storm's coming." I point at the clouds and call out to her over my shoulder, "Get Miss Stranje. Hurry! We may need her."

It is a narrow, and in some places nonexistent, path winding down Queen's Cape cliff. It zigzags down a one-hundred-thirty-foot drop and requires extreme caution. I employ my hands, as well as my feet, and heartily wish I had on a pair of sturdy half boots rather than these thin-soled slippers.

Although Queen's Cape is the cliff situated closest to Stranje House, it is also the steepest and most treacherous. That is why we usually go to and from the beach, using the broader, less dangerous switchback path lower down to the west, near the caves and inlet.

As I make my way down, I notice several displaced boulders and numerous broken spikes of tall seagrass. At the halfway mark, I stop to catch my breath, and glance up to where I first saw the object dislodged. The sheer incline above the outcropping is full of notches and loose soil. Below that, is a fresh rockslide. All this confirms my suspicions.

I continue another seventy feet down the steep path and there, glinting in the sun, sits the brass object I was seeking. A small sailor's telescope resting against a mound of flowering cliff daisies.

I retrieve the spyglass and turn it round in my hand. We have one very similar to it in our workroom. This one, though, has grimy fingerprints evident all along its length. Extending it, so that sunlight catches on it, I read the elaborate maker's inscription engraved on the eyepiece. My breath catches.

Dollond & Son, Paris, France.

My steps grow far more hesitant now. There, behind a boulder, barely noticeable in the shadows, lies the edge of a leather shoe. I stoop down to investigate.

Brown. A man's shoe. Well-worn leather, full of saltwater stains.

Judging by the look of this shoe, it belonged to a sailor—a French sailor ordered to spy on us. It's lodged against the boulder as if thrown there with substantial force.

How?

Up to the right, fifteen feet above my head, juts a sharp-angled rock overhang. The beige sandstone cliffs have been polished smooth by the salt and wind. The dark red stain on the corner of the outcropping can't be natural. It looks like blood. I back up, squinting to see better. If a man fell, slid from his perch at the top of Queen's Cape, his foot might have struck that jagged ledge. A fall like that could very easily have knocked his shoe loose. And it would've flown off toward this boulder.

Poor fellow!

I grimace, picturing his violent tumble earthward. It plays out in my mind, and I can almost hear the crunch of bone as his foot hits the ledge and his leg bones shatter. Instead of continuing to fall straight down, the impact would've thrown him opposite the flight of his shoe.

East.

Walking that direction, I tread warily, searching for anything out of place. This section of the beach is covered with smooth knobby stones. Teetering to keep my balance, I come to a standstill beside a pile of jagged rocks at the base of the cliff.

This is the place.

He landed here. The sickly smell of rust and rot is unmistakable.

Blood.

And by the looks of it—quite a bit. It's as if someone splashed a bucket of burgundy red paint across the stones. A goodly amount would have run under these rocks, between the pebbles, and leached into the sand. Surely, whoever left this much blood could not have survived for very long.

If at all.

The thick sludge is drying in the sun and beginning to crack and clump. Flies buzz around it, drawn to a feast of decay.

Yet his body is not here.

How can that be?

I suppose if his legs struck these rocks first, rather than his head, it's conceivable he might have hobbled away. Highly unlikely. There's only one way to find out. I wrinkle my nose. But there's no point in running from a task that requires doing.

Picking up a long thin stick, I stir it into the grisly remains pooled between stones. Then, nearly gagging, I fish out a wad of something drenched in the reddish slime and scrape it on a nearby rock. I lean closer to make sure I'm not leaping to conclusions. The smell alone, forces me to gulp back a wave of nausea. The hideous mass on the rock appears to be a gob of stringy blood-soaked hair.

My stomach lurches.

I drop the stick and turn away, leaning my forehead against the cold hard cliff wall. Breath comes in shallow bursts as if I'd run for miles. *Think,* I order myself. *Gather the facts.*

Head wound.

Puddle of blood.

Fractured leg.

Where is the body?

A new thought grips me. One so horrid my shoulders tremble. If Tess hadn't come and found me at the cliff top today, Miss Stranje and the others might have found *my* hair and blood splattered on these stones.

In a painfully vivid flash, I imagine my friends' horror at finding my body in a broken gory heap. Their shock. Their grief. Their anger. A moan resonates deep in my throat.

Some childish part of me wants to lay the blame on my parents. It's their fault.

How could they have been so cruel?

How could they have abandoned me?

Another thought whispers across my mind. This one quiet yet as forceful as wind, and it asks, *did you not intend to abandon your friends? Was that not cruel?*

I wince. It's true. It wouldn't have been my parents who wounded those here who love me. It would've been me—my fainthearted choice—that hurt them. When faced with the choice of running from life or staying and facing my problems, leaping had seemed such a clear solution, so easy. And so... I squeeze my eyes shut, flinching beneath the weight of shame... *so cowardly.*

My eyes flash open. Daneska is right. *I am the white mouse.*

A tear burns down my cheek, an acidic whip that stings my soul.

No more.

Not today, anyway.

I dash the tear away. "I *didn't* jump." I say aloud to the deaf stones surrounding me. "That counts for something!" They don't answer. The wind fans against my face carrying salt spray with it. "It counts," I insist.

Overhead, a gull squawks in agreement.

"Thank you." I tilt my head. "And now, orphaned pauper or not, I have work to do."

I turn and scan the shoreline. *Confound it all! Where did this spy disappear to?*

Nothing!

There's nothing amiss in either direction. I half expect a bloodied stranger to come limping out from behind the bushes that rim the cove. Or crawl out from the shadows along the cliffs. Except the beach remains silent but for lapping waves and birds screeching into the wind as they soar overhead.

Where is he?

How did he move from this spot? It's too high on the beach for the tide to have carried his remains away. So, either he limped away, or he is still nearby. Except there are no footprints, nor is there a discernible blood trail.

Impossible.

Think, Sera, think. It only *seems* impossible.

An unbidden ripple of excitement races through me. I'm ashamed to admit it, but my heart thrums too excitedly to deny it. The challenge of an *impossible* mystery should not thrill me. And yet...

It does.

With grim determination, I squat down and study the scene harder. There, off to the right... that is a footprint in the pebbles. It's faint and perhaps I'm imagining things—

"Halloo!" A distant call startles me.

It's Miss Stranje and the others, hurrying along the shore from the direction of the inlet. They wisely took the safer path down to the beach. Miss Stranje leads the pack— Tess, Georgie, Maya, and Lady Jane hurry toward me.

I stand, watching their approach, and peace washes through me. They radiate goodness as brilliantly as the morning sun scatters gloom. Like the power that moves the sea, their inner happiness rolls toward me in waves. Lady Jane raps Georgie on the shoulder and her laughter catches in the wind like gentle chimes. Maya glides a little off to the side and holds her hand out as if testing for rain. At Jane's laughter she turns briefly, but then alerts in my direction as if I, too, am emitting a sound. Her hand shoots into the air in a quick wave of salutation, and amber sparks swirl through the air.

It baffles me that most people cannot see how emotions send vibrations whirling in every direction. It happens as surely as tossing a stone in a pond creates ripples. Maya told me once that she hears people's feelings like a song, vibrating like musical instruments. I wonder what that would be like. All I see are the colors.

Even from this distance, my friends' approach causes a

tumult in my chest.

It's the contrast.

In slinking gray shadows my parents sailed away from me—without so much as a *fare-thee-well.* Yet here, hurrying toward me with noisy sunlit greetings, my *real* family approaches—full of bright light and love, they race up the beach toward me.

And I cannot bear the thought of leaving them.

I can't do it. I won't.

Not now.

Not ever.

This is where I belong, here at Stranje House, with them! I'll do whatever it takes to stay. *Except, how?* It would be wrong to throw myself on Miss Stranje's charity—to burden her with the expense of my upkeep and housing.

What then?

How shall I pay my tuition?

Lady Jane insists there is always a solution if we look hard enough. That isn't always true, except maybe this time she's right. In that brief moment, watching them walk toward me, hands raised in greeting, a solution arises.

I know exactly what I must do.

CHAPTER 4

THE CASE OF THE MISSING CORPSE

IF I WANT A FUTURE here, I must purchase one. And now I have an idea how I can do that.

But first...

I must stop Miss Stranje and the others from trampling clues. Tess brought one of our wolf dogs. Tromos lopes alongside her, chasing and splashing in the waves. If they come much closer their footprints will mar our investigation.

"Stop!" I shout and quickly pick my way toward them, fanning my arms. "Don't come any closer."

Their steps slow, and yet they don't seem to understand.

"Stay near the waves!" The wind muffles my shouts of warning. I lengthen my stride, trying to choose footfalls that will not ruin any other possible footprints. It is Georgie who first perceives my meaning. She runs out in front of the others, arms spread wide to stop them. Tess immediately marshals Tromos to her side.

As soon as I reach the damp part of the beach, where waves have already destroyed any evidence, I break into a full run. Out of breath and with my skirts splattered with mud and sand, I finally reach them. Wordlessly, I extend the telescope to our headmistress.

Miss Stranje turns it over in her hands. Georgie leans in to study the small brass spyglass. "That's not one of ours."

Miss Stranje reads the inscription and looks up. "Decidedly not. Where did you find it?"

"It fell from a tuft of Marram grass about twenty feet below the crest of Queen's Cape." I point at the cliff head towering behind us.

"That means Ghost has been spying on us." Lady Jane squints up at the cliff. "From that vantage point, they would've noticed candles and lamplight during the night and the curtains partially drawn during the day."

Georgiana shades her eyes and studies the precarious perch. "And easily guessed which room Lady Daneska was in."

Miss Stranje secures the spyglass in her pocket. "We'll move her tonight."

"We've another quandary." I explain about finding the blood, the shoe, and how the spy's body is missing. "He can't have survived, yet he seems to have simply disappeared. Come let me show you where he fell, but mind where you step. I may have overlooked some clue to his whereabouts."

"I doubt it," Maya reassures me in a soothing tone. "Unless something was intentionally hidden, you would have noticed it."

Ever since our adventures in Brighton, she treats me as if I am her sister. Her confidence in me, even though it may be misplaced, makes me smile. "I warn you, it's a ghastly sight, but you must see for yourselves if you think he could've survived."

I lead them to the pool of drying blood. As soon as they stop grimacing, I point out the significant seepage between the rocks, and that even more blood must have seeped into the sand below.

Lady Jane covers her nose with a handkerchief. "I don't see how anyone could live after losing that much blood."

"Mmm," Tess mutters while struggling to hold Tromos back from the gore. "It's not impossible."

Georgie inspects the puddle with a stick, much as I had done earlier.

Lady Jane turns away but almost immediately cries out.

"Good heavens! What is on that rock? Is that a clump of…" She draws back, pointing her finger. "It's hair!"

I steady her on the slippery pebbles. "Yes. He must've hit his head. Another reason I expected to find a corpse nearby."

Lady Jane continues to stare at the sticky mess smeared on the nearby stone. "And you—you fished this out of *there*, didn't you?"

I let go of her and glance away, feeling a bit ashamed of such callous behavior on my part. "Well, yes. I—I had to… to ascertain whether he was likely to be alive or dead."

"Ugh." She covers her lurching throat.

"Don't be missish, Jane. It had to be done." Georgie straightens and tosses away her stick "How could he have walked away having lost this much blood?" She peers up and down the beach, as if there must be a dead man strolling nearby.

"Ahem." Miss Stranje stares sternly at each of us in turn. "The first rule of a proper investigation is…?"

Georgie answers like the prize student she is. "Do not rely upon assumptions. Take stock of the facts and proceed from there."

"Correct." Miss Stranje studies each of us, making certain we're attending properly. "However, unlikely, there are stories of people surviving massive wounds and extensive blood loss such as this. Our own Lord Ravencross for one. Gabriel was gravely wounded and survived. His brother Lucien was assumed dead for the very reason you cite. Too great a blood loss. I attended his funeral. And we all know how that turned out."

Tess who acknowledges this truth with a grim sniff. "Ghost."

"Precisely. Which is why we must evaluate based on facts alone." Miss Stranje taps one finger against her palm. "We know this: the tide only rises this high during storms. We had no storm last night. Ergo, if he died, his body would still be lying right here. Unless...?"

"Unless he was not alone." I answer absently, my eyes straying to the surrounding area.

"Exactly." She nods to me. "We cannot rule out the idea that there may have been more than one spy. It is possible his cohort, or cohorts, carried him off or helped him escape in a skiff."

"I considered that possibility." I point out the lone footprint-like depression in the pebbles that I'd noticed earlier. "Other than this rather vague shape, I didn't see any other tracks or bloody footprints, although I'd only just begun to widen my search when you arrived."

"If that is his shoe—" The rising breeze whips Tess's long dark hair across her cheek. She flings it back and strokes the black fur behind Tromos's ears. "Let Tromos smell it. She can track him."

"Brilliant idea!" I retrieve the spy's shoe and hold out the shoe to her. "Do you think she can follow his scent even in this wind?"

"Of course." Tess snatches the shoe away from me.

"Her nose is much sharper than any hound. Wolves can smell even the faintest drop of blood from a furlong away. Why do you think that puddle over there has been driving her to madness?"

I nod to our guardian wolf. "My apologies to you both."

Tromos yips as if she understands, trots straight to the ghastly pool of blood, and laps at the edge of it.

"Ew," Lady Jane grimaces.

I wave Tromos away. "No! Stop her."

Tess shrugs. "What do you expect? Wolves like blood." She tugs the wolf dog back and holds the shoe to Tromos's nose, whispering something in ancient Welsh. Tromos's ears are alert, and she grunts as if she understands.

"Find!" Tess commands in a louder voice, undoubtedly said for our benefit because Tromos already has her nose to the ground sniffing back and forth across the stones and sand. She heads off at an angle toward the waves, abruptly turns left through a gully and halts at a divot in the stones. Pawing and sniffing at it quizzically, she lifts her head and turns to Tess as if she has a question.

It *might* be a footprint, misshapen to be sure. A stride's length ahead there appears to be another depression that also might be a footprint. I signal eagerly at Tess. "Have her follow the new scent. Someone else must've carried him."

Tess nods with a soft whistle, and the wolf dog eagerly lunges forward, zealously tracking our missing corpse. I'm in awe. There must be thousands of scents on this beach—seaweed, turtles, sand crabs, dead fish, live fish, bird-droppings—and yet, Tromos seems absolutely certain which direction to go.

Still angling east, she heads around a berm at the base of one of the smaller cliffs and picks up speed moving away from the water toward the upper shore. Her tail, previously held curled upward, suddenly wags excitedly, and she lopes toward a heaped-up pile of driftwood. She digs furiously beneath the sticks and branches, her big paws sending a spray of sand arcing through the air.

Something moves within the tangled pile of wood. I cannot tell if the gray vapors I see swirling through the branches are a mirage or vaporous beings.

I shake my head, trying to clear the vision. It isn't a ghost—yet it reminds me of death. Which might mean—

Oh no!

I race to catch up, shouting at Tromos, "Stop! Stay back."

The wolf dog is too enlivened by the hunt to heed my command, but she stops suddenly and growls.

I reach in to clasp her by the thick ruff of fur on her neck, but I'm startled by a human hand protruding from the sand.

"Back," I command. Tromos obeys, but our ever-vigilant protector issues a low warning and yips.

The hand twitches.

A gray wraith eddies above it.

Reflexively I jump back, afraid my eyes are playing tricks. A muffled groan comes from deeper beneath the wood. He's alive.

"Help!" I shout and wave frantically to the others. "Help!" I yell while flinging boughs of driftwood out of the way of our missing corpse.

No! Not a corpse.

This man is not dead. At least, not yet. He's a living, breathing soul buried under these crisscrossed branches of wood and a mound of sand. Someone intentionally hid his grave.

Tess is the first to reach us. She pulls Tromos back. "He's alive?"

"Yes." I wipe grit and silt away from a nose that barely protrudes from the sand. As soon as I brush the sand from his lashes, a pair of eyes blink anxiously at me.

"It's all right." I try to calm him, smoothing my fingers across his brows. "We'll have you out of here as soon as possible."

Tess tosses more wood out of the way, and sets to work across from me, digging him out.

"What in heaven's name!" Georgie falls to her knees beside me and immediately begins excavating his legs. "Someone buried this poor devil alive, didn't they?" She doesn't wait for an answer. "What sort of person would do such a thing?" She flings away a fist full of sand.

"I expect it's the sort who kidnap princes and shoot young women who get in their way." I carefully brush sand away from his eyes, nose, and mouth. "Don't be afraid." I try to soothe him. "You'll be all right. We'll have you out in no time." Except he's still afraid. Shivering gray terror blooms in the air around him like a nervous storm cloud.

Georgie sends me a raised eyebrow and a quick shake of the head, warning that he may yet succumb to his injuries. "It's a miracle he's still breathing."

"Daresay someone must've missed that little detail." Lady Jane brushes her skirts back and kneels between us, rapidly digging out his arm. "Either that or whoever did this thought him near enough to death that they buried him to finish the job. Which is it, mister?"

His eyes blink open and shut as if the sand might be stinging them, despite my being cautious. I brush the rest away with my shawl.

"Well," demands Jane. "Which is it? Were you unconscious, or did they bury you alive?"

The gloomy cloud lingering over him spikes with red. So, I have a rather strong suspicion he prefers to not reminisce about being stuffed into a hole, covered with sand, and left for dead.

"Good heavens!" Miss Stranje strides up, takes one look at our partially buried spy, and starts issuing orders. "Maya, we'll need my medical kit—the bag with bandages. Lady Jane, go back to the house with her. Tell Greaves we require his immediate assistance. Have him bring the stretcher, a blanket, and a footman, preferably Phillip, to help carry the patient. Find the stable lad and send him to fetch the doctor. As soon as you've dispatched them, a courier must be sent to Lord Castlereagh and Captain Grey informing them that we've captured a spy. Go!" She claps her hands, springing Maya and Lady Jane into action. "Hurry!" She then drops down and starts digging around the spy's head.

Georgiana vigorously scoops sand and dirt away from the spy's lower extremities. "Bone!" She points. "A tibia, I think. Looks as if his shin bone snapped right above the ankle. Lots of blood in the sand. Uh-oh. Here comes more," she yelps. "The sand must've applied pressure and slowed the bleeding." She yanks the fichu out from her collar and wads it up to press against the spurting wound. "If we free him before Maya brings back your bandages, it's quite possible he could bleed to death."

"Yes." Miss Stranje sits back from her work. "Luckily, judging by the amount of blood in the soil next to his head, this gash may not be as severe as we thought. Head wounds can be deceptive, even small ones bleed profusely at the start. Even so, you've a valid point Georgiana. The pressure and salt in the sand may have saved his life."

We all stop working. Georgie purses her lips. "But if we don't dig him out soon, the muck and rot in the sand may claim him with an infection."

"A chance we have to take." Our headmistress drags her finger around an area around his head. "I'll leave this section pressing against his head until they arrive with our bandages. We can dig the rest of him out but stop if you meet with more injuries."

Tess and I return to the task of freeing him. "I know you can hear us," I say while gently brushing the remaining grains of sand away from his cheeks and forehead. "Don't be afraid. We won't hurt you. We've sent for a doctor."

He blinks his eyes open and stares at me warily.

"*Parlez-vous Anglais?*" I ask, watching his expression intently.

"*Non.*"

He lies.

A twitch gives him away—that and the quivering gray ether surrounding him shrinks as if it wants to hide from me. I shake my head at Miss Stranje, pursing my lips in such a way that she understands he is lying.

She sighs loudly and sits back on her haunches. "Then he is of no use to us," she says this firmly, using remarkably distinct English. "Why should we go to all this trouble? He is nothing but a vile unscrupulous spy. We may as well cover him up again and leave him here to die." She plops a double handful of wet sand onto his chest.

What little color remained in our vile unscrupulous spy's face instantly pales to ashen white. They can all see that as well as I can. The thing the others probably cannot see is the sudden wash of mustard-colored fear that floods his shivering gray cloud.

Georgie gapes in disbelief at our headmistress, but before she can voice her objection, the man cries out.

"*Non!*" His eyes widen with fright. "*Non!* Do not. *S'il*

vous plaît."

Tess crosses her arms and slants her head. "It seems you *do* understand some English, *monsieur.*" Over her shoulder, Tromos growls dangerously.

"*Oui.*" He confesses quietly and turns a shamefaced gaze back to me.

"You serve the Iron Crown, do you not?" Tess leans over the Frenchman, allowing Tromos to push in and bare her teeth in his quaking face. Tromos is huge, black as night, with a wolf's wide ruff and fearsome yellow eyes. She is enough to make the heartiest of men quake. Especially one buried alive in the sand.

His answer was scarcely audible, but unmistakably, "*Oui.*"

Tess growls as fiercely as Tromos. "Ghost sent you, didn't he?"

Our spy moans. Perhaps out of pain, but more likely in fear of betraying a man to whom doing so means certain death. He squeezes his eyes tight before giving us a barely perceptible nod.

Tess leans closer. "Did you tell them which room is Lady Daneska's?"

His gaze darts from her and strains to find me, yammering, "*J'ai obéi aux ordres.*"

"Did you tell them?" Tess demands. Tromos snarls a ferocious warning. Clearly, at Tess's signal, the wolf dog would rip this poor man to pieces.

"Yes. He did," I answer calmly because I can see it in

his eyes. And because the atmosphere around him is spiking and fragmenting with fevered yellow panic. I can almost smell his urine leaking into the sand. "You are frightening him to death. Let the poor man rest. He's told us all he can."

For now.

"Has he?" Georgie resumes scooping away sand with her free hand but stops for a moment. "Is it possible he knows where they're keeping the Prince Regent?"

I turn, watching his face for signs of concealment.

He knows something.

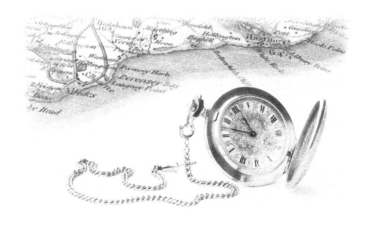

CHAPTER 5

FATALLY UNIMPORTANT

MISS STRANJE WALKS BESIDE ME as we follow the stretcher up the cliffs. To the west of us sits the mouth of a smugglers' cave that runs beneath Stranje house. In that cave is a tunnel connected to our cellars and dungeons and an entrance into the secret passages. Georgie leans out trying to peer into the dark narrow opening, not that anyone can see much at high tide. I'm sure she's hoping to catch a glimpse of a rowboat or perhaps even a puff of smoke from Mr. Sinclair's small steamship prototype. That would mean her fiancé, Lord Wyatt, might be aboard. This is the entrance he and Captain Grey prefer to use since it keeps their comings and goings secret.

"Mind your step, Georgiana!" Miss Stranje scolds. "The last thing I need is you taking a tumble. I've enough to do with patching up Lady Daneska and now this fellow."

Georgie's shoulders sag but she carries on obediently, marching up the switchbacks. Miss Stranje takes my hand and quietly asks, "How are you faring after the news about your family?"

"Better, now that I've had a chance to think it through," I say with budding confidence. "I have a plan."

"Do you now?" She sounds as if she is smiling, except her lips remain fixed.

"I do." I don't mean to gulp. I'm not nervous. Not at all. So, I press on as if I'd been gulp-less. "Ever since Alice's betrayal, you've been short a housemaid, have you not?"

She doesn't say anything. There is no sound except our steady footfalls crunching against the gravel on the path. Finally, she lifts her chin and says, "Yes, but what has that to do with you?"

"Well, I would like to apply for the position."

Her feet stop suddenly, and she lets go of my hand. "Housemaid?"

I dare not meet her gaze for I can already feel the stern disapproving look she is casting upon me. My lips feel unaccountably parched.

"I will not accept your charity." Even to me my protest

sounds like the peep of a motherless chick. "Ahem," I clear out the squeakiness, and straighten my back, fighting for a tone that lands somewhere between frank and mature. "I am alone now. And I must find my way in the world. You need a housemaid and I need employment."

"Hmm." At least, she did not say *no*. Except her eyes harden and turn beady and cold like a hawk staring down a white mouse. "Hmm," she says again, and my throat begins to tighten.

She walks on, and I scamper up beside her. "Peggy and Cook can teach me how to go on as a servant. Rest assured, I shall attend to the duties diligently. And I can still keep up my studies. I shan't be a bother. Peggy is getting on in age—you know how her joints pain her. She could use the help."

"I am well aware of Peggy's condition." Miss Stranje turns sharpish on me, bestowing a brief glare upon me, and then she continues walking. "If you must know, I have already interviewed two young women for the post."

"Oh." My stomach sinks and seems to thump along behind me in the gravel. I try to swallow, except there's no moisture left in my mouth. "I see."

We trudge along in silence. If you can call me dragging my feet along with my thudding heart *silent*. Not to mention my lamenting soul—which seems to me obscenely loud. So loud that even though Maya is two switchbacks ahead of us, she leans out and looks back at me as if my inner weeping echoes from the clifftops.

"However, if you are looking for employment..." Miss Stranje interrupts my thoughts cheerily, just as if she hasn't dashed to pieces my plans of becoming her housemaid. I stumble and she clasps my arm.

"Well... yes, I *was*."

"How very fortuitous. I happen to be looking for someone to fill a position at our school. A position for which you are far more qualified."

Luckily, there is no one behind us because I stop walking. Her countenance shimmers exactly as it does when she is laughing. Except she isn't—at least, not outwardly.

"What position?" I ask skeptically.

"It is a matter of some urgency and involves the exchange of sensitive information. Which is another way of saying I must rely upon your complete discretion."

"You have it." I nod vigorously. "Always." And even though she already knows this, I watch her reaction closely. She is not laughing. There's not even the hint of a smile, and yet, something is definitely setting her energy flickering. I narrow my gaze. "Go on."

"Very well." Her pace quickens. "This incident today proves beyond a shadow of a doubt that our situation here at Stranje House has grown even more perilous. It is incumbent upon me to hire an assistant whose duties will include remaining alert to any security breaches. I require a protector of sorts for Madame Cho, and myself, as well as you and your fellow students—a security advisor, if you will. This person must have the ability to pay keen attention to details, details that may seem insignificant to others but have a bearing on our safety. She will counsel me regarding anything, *anything at all*, that signifies an enemy may be approaching or infiltrating our perimeter. My security advisor must also be skilled at interviewing suspects and have the ability to ferret out reliable information despite a subject's unwillingness to divulge the truth. In short, this person must be a stalwart guardian of our objectives and serve as a protector for all the residents at Stranje House."

I stare at her.

She is serious.

Or pretending to be.

If I were the sort of impetuous girl who stamps her foot, I would do so at this very moment. "You know perfectly well that I already do those things. *All of them.*"

"Hmm." She blinks, feigning surprise. "So, you do." She turns and strides up the path. "Then I suppose it is high time I began paying you for your services. Shall we meet later to negotiate your salary? Shall we say in an hour or two, depending upon how long it takes me to patch up this unfortunate spy and keep him from dying before the doctor arrives."

"Hmm." I mimic her stern secretive manner and march up the path at her side.

She may *think* this is a clever trick to foist charity upon me. But the fact of the matter is, she truly does need a security advisor. Today proves it, as do dozens of recent incidents. So, I will take this quasi-position she is offering. Furthermore, I intend to earn every penny she pays me, and then some. I will make it my mission in life to keep everyone at Stranje House safe.

"I accept," I announce to her and the world rather louder than I'd intended.

"Delighted to hear it." She shakes the dust from her skirts as we step up over the final rise at the top of the cliffs. Her smug delight withers too quickly. Something in the distance wipes the half smile from her lips. "What is he doing here?"

The last person in the world I expect to see walking across the grassy plateau toward us is Mr. Quentin Chadwick. Yet this is no mirage or trickery from my eyes. He is still some distance from us, yet his confident stride is unmistakable.

Not only that, but Mr. Chadwick radiates an unusually expansive purple ether, spun of noble decency and vibrant intelligence. There is a tranquility about him that defies description. I credit this to his having had too happy a childhood.

Far too happy to suit me.

How can I truly love a man who isn't brooding and wounded? How can a man who has known so little of the evil that infests our world understand me?

Impossible.

More than that, *why* would such a man ever *love* me?

"This cannot be good." I mumble and look away,

dreading that I will have to explain about my family abandoning me and end our courtship.

"I agree," Miss Stranje says, and I worry for a minute that she can read my thoughts. "That's young Chadwick. Something must've gone awry. Captain Grey did not send word that he would be coming." Her concern instantly bites into the air.

The closer Quinton gets, the more that rosy pink swirls through his purple mantle. Even from this distance I can feel his warm gaze upon me. "Although," I comment offhandedly, "he does not appear to be distressed." No need to mention the amorous pink frothing through his countenance.

"You can tell that from here?"

"Yes."

"Remarkable." She pats my shoulder. "You will make an excellent security advisor."

He stops beside Georgie and Tess, probably asking about the man Phillip and Greaves are carrying on the litter. I brush a gnat away from my ear. "He appears to be excited now."

Miss Stranje chuckles. "Yes. Even I can see that."

He sprints toward us, white light flashing within his gleaming purple. I try not to smile, but it is hard. He reminds me so much of a beautiful colt, blithely galloping toward us.

Strong. Joyful. Untroubled.

Hat in hand, his brown hair catches on rays of

sunshine. If I were someone else, I might run to meet him and let him sweep me up in his arms and gaily whirl me around.

Ah, but I am not someone else. I am me—*Seraphina the terrible*. There is too much brokenness hidden in my soul to indulge in such frivolity.

Miss Stranje picks up her pace, and I stay close to her. He leans forward when we meet, bowing I suppose. Either that or catching his breath.

Oh yes, he is bowing. First to her, then to me.

So very proper.

I do so wish his cheeks would not flush so brightly when he grins at me. Mine tend to follow suit. It's not my fault. *Empathetic blushing*—that's all it is. I study the grass at my feet waiting for my stupid cheeks to stop burning.

"Miss Stranje!" he exclaims. "You've caught a spy." I admit I am quite fond of his voice. Anyone would be. The tone is a marvel. He makes everything sound jubilant, as if he magically infuses each word with blue skies. "Captain Grey and the Minister of Foreign Affairs will be extremely pleased to hear of this."

Miss Stranje nods at his praise. "Lady Jane sent word to them by courier, but our prisoner is injured rather badly. Even if he survives, he may not be able to tell us much. We shall soon see."

Her manner shifts abruptly. Although still cordial, she tilts her head, and her eyes narrow at him. "As delighted as we are to see you Mr. Chadwick, I must ask, what brings you here?"

"Oh, yes. *That.*" He glances nervously in my direction and then stands very straight. "I've had my first assignment, you see."

"Have you now?" her shoulders stiffen. A flurry of questions flit anxiously around her. They are like ripe limes of curiosity bubbling in the air above her. Instead of asking any of these biting questions, she calmly congratulates him. "I am impressed, young man. You must've run through your training very quickly."

"Quickly? Er, sadly, no." He winces and glances away before explaining. "My education still lacks a great deal. This assignment owes nothing to my having excelled. But rather it is a case of dire necessity."

Her lips press tight.

"Go on," I urge.

"Yes, yes, of course." The rosy pink fades entirely and his purple darkens. He hesitates for a moment, turning his hat over and over in his hands before plunking it back on his head. "The long and short of it is we've run out of leads."

Miss Stranje draws a deep breath and waits for him to continue.

"Ghost and Prince George seem to have vanished without a trace. Lord Castlereagh's contacts on the continent have not seen or heard so much as a whisper of their whereabouts. Captain Grey's men have not yet been able to even locate where they docked, much less their current location. The Foreign Minister is at his wits end. So, they came up with a plan."

"A plan," I ask, wariness causing my stomach to tense. I glance up and see the same worry lacing his luminous purple with dampening strands of black funeral crape.

"They need someone to infiltrate the Iron Crown—a man to pose as a traitor." His voice cracks slightly. "The scheme requires a fellow the Iron Crown won't recognize. As luck would have it, my French is the boot that fits. I'm fairly fluent, you see."

Miss Stranje nods, holding her breath now. Her bright green questions have all shriveled to dust.

Mr. Chadwick whips his hat off again and fiddles with the brim. "The traitor has to be someone who knows French well enough to understand what he's overhearing. Naturally, Lord Wyatt would be ideal, except he is too well-known in the enemy camp. So, you see, the assignment fell to me by default."

"No, Mr. Chadwick. That is not so." Miss Stranje hardens into a golden saint, radiant in the sunlight. Her back locks in as straight as any battlement, and her voice, although gentle, is immutable. "I know Captain Grey very well. He does not do anything by default. It is not his way. He has confidence in you, otherwise, even if you were the last French speaking man in England, he would not have sent you."

"No, I suppose not." He swallows and faces her squarely, setting his hat firmly back on his head. "I am here today because he gave me leave to inform you of the plan and to explain the situation to my parents, in case they hear of my supposed treachery and mistakenly think it is true. Also..." He glances at me. "To make my farewells. In case, well... in case..."

In case he gets killed.

No, no, no! People like him do not die.

Do they?

The grass and trees suddenly grow dull and blurry. I can't seem to see them at all. A cloud must've covered the sun. I realize he is staring at me, and I am murmuring, "No," out loud.

Miss Stranje is saying something.

"In case," she repeats, this time loud enough to startle the sun into coming out again. "In the unlikely event that you need to be away a trifle longer than expected."

"Just so," he says cheerily, as if they aren't talking in cloaked terms about him dying.

"Very well then." She claps Mr. Chadwick on the arm. "Now, I'm afraid I must leave you and attend to our wounded patient. Miss Wyndham, you may have a quarter hour, no longer. I require your assistance."

"Wait." Quentin stops her. "Before you go. Would you allow me to question the spy? Perhaps I might try questioning him in French—"

"Yes, of course, you may." She turns back briefly. "However, I want my security advisor to interview him first."

"Your security advisor?" He steps back blinking. "And this advisor of yours, does he speak French?"

"Yes. Not only that, but my advisor is an expert inter-rogator, which is why she must question the spy before anyone else inadvertently muddies the waters."

"Splendid!" He rubs his palms together eagerly. "I would very much like to observe your expert at work. No doubt, I shall learn a trick or two."

"I've no objection, so long as you obtain her permission first."

"And this security advisor of yours, where would I find—"

Not waiting to answer, Miss Stranje waves to him over her shoulder and strides toward the house.

"Ohhh." He turns to me with a sheepish grin. "It's you, isn't it? I should've known. I remember your uncanny abil-ity to know whether someone is telling the truth."

We stroll amiably through the grassy field. "She of-fered me the position, and since I find myself in need of employment." I shrug, not wanting to explain more. "I de-cided to accept."

"In need of employment? I don't understand. What of your parents?"

I shrug. "Those clouds appear to be building toward a storm, perhaps we ought to return to the house."

Mr. Chadwick is too curious by half. The only son of a perfect family, it is no wonder he cannot let it go, and persists in asking, "If you are in need, can you not appeal to them?"

I don't expect you to understand. "No."

"I fail to see why not. It is one thing to do covert errands for Miss Stranje. It is altogether another matter to enter into her employment. Surely your parents cannot wish to have their daughter go into service. It just isn't done. Perhaps if you wrote to them?"

May as well tell him and have done with it. Lengthening my stride, I state the facts as succinctly as possible. "If you must know, Mr. Chadwick, my parents have abandoned me."

"What? How can it be?" He stops short and grasps my arm. "Why?"

"Salient questions, to be sure. Except I have no answers for you." I shake free of his grip. "I only know that without sending word, they seem to have emigrated to America and left me in a rather awkward and penniless state."

"There must be some mistake." He frowns and shakes his head. Disbelief does not sit easily on his features. "Surely, they will send for you?"

"Doubtful."

"It must be owing to a mishap of some sort. Yes, that's it, a lost letter or a delay in the mails. That sort of thing."

He has no way of comprehending this.

I've met his parents; they are kind, levelheaded, and brave. Most assuredly not the sort who would run away from their son or daughter.

"No, Mr. Chadwick. It is not *that* sort of thing. They will not send for me. There is no delayed letter coming to my rescue. There you have it—a *fait accompli*. So, you see, I am no longer suitable for anything other than a lifetime in service."

"Nonsense!" He sputters and kicks at the grass. "You are worth a great deal more than any of those flibbertigibbet debutantes on the marriage mart. A *great deal* more." Scarlet blooms through his purple aura. He mutters something I cannot hear and whips off his hat. "Look here, Miss Wyndham. Were it not for this wretched assignment I would offer for you right here on the spot."

"No, no, you've misunderstood me, Mr. Chadwick," I back away. "You needn't say such things. Please, do not suppose I told you this to solicit a proposal. Nothing could be further from the truth. I merely thought you ought to be informed." I cannot bear to look at him while I explain the rest. Nevertheless, it must be said. The facts must be laid bare. "I only tell you this so that you might place your future, um..." I rub my forehead trying to find the right words. "Erm, so you will place your future *expectations* elsewhere. What I mean to say is, *if* you harbor any intentions in my direction—" I cover my face with my hands. "Dash it all! This is horribly embarrassing."

"You've nothing to be embarrassed about." He brushes my hands away and lifts my chin. "I'm sorry your family dealt with you so poorly. It was wrong of them. Very wrong. And truth be told, I do have intentions in your direction. You must know that. And this changes nothing."

"It does." Throwing my hands wide, I ask, "Don't you see? It changes everything. I have no family connections. No dowry. No—"

"It changes nothing. Nothing at all. I have no need of a dowry. You are my brilliant Miss Wyndham, the brightest diamond in the kingdom. To be frank, you are of greater worth to me than any dowry, no matter how lavish it might be—"

"Stop." I shake my head. My cheeks burn with heat. I cannot help but like him quite well for spouting such nonsense.

The brightest diamond in the kingdom.

I'm quite sure it is complete balderdash, and yet I shall treasure those words until the day they lay me in the ground.

He clasps both of my hands in his. "If my situation were any different, if this mission were not so extraordinarily crucial, I would offer for you at once." He gently toys with my fingers, stroking them with far too much familiarity. "Upon my return, Sera—"

"No, please. You mustn't say anything more." Tears of embarrassment sizzle down my cheeks. "This is all very kind—"

"Kindness has nothing to do with it." He holds my hands tighter and tugs me closer. Then as if remembering the proprieties, he lets go but does not step back. Instead, he is so close his words are like a soft breath on my cheek. "Look here, Miss Wyndham, now that nothing is hidden between us. I mean to request something of you."

Nothing hidden?

Au contraire. There are a great many things hidden between us. Things that I daresay would terrify you.

He misses the apprehension on my face. He is too busy glancing furtively at Stranje House in the distance, as if he expects someone to come running in our direction.

"What request?" I choke out in a husky whisper.

He swallows hard and glances at the storm in the distance before facing me. "Er, you see, given the fact that I might conceivably be away from England somewhat longer than expected..."

He's hedging around it again–his impending doom.

"Meaning you might die."

"Well, yes. I wouldn't have put it quite so bluntly, but in light of that possibility..." He whips his hat off and fiddles with the brim. All the while, I am wishing he was playing with my fingers again instead.

"If it wouldn't be too presumptuous of me to ask," he begins. "Might I impose upon you to... to have the honor of–" He shakes his head and rakes a hand through his bronze curls. "No, that sounds all wrong. Allow me to rephrase. Perhaps *permission* is the appropriate word."

"Appropriate word for what?"

He lifts his chin, a mixture of wildly vibrant colors swirl around him. "May I have permission to kiss you farewell? One brief kiss, that's all I ask. I know it is highly improper, but under the circumstances..." He rattles on, jumbling my emotions, weaving them into an indecipherable tangle.

The air around him drifts towards me in such beguiling caresses that I am sorely tempted to grab him by the ears and plant my lips on his.

He fidgets with his wretched hat. "I assure you my intentions are wholly honorable and—"

"I rather think at this point, considering the fact that I have not run away screaming, you might stop asking, and simply do it."

He stares at me, as if I slapped him instead of granting him permission. "Oh."

Oh. Indeed.

His whirlwind of too many colors instantly bursts. Clearly, I have put a damper on whatever ardor he may have felt.

Except, no...

His cheeks flush, and outwardly a deep rose bursts in the air between us. He tosses his hat to the ground and wraps his arms around me, holding me so close I can scarcely breathe. Gazing intently at my mouth he whispers huskily, "I confess, I have never done this before."

Breathe.

Except, I can't.

Instead, I hold perfectly still—*waiting.*

His arms relax, ever so slightly, and the air around us

deepens to a rich wine. Now I breathe, drinking it in, savoring the way it flows over us and around us, a waterfall of spellbinding sensations.

"Nor have I." The words barely escape before he covers my lips with his.

Kissing is wondrous.

If only there was some way to bury myself in its glorious warmth forever. I close my eyes. Too soon, he lets go. His sharp intake of breath startles me. Kissing him made me feel as if I was pleasantly melting. Small wonder—I open my eyes to discover Quentin Chadwick is blazing like a bonfire. I blink, trying to make sense of it.

Is he angry?

Confused, I ask, "Did you not like it?"

His head tilts oddly. He says nothing but seizes me and, *praise heaven*, he kisses me again.

He must've liked it.

Yes, yes, I'm quite sure now. He covers my mouth as if he is a starving man and I am a feast. His one kiss turns into two and then into ten. I grow more and more intoxicated with each one and am no longer certain I can stand on my own.

"Ahem."

A foggy portion of my brain asks, *Who said that?*

"Ahem!"

Georgie.

Uh-oh! A rush of embarrassment restores feeling to my limbs and mortification to my cheeks. Mr. Chadwick and

I reluctantly ease apart.

A teasing smirk dances across Georgie's features. At least she has the good grace to pretend she's looking at the ocean. "Miss Stranje sent me to collect you. The spy may not survive the hour. You must come straightway and question him."

Our blissful haze explodes into a million glittering shards, and I break into a run. Georgie and Quentin follow hard on my heels. But I must race death, and that makes me faster than anyone expects.

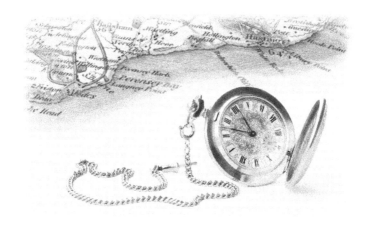

CHAPTER 6

THE TROUBLE WITH LIES

WE DASH INTO THE HOUSE through the side door. Greaves stands at the foot of the staircase, somber and butler-stiff, pointing grimly up at the second floor.

If we are too late, how shall I ever forgive myself?

We thunder up the stairs and dash down the hallway. *I should not have dallied so long with Quentin.* Skidding into the bedroom, I expect death to have already claimed our spy, except it has not. The man's light remains, albeit weak and flickering like a guttering candle. "He's alive." I stoop to catch my breath.

"Barely." Miss Stranje takes my arm and guides me forward. "Find out what you can."

She doesn't see the other presences in the room. I balk, but then bolster my courage and let her tug me forward. I should be used to such things by now. Three minions of hell are visible to me. And two beings of light are also there, although I cannot see them. I only sense their presence. Miss Stranje's jaw is clenched tight, and her expression is so fierce, it is as if she's charging into battle. It makes me wonder if she senses them. She is wise to be on guard, considering the war waging over this man's soul and the fearsome unseen beings inhabiting this room.

The dying man's eyes dart about as if he, too, sees the visitors hovering about, ready to take possession of his soul. Sadness claws at my heart for him. This spy is not really a spy at all. His clothing and tattoos are the trappings of a lowly sailor, a hapless pawn sent on an assignment for which he was woefully ill-equipped.

Poor fellow.

If only I had Maya's ability to calm fears with her voice, her gift of persuasion. We need her now. "Where is Maya?"

Miss Stranje, grim as a raven in a cemetery, shakes her head. "Lady Daneska awoke in pain. She and Tess are tending her."

Hoping someone could help him before it's too late, I ask, "Any word from the doctor?"

"Not yet." Her guarded expression tells me that even if

he arrives within the hour, it will be too late. "You must question him now."

"I understand." I struggle to slow my galloping pulse and pull a chair to his bedside to sit. I lower my voice to a gentle whisper. "Do not be afraid. Those you served in this life can no longer hurt you."

The demons rattle the air in a flurry of anger. The sailor's eyes widen in terror. Even though no one else seems to notice, he must feel their presence. Does he not sense the other beings? I cannot quite fully see them either, save for a faint glowing outline now and then. I may not see them, but I certainly feel them. They stand nearby radiating power, solemnly waiting, yet he never even glances in that direction, nor does he plead for their help.

I do, though. I stare directly at them, straining to see, glimpsing only the slenderest shimmer of light. Not that it matters, I *know* they are there.

Do something, I silently plead. *Please.*

They move closer to me.

Not me. Help him! This poor dying sailor is the one who needs help.

Please.

They seem to look at him more intently as if waiting for some sort of acknowledgment from him. Whereas the dark ones pester him mercilessly, poking at him, scoffing at my attempts to help. I grit my teeth and swing my arm in a feeble attempt to brush his evil tormentors away. They merely dart out of my reach.

"Get on with it." Miss Stranje says and frowns sternly at me.

In French, I say to the man, "Quickly, *monsieur*. I cannot protect you unless you unburden yourself. *Allez, dis-moi la vérité*. Tell me the truth. Where have your masters hidden Prince George?"

Fear nearly quenches what little remains of his fading life force. I rest my hand lightly over his heart, hoping to lend him warmth and maybe even a morsel of comfort. He draws in a weak breath, and life seems to flow back into his lungs. A tentative trickle, but at least it is something. He exhales, and there is a hint of gratitude on his lips.

I urge him again. "*Mon ami*, you have very little time left. *S'il vous plaît*, please tell me where in France they are hiding?"

"*France?*" He squints at me and tilts his head slightly. That small gesture triggers a wince and a ragged gulp for air. "*Non—*" Before he can speak, the dark ones *whoosh* past me and bend close to his ears, muttering.

Leave him be, I say in a nearly silent command.

The demonic creatures pay me little heed. A hiss, a sneer, and they turn back to their victim. I try to shoo them away, except their vaporous forms seem to move around my arm as if it is simply a boulder in their stream. So, I grasp his hand and plead loud enough to be heard over their vicious chatter, "Not France? Then where?"

Miss Stranje leans in beside me and demands sharply, "Antwerp! Are they in Antwerp?"

The sailor's eyes flash to her.

Quinton stands at her shoulder and pushes closer. "We considered the Netherlands. Try that?"

The man's energy is draining fast. A piercing cold seems to wash through him. My fingers whiten trying to fight off the frigid chill enveloping him. I can no longer hold back death. I withdraw my hand and glare at the shadowy beings gobbling at this unfortunate man's ears, nattering like hungry cockroaches at midnight.

"Muid"—the sailor gasps, his eyes blinking and watering in desperation—"M-den."

"What did he say?" Quinton demands. "Did he say murder?"

"No." Georgie stands on the other side of the bed. "I believe he's trying to tell us the name of a port."

With a garbled rasp, the sailor stammers, "M-Muiden."

One last lie.

The demons withdraw, satisfied, and their incessant chattering stops.

Sneering vultures.

As soon as the sailor finishes speaking, his eyes flash open in a white-hot jolt of pain. He arches—pain too massive, too sharp, too intense to allow even a scream, then he collapses with a wheeze.

It is over.

Stillness blankets him as surely as will the dirt of his grave. I step back, turning away, not wanting to witness what I suspect will happen next.

Everyone else seems oblivious to the turmoil in the room. They do not sense his spirit being carried away captive into darkness. How fortunate for them. I close my eyes and all but cover my ears to blot out his terror.

Think of other things. Anything else.

Sunrises over the sea.

Kisses.

I peek at Quentin, wishing he understood, wishing he would hold me until it passes. He smiles at me, a frown flickers through his features as if he recognizes my distress. Just then I turn and look back at the dead man.

The room is suddenly still, empty of demons and lost souls.

I realize I've been holding my breath, and let it go. The worst is over. Breathe. I turn back to Quentin. Except now he is Mr. Chadwick again. His noble purple is in full bloom as he dives into a discussion of strategies with Miss Stranje and Georgie. I step back, leaning against the wall for support.

He smacks his fist against his other hand. "Captain Grey suspected they might have taken the Prince Regent to a port north of France. We sent a man to investigate in Amsterdam, but we didn't even consider Muiden. Why would we? It's little more than a fishing harbor. This changes everything."

"Does it? I wonder." Miss Stranje rubs the back of her neck. "It seems odd to me. One would think France the safest place for Napoleon to hide a kidnapped monarch. I should think carting the Prince through the Netherlands would make it rather difficult to keep their location secret. There are still so many nobles loyal to William I in that region."

"True enough, in the past." Mr. Chadwick argues. "Now, though, Napoleon maintains firm control of that region. Aside from that, Muiden is so small they may have slipped in unnoticed."

Georgie taps her finger on the bureau, thinking aloud. "Napoleon's grip on middle Europe is stronger than ever, and yet no one has reported seeing him in the last few weeks. Why? I should think he would be parading around as if he's invincible? Especially since he still has our allies and Wellington's troops hemmed in at the Russian border. If he has the Prince Regent, why hide at all?"

"What's ado?" Lady Jane bursts into the room and gapes at the spy on the bed. "Oh. I see. The spy has expired."

Expired? I blink, stunned as always by Lady Jane's pragmatic view of the world. *What a tame way to describe the rawness of death.*

She turns to each of us and lands on me. "What did you learn?"

I look down, staring at the worn carpet beneath my feet. Thankfully Georgie answers for me, and the four of them continue their debate. I remain mum edging quietly toward the door.

"Sera!" Miss Stranje wheels on me. "What's vexing

you? You're crossing and uncrossing your arms, and I daresay you're on the verge of gnawing your knuckles raw."

I snatch my hand away from my mouth and whisk it behind my back. "I hadn't realized."

"Obviously not. You were frowning at the floor as if you were trying to puzzle out a knotty mathematical equation."

If only this quandary were as straightforward as a math problem.

"Out with it," she demands.

I cannot possibly tell her about the dark shadowy beings that lurked around her so-called spy. Nor can I tell her about their vicious whispering in his ear. Nor how they gloated after he uttered his last deceitful words, their triumph at his demise.

"Was he lying?" It is my stern headmistress who crosses her arms now, impatience shooting orange daggers at me.

I cannot bring myself to look directly at her. So, I duck my head, avoiding her whiffs of irritation. "Not entirely."

"*Not entirely*—but in part." She adopts her customary badger-like shrewdness. "Which part?"

I shrug. "I do not think he was being honest about the port."

"What makes you say that?" Quentin peers hard at me. "What signs of deception did you see? I observed him as closely as I could and saw no indication that he was lying. In point of fact, I felt certain you had wrested the truth out of him—a deathbed confession."

I bite my lip. All four of them wait expectantly, staring at me. Now, I must lie. I detest lies. Yet I cannot tell them the truth. Mentioning demons would sound mad. Insane. They would send me away to an asylum or lock me away in the dungeon and throw away the key.

Miss Stranje taught us that if we find ourselves in a position where we have no choice but to prevaricate, we ought to weave our story as close to the truth as possible.

Lie.

Only after what I just witnessed, how can I? It turns my stomach to even consider it. Instead, I hunt for the truth that I can tell. "He exhibited a few small indications."

What had I seen?

I close my eyes and recall the dead man's face during those last moments. "He avoided looking at me. When he tried to answer, his left eye twitched faintly, his skin color shifted slightly, and the pulse in his neck quickened. There were a few more subtle indications. Admittedly none of these are conclusive, and they were hardly noticeable, but—"

"But *you* noticed." Mr. Chadwick draws back, rubbing his chin, his purple aura draws inward, shrinking and losing some of its radiance. He's confused, I suspect he is wondering how he missed those details. They were there, each one.

He did miss them.

Nevertheless, I don't want him to feel bad. "I had the advantage of a closer view of the sailor."

"Spy," Mr. Chadwick quietly corrects, still not looking as if my explanation has mollified him. "I suppose. I tried to watch him from over your shoulder."

"I'm sure you would've noticed if you'd had a closer vantage point." I try to keep the relief out of my voice. It's nearly impossible. I'm so happy that I needn't mention beings that no one else can see.

Breathing easier, I gather the courage to explain, "Those indications gave me serious doubts that some parts of his confession were genuine. I'm sure you noted that he accidentally exposed his confusion when I asked where they were holding the Prince in France. Clearly, they are not there. That much seemed sincere. After that..."

I clamp my lips tight recalling the way those spiteful creatures had crowed to each other after they made him tell us Ghost and Napoleon made port in the Netherlands. That's how I know without a doubt that Muiden is NOT where they are hiding Prince George.

If not there, then where...

Clues begin knitting together in my mind. Ragged bits and pieces take on elusive importance. The sailor's reaction when I mentioned France—why should that surprise him? Unless...

Unless he thought I knew where they were.

And what of the ease with which whoever buried him escaped the beach without a trace. There should have been signs, evidence that someone else had been there. Not only that, a man put ashore and stationed at a lookout post would surely have bought supplies with him.

I rush back to his corpse and search the bedding beside him. Failing to turn up anything, I run my fingers around his cloth belt, hunting for something that might be concealed in it.

Nothing.

Turning to the others, I ask, "Did anyone find his haversack? Or any small pouch hanging from his sash or buried in the sand beside him? A satchel? A kerchief holding possessions? Anything?"

"Nothing of the sort." Miss Stranje turns to Georgie. "What of you, Miss Fitzwilliam? You were digging out his legs."

"I didn't run across anything other than what you see here." Georgie grimaces at the dead man and shivers. "Whoever buried him must've taken his belongings with them."

"I suppose." I rub my palms, trying to brush off the scent of death. Surely he would have stowed certain items for the trip, hidden them on his person as sailors are wont to do—a flask, a pipe, a morsel of dried meat—the accouterments of a man away from his moorings.

Unless...

My stomach twists uncomfortably as these new clues burrow into the frayed edges of my mind. I swallow, except I can't. My mouth has gone dry. I think I know where Ghost and Napoleon might be, and it is a most unsettling prospect. My heart pounds madly against my chest. If I were to propose such an idea, they would all scoff at me, or worse, lose confidence in me entirely.

I shake my head at the far-fetched notion. I must be mistaken. *Not even Napoleon would be so daring.*

Without solid quantifiable proof, this conjecture is nothing but a wild hare—the musings of a madwoman. If only this wild hare wasn't beginning to feel like a monstrous truth.

For a split-second, a second that seems to explode and suck up all the air in the room, I consider telling Miss Stranje the whole of it. Risking everything. Endangering my last and only place in this woefully tangible world.

"Hmm," she stares at me, squinty-eyed and suspicious. "Why do I have the feeling you are not telling me something?"

She is annoyingly perceptive.

"It's nothing." I clamp my lips between my teeth.

On the other hand, it might be something. A terrifying *something.*

But no!

I haven't a speck of physical evidence. I dare not say anything until I have investigated and found tangible proof. I breathe in steadily and evenly, banishing the shakiness in my legs. I stand straight and erect, daring to meet her gaze. "Nothing of substance."

Yet.

Tonight, however, I will sneak out and find out if these are merely fanciful theories or...

A very real nightmare.

I hurry from the room, and Quentin follows me into the hallway. "Wait." He grasps my hand. "That was impressive—the way you saw through a dying man's lies."

I stare at my fingers wrapped in Quentin Chadwick's palm. He has lovely big hands. I like the warmth of them when he holds mine. He's so full of life; I cannot help but smile.

He smiles back. "I will leave shortly and ride with all haste back to London. Captain Grey and Lord Castlereagh need to know that Prince George was not taken to France. They'll want to begin searching in Muiden immediately."

"No, don't," I blurt. "That is, er, what I mean to say is, must you rush off? As I said, I don't believe they're in the Netherlands either. In fact, I'm quite certain of it. Napoleon was wounded, and so was Ghost. It's possible they made port elsewhere, somewhere closer at hand. Can you not give me just one day to find out more?"

"That spy's dying words are our first lead after two weeks of utter frustration. It is the first and only hint we've had at where they *might* be. Not only that, it could mean I don't need to go to France and ingratiate myself into the Iron Crown." He stares hard at me. When I don't immediately agree, he lets my fingers slip from his grasp. "But you know something more, don't you?"

I look down instead of answering, at hands that are all alone in this world, at fingers that must remain strong.

"Sera, what are you not telling me?"

I wet my lips and step back. "I have a theory, that's all. If you will only give me a little time, I will find proof one way or the other." I hunger for his steadying touch and my hand drifts toward his, but I retract it and force my lips into a rigid attempt at a smile. "One day—that is all I ask. Grant me twenty-four hours and I will have more information for you to take to Captain Grey. Reliable information."

He hesitates. Strands of gray confusion muddy his aura, and his delectable mouth presses into a hard vexatious line.

I heave in a breath, fighting to accept his decision. "Do what you will. I need to return to the beach and search while it is yet daylight."

That is a partial lie. I will, indeed, search the beach again, but it is the darkness I truly need. He blinks. His eyes, ordinarily wide and bright, narrow at me. He knows I'm hiding something important. I turn away, fighting the urge to cover my face in shame.

I had to hedge.

No choice.

If I'd babbled to him about demons whispering in the sailor's ear, it would be a thousand times worse. If he were to hear that, he would look at me with an eye to putting a sack over my head and hauling me off to Bedlam.

No one looks kindly upon madness.

Certainly, never with love.

Usually, they look at me with soul-searing disgust.

Toward the end, my mother found a way to look right through me, as if I wasn't there at all. As if pretending I didn't exist would make it so. Perhaps that's what happened with my family. They pretended I wasn't alive so often that eventually, they simply forgot me entirely.

"Very well," Quinton says to my retreating back. "I'll visit my parents and return tomorrow. No doubt my father will return with me to do his magistrate duties and assist the coroner in the matter of the dead spy. Let us give this twenty-four hours and see what turns up. I don't suppose Britain will collapse in one day."

Let us hope not.

I pause, touching my fingers to the oak paneling in the hallway, grateful he is letting me escape. I can't turn around, or he might notice my turmoil.

"Thank you," I mumble, wishing I could tell him everything, all the unbelievable mad fantastical things I see—horrors and marvels alike.

Maybe I will.

He claims he wants to marry me. Shouldn't he know the truth about it all? If he is eventually going to run away in revulsion, wouldn't it be better if he does so now, rather than later when our hearts are more entwined?

I stop and turn around. But Mr. Chadwick has gone back into the dead man's bedroom to speak with Miss Stranje, and the door clicks shut.

CHAPTER 7

PUTTING THE PLAN INTO PLAY

THE AFTERNOON BRINGS with it cold grit in my shoes and salt spray chafing my lips and arms. The sun no longer warms the beach. Instead, she sits low in the sky, a hazy orange ball barely visible through the clouds. Wind whips cold fingers through my hair as I climb up the steep cliffs, making my way back to Stranje House.

When I finally reach the crest, I see Maya striding through the calf-high grass toward me. I try to brush out my skirts before greeting her, but it is futile. I'm sticky with salt and sand and parched as a baked fish.

"Miss Stranje sent me to fetch you. The dinner hour approaches." Then, as if anticipating my sorry state, Maya hands me a flask of water. "Did you find anything?"

"Nothing of much use." Tilting the jug to my lips, I gulp down several reviving sips and replace the cork. "Thank you. I scoured the beach and found a button that must've been torn from the sailor's trousers when he was dragged to his grave."

"A button?" she says, as if this is vastly interesting news. But I know that look, and the way she tilts her head as if she's listening to more than just my words. The air around Maya swirls with rich pomegranate and wild orange, yet these heated atmospheres are interwoven with contrasting blue. The most intriguing part is the way everything around her seems to vibrate, almost as if an invisible rhythm pulsates within her.

"Here." I show Maya the tarnished brass button. "It matches the others on his trousers. I also ran across a sizable leafy branch, still green, and freshly torn off a thorny gorse bush. This scrap of fabric was stuck on one of the thorns. It's cambric. Which means the thorn must've snagged on one of their shirts while whoever buried him used the bough to sweep away their footprints."

"Astonishing." Her eyes grow overly large and bright, dancing with humor. "Do you mean to say that you found proof the spy did not bury himself?"

I thrust the water jug back to her. "Amused, are you?"

"Mildly." Still smiling, she loops her arm through

mine and peers closely at me as we walk. "What *are* you searching for exactly? I do not think it is buttons or broken branches."

I shrug. "I'm not quite certain." It is not a lie. Not really. I hadn't actually expected to find much on the beach. Unfortunately, I cannot begin the more critical search until everyone at Stranje House is fast asleep.

"But you *are* looking for something." It is not a question, even though she expects an answer.

"I–I had hoped there might be something." I carefully avoid meeting her gaze. "Hadn't we better hurry back to the house? How fares Lady Daneska?"

"She will live, I think." Maya lets go of my arm, and we walk faster. "Her fever finally broke."

"That's a relief." Lady Daneska may be callous and excessively selfish, but I have no desire to see her suffer. "I'm glad she's finally recovering. Although, I doubt she'll be able to tell us anything useful."

"No? Why do you say that?" She squints hard at me while I silently curse my foolish tongue. It was a small slip, but with Maya, even a small slip is too much. There's no need to look at her. I feel her needling into my mind.

"I meant nothing by it." I try not to sound snappish. "It's just that Ghost did not return to France to hide Prince George. You may not have heard, but the sailor we found told us that much before he died."

"The spy, you mean. Yes, I heard."

"Well then, now you see. It is unlikely Lady Daneska

would have any idea where they've gone. How could she?"

Maya tilts her head sideways, frowning at me. "Sera!" she snaps. "You *are* hiding something." She says this as if she just caught a rat sneaking through the larder. "What is it?" She pokes my arm.

I stop, close my eyes for a moment and exhale loudly before turning to her. "You know perfectly well that I am *always* hiding. You have said so yourself at least a dozen times." And with that, I stride forward.

"True." She glides effortlessly along beside me. "But today is different. You are hiding more than usual."

"It has been a rather trying day." I number those trials in my head.

My parents abandoned me and left me penniless.

Mr. Chadwick kissed me.

And...

"I watched a man die," I say vehemently. As if *that* tops the list. Which it doesn't. That honor is held by my wretchedly unprovable premonition that Ghost, Napoleon, and their band of Iron Crown cutthroats may be encamped much closer than anyone imagines.

"That must've been awful for you." She sighs. "Very well. I will not press the matter today, but tomorrow is a different matter."

"*If* there is a tomorrow," I mutter.

"I heard that."

We walk in silence toward Stranje House. Wind ripples through the broad clifftop, robins whistle their evening overtures across the treetops, and crickets accompany them from hiding places in the tall grass.

Maya rests her hand lightly on my arm and interrupts this chaotic chorus. "Sera, you do know, do you not, that I will keep your secrets should you ever wish to confide in me?"

"Yes," I answer softly, brushing hair out of my eyes. If there is anyone in this whole wide wobbly world that I trust, it is Maya. Trouble is—my secrets are not ordinary—they're the kind that make people back away wearing nervous expressions.

"Ah." She nods and keeps pace with me. "I see."

"What do you mean?" I halt suddenly, nearly stumbling in a rabbit hole. "What do you see?"

"I *see* that you intend to keep hiding. I hear you running away." She smiles as if she already knows far too much. "I do not mind. We are sisters. I will listen whenever you are ready to come out into the sunshine."

"*Sunshine*," I mumble and begin walking again, kicking grass out of my way with every step. "I am *not* hiding."

Well, perhaps I am.

Except it isn't hiding, it's retreating to a place of safety deep inside. I am simply being prudent.

She doesn't answer, but I see her chuckling quietly and that preposterous aura of hers twirling merrily about.

"I'm not hiding."

ૐ ૒

I dare not talk to her the rest of the way home. I change my dress, wash up quickly to hurry down to dinner. It's a casual evening, and everyone else has already been seated. I apologize for being late and take my place in the empty chair.

It surprises me to find the doctor dining with us. For the first five minutes, there is nothing but the muffled *clinks* of silverware against the plates. The doctor clears his throat and punctures the silence. "May I say, this is a splendid repast, Miss Stranje. A delectable roast. Splendid. Simply splendid. Thank you for allowing me to stay the night. Of course, I would have willingly journeyed home were it not necessary for me to remain here until the coroner can arrive in the morning to investigate the death."

"Yes, of course. It is all a very complicated matter. What a comfort it is to have you here," she says all this without an ounce of the customary firmness in her voice. "Were it not for you, I would have no idea what to do."

I practically choke on my buttered peas. *She knows exactly what to do. Always. No matter what.*

"Nothing to concern yourself with, my dear lady." The doctor preens and sniffs haughtily. "It's a formality, that is all. All a matter of dotting the i's and crossing the t's. No need to worry. I've dealt with this sort of thing dozens of times. Nevertheless, I apologize for the inconvenience."

"Not at all, Doctor." Miss Stranje's smile is forced. His being here most certainly is *an inconvenience*. She dislikes any intrusion on our privacy. Even so, she remains the

KATHLEEN BALDWIN

epitome of graciousness. "We appreciate you attending to the matter."

He nods. "You mentioned the magistrate's son, young Chadwick, arrived here not long before that fellow di—" He glances around the table at the young ladies surrounding him, and jams a forkful of roasted pork and potatoes into his mouth. His Adam's apple bobs up and down as he thoughtfully chews and finally swallows uncomfortably. "Before he, uh, before the fellow stuck his spoon in the wall? Begging your pardon, Miss Stranje. Delicate ears and all." He nods at all of us.

"Think nothing of it, Doctor. My young ladies are not the missish sorts. In point of fact, it was our brave Miss Wyndham, here, who found the unfortunate fellow." She gestures to me far more flamboyantly than I deserve. "Poor man was lying on the beach, half buried in sand."

Half buried?

I lower my eyes to my plate and load my fork, wishing she hadn't mentioned me. If the doctor decides to question me, I'm not sure I have the capacity to spin lies today.

"Tragic." Miss Stranje shakes her head. "And quite frightening, when one thinks on it." Her hand flutters up and covers her open mouth. "Oh, Doctor! You don't suppose smugglers set upon him, do you? Or... God save us, *pirates?*" She gulps such a wide-eyed shaky breath that I almost believe for a split second our intrepid headmistress might actually be afraid.

Except I know better.

Not our headmistress.

There isn't a pirate on earth she'd be afraid to clash swords with.

Miss Stranje's inner workings are made of solid iron. I doubt she has a fearful bone in her body. She's merely making certain the doctor won't suspect we have anything to do with that sailor's death on our cliffs.

Shrewd.

The doctor succumbs to her ruse and straightens in his chair. "No need to fear, Miss Stranje. I'm certain it will all turn out to be an accident of some sort. And as for pirates or brigands—I shall be here sitting watch over the corpse all night. Not only that, but I'm sure there are plenty of footmen to protect you and the young ladies—not that it will be necessary, of course."

Plenty?

Lady Jane and Georgie exchange smirks.

One green footman and a rather elderly butler?

And neither of them would last two minutes fending off our enemies. Tess and Madame Cho would stand a far better chance. And of course, Miss Stranje. She would prime her pistols and defend us to the death against Ghost and his murderous band of cutthroats.

"What a great relief." She sighs with just enough mewing noises to make the doctor pity her.

Well played.

"More wine, Doctor?" He accepts, and she turns to Maya. "The footman seems to be in the kitchen, would you be so good as to fill the doctor's glass?" This is an odd request, normally she would pour the wine for a guest herself. But then I note the way her eyebrow arches as she hands Maya the doctor's glass. And Maya adjusts her poison ring. They intend to drug our guest.

This is the perfect moment for me to excuse myself. My investigation tonight is sure to prove long and arduous, so I'll need a short rest before venturing out. But first I must gather a few necessary supplies. To wit, I conceal a piece of bread in my handkerchief and tuck it in my pocket. Now comes the tricky part. I am no good at play-acting but there's no way around it. "Ahem." I clear my throat. "Begging your pardon, Miss Stranje."

"Yes," she blinks at me in surprise.

I lower my head hoping she cannot see the heat rising in my cheeks. She has known me long enough to know I always blush when I'm about to do something she wouldn't approve of. I rub my forehead. "I am very sorry, but it seems today's events have left me woefully fatigued and battling a rather bad headache. I would very much like to go to the dormitorium and rest. That is, if I might be excused, please?"

"Certainly, Miss Wyndham. It has been a stressful day." She squints at me with genuine concern. "Oh, but you've hardly touched your food. Would you like a tray sent to your room?" White ribbons of compassion waft out and brush soft against my cheek, making me feel even guiltier.

"Thank you, no." I shake my head, keeping my eyes cast down. "Sleep is the only remedy I require."

Madame Cho glances sideways at me. "I shall come and check on you later." She phrases this as if she too is concerned, and there is nothing caustic in her tone, but our Master of Defensive Arts is glowing with suspicion. There are no white ribbons coming from her, only orange spikes of distrust. She thinks I'm up to something. How she knows, I cannot guess. I didn't lie. It is true; my head is throbbing, and I definitely require a short nap before I go to work. If I'm to serve as Miss Stranje's security advisor I must tend to my duties properly, and that means finding out if my theory, no matter how outrageous it may be, is valid.

Later that night, Miss Stranje visits me in the dormitorium, bringing a glass of lemon and ginger water. "I always find it reviving," she says, checking my forehead for a fever.

"I am all right. I just need some rest."

"Do you wish to talk about anything?"

I wish to talk about a great many things. None of which I dare to speak aloud to another human being. I know the stir it causes. So, I simply shake my head, sip the lemon water and set it on the bedside table.

"Very well." She sighs and pats my shoulder. "When you're ready, my dear." And the white ribbons sail out again, covering me like wings, brushing ever so softly against my hair. "You've had a distressing day. Tomorrow will be better. You will see."

I smile, hoping she is right, although I have serious doubts. If I am right, tomorrow may prove to be a very bleak day for all of us. In either case, I will find proof for her, no matter the cost. She and the other girls mean more to me than life itself. And for their sakes, for all our sakes, I pray I am wrong.

True to her word, two hours after all the other girls have gone to sleep, Madame Cho stealthily opens the door of our dormitorium. I anticipated she would choose this hour, the hour when we sink deep into sleep. I face the wall, pretending to sleep. I have been a student at Stranje House for enough years to recognize the way she pads quietly across the floor instead of stepping. Hers is an ever so slight brush-brush step.

If Tess were not playing nursemaid to Lady Daneska, Madame Cho would first stop, as she always does, to smooth her hand over Tess's dark curls and mumble a hushed prayer. Tess's dreams often help us, but Madame knows they are torture for Tess, who night after night relives the pain and horror of other people's deaths.

Tonight, though, Madame Cho stops at my bed, and stares down at me. I feel her sharp eyes boring into the back of my skull. Silent as a wraith, she stands and listens to my heavy breathing, waiting for any false sounds to come from my throat. Lady Jane jests that Madame Cho can detect a fake snore from across the house. An exaggeration. Nevertheless, I force slow even breaths. A less wise part of me itches to look up at her and grin—just so I can watch her eyebrows fly up and her face pucker knowingly, like a cat having caught her misbehaving mouse.

Why does she suspect me tonight, I wonder?

She is so crafty. Perhaps I ought to ask her to accompany me on this perilous search. If I have guessed correctly about all this, it may prove vital to have a warrior along. And there is none better than Madame Cho.

But she would not come.

Instead, she would rap me with her bamboo cane, give me a stern lecture, and send me back to bed. Then, she would sit guard all night long just to make sure I did as she commanded. So, I sniff and rustle as if something has disturbed my dreams.

Still, she waits.

And waits.

Madame Cho is fond of saying, "Patience is our greatest weapon." It most certainly is hers. At last, she issues a mumbled *humph*, and tucks the blanket up over my shoulder. She smooths it down, and for one brief moment I can imagine what it might feel like to have a mother who loves me. I smile, listening as she pads stealthily across the floor.

When the door finally closes, the room grows colder, lonelier, darker, and I am almost sad she did not catch me.

Almost.

I have work to do.

I change into a serviceable work dress, load the pockets, and tiptoe to the hidden door of our secret passage. The oak paneling often creaks, which makes it tricky to open without waking the others. Little by little, I inch it open, a crack barely wide enough for me to slip through. Punch and Judy, our pet rats, scamper after me, but I cannot have them following me tonight. So, I toss them bread I'd hidden in my pocket and slide the door shut, locking them in the dormitorium.

Darkness closes around me.

I collect a small oil lantern and striker I'd stashed in the passage earlier in the evening. The lamp only holds a small quantity of oil, which I will need later, so I cannot light it yet. Nor do I dare risk the glow being spotted or the smell of burning oil detected through cracks in the paneling or fissures in the wattle and daub walls. Accordingly, I place the lantern in my pocket and proceed carefully, feeling my way along the wall, squeezing sideways at times, mindful of each footstep, knowing the slightest stumble might alert a member of the household to my presence. Moving tortoise slow, I focus on each limb, wary of crumbling plaster that can trip one up, of split timbers with sharp edges that might snag an ankle, and exposed nails that can rip into one's shoulder.

An invisible map of Stranje House and her secret byways unfolds in my mind.

These hidden passages are hollows, furrowed out in the thick gap between the outer walls and the inner walls. Extremely narrow, and when descending one must sometimes duck under a window box or climb over a door lintel. At key intersections rough-hewn steps lead up or down to various levels of the house. Built in Queen Elizabeth's day, some routes open into priest holes, small cupboards where fleeing priests used to hide. Some passages wind deep into the bowels of the house and lead to underground escape tunnels, heading out through the sea caves, the stable, or other places.

Last spring, despite the exterior entrances being camouflaged, Ghost snuck in through one and freed Lady Daneska from our dungeon. They kidnapped Tess and nearly killed Madame Cho. After that we barricaded those exterior entrances. Except there are other passages, long forgotten underground escape routes, narrow tunnels thought blocked off or caved in years ago. It is one of those I want to inspect tonight.

If Ghost and his men plan to rescue Lady Daneska, this is the passage I think they might use.

CHAPTER 8

WHAT LURKS IN THE DARK

SPIDERS SCURRY OUT of my way, as I duck my head and wriggle past their cobwebs. *Ugh!* After each web, I stop and rub my hair vigorously. I cringe at the thought of having collected a sticky web full of dead insects. Or worse, one of the eight-legged killers themselves.

As I rake my hands through my hair, mice patter into hiding spots and peek out at me. Odd, the way such small creatures still give off an observable essence—tiny yellow puffs of nervousness and curiosity surround them. And odder still, despite this murky darkness, I begin to feel as if I can almost see.

Am I actually seeing or merely sensing these presences?

I cannot tell.

Thankfully, there are fewer and fewer webs as I continue on. Moving by memory, I feel my way through the maze tucked inside Stranje House's inner walls, marveling at what one can perceive, not with one's eyes, but by other senses—

Eewwh!

A horrid smell drowns me in bitter black broth. I open my eyes as wide as I can and strain to see into the stinking murk. "What—?" I sputter without thinking.

I regret it the minute that whispered exclamation slips out of my mouth. A caustic stench coats my tongue and stings the back of my throat. I stifle a cough and pinch my nose. The choking smell burns my eyes.

This can only be one thing.

Bats.

That explains why there were so few spider webs in this section of the house. First thing in the morning, I will let Miss Stranje know a family of bats have taken up residence in this lower east corner of the walls.

That is *if* I survive this night.

The odor is brutal. If there was a different route, I would most certainly avail myself of it. Unfortunately, this is the only path I can take. The stink grows stronger and more stifling with every step until I am directly beside their roost. Several dozen faint orange pinpricks glitter in the inky blackness. Bat eyes, I think, shifting along in the woodwork, rustling in the cross beams. The adults must be out hunting. It seems only the young bats, the pups, remain here in the nest. They flap their tiny wings and chitter nervously at me—so anxious are they that fear blooms around them in barely perceptible pinkish gray.

To avoid the bat droppings, I must chance a broad leap. Bat feces are like putrid tar. Not only can the stuff make one dreadfully sick, but it is also stickier than glue. I would rather not wear it forever on the bottom of my shoes, so I lift my skirts and jump. But that small space is treacherous, and splinter rips through my left stocking and scrapes my leg. I suppress the urge to yelp aloud and clutch the wound, hoping there were no droppings on that wretched splinter.

Saints above! I need air.

On the verge of gagging up what little dinner I had, I stagger forward. The gash on my leg smarts, but my lungs ache and all I can think about is getting to where there is breathable air. The adult bats must have flown outside to hunt insects, so there has to be a hole in the outer wall nearby.

Ah, there it is.

Although not much bigger than a walnut, the gap allows in a welcome whiff of fresh night air. Taking in several desperate gasps, I stoop down and squeeze the wound. It is imperative that I bleed out any impurities. As soon as warm blood soaks my stocking, I'm satisfied that, for now,

I have done all I can.

I press on, grateful to escape that caustic stench. The passageway dips significantly for a few yards. The opening I expect to find should be up ahead only a little farther. An influx of cool air alerts me to the junction's proximity.

There it is.

I duck under a low beam and enter an even darker world. Not so much as a speck of light creeps in here—not in this section. I've entered a crumbling dirt tunnel, only braced here and there with rotting wood timbers. No longer part of the house, there are no windows bisecting the walls, no doorways allowing moonlight to slither in around uneven seams or warped doorframes.

Hunched under the even lower ceiling, I tread with extreme caution. This cloying darkness and clammy air begets a suffocating fear. And like those anxious baby bats, I suspect my own aura shrinks to a timid gray. Straining my senses, I hunt for signs of life. Desperate for even a morsel of light, whether it belongs to this world or the other. I swallow, and despite the humidity, my throat feels dry and raw.

I know where I'm going.

This is what I tell myself to quiet the pulsing panic rising from my stomach.

There's nothing to fear.

There might be.

Think about the diagrams. Visualize the path ahead.

Yes, very well, I will think of maps.

Maps are steady things—predictable nonthreatening things.

I close my eyes and picture the way ahead. This is one of the older passages, abandoned long ago. It leads to a small stone turret perched on the edge of the cliffs. I picture it in my mind, the hand-hewn stones slick and smoothed from the weather. It sits on the border of Lord Ravencross's estate, a crumbling old structure perched at the edge of the cliffs. It is in disrepair now, but once it served as a lighthouse of sorts—a signal house used by smugglers back in the days before Parliament removed the taxes levied on imported goods such as tea and chocolate. There are rumors that back when exporting wool was prohibited, the old Lord Ravencross made a fortune smuggling out wool from these shores.

I stumble over a mound of dirt that has fallen in the path. My forehead bumps against a large root growing across the tunnel. The inky air is thick with the scent of mud and stagnant water. There are noises, too. The *plunk, plunk, plunk* of water seeping from the damp earthen walls. And a mournful moan, as if the wind blowing through trees and grasses above ground causes this lightless world to groan in envy.

Twisted roots dangle everywhere, grasping for water. They catch and tangle in my hair forcing me to stoop even lower as I make my way deeper and deeper into this black gloom.

I jump—startled by a squeak.

It, *whatever it was*, scampers away, and I shiver. There could be all manner of creatures in here. Moles. Rats. Perhaps even badgers and—

A slithering sound stops me from taking another step.

What if there are...

Snakes?

There could be. This is a hole in the ground and that's where they like to live.

Oh, no!

No, no, no. Please, not that.

I huddle down, hugging my quivering arms around me.

This was a bad idea.

I should never have come.

Part of me screams, *Turn back! Turn back, now.*

Except I can't. I have to find out if my suspicions are right. Too much depends upon it.

But there could be snakes.

There are worse things than snakes.

Worse than adders? Adders with venomous poison, slinking along in the dark, striking without warning, worse than that?

Much worse.

Ghost is worse.

Was that another slither? I thought I heard something slinking on its scaly belly over dirt clods.

I hunker down and listen.

Is it getting colder?

Why is it getting colder?

It shouldn't be. Not here, not underground. My inner sight dims to nothing. Nothing at all. I'm blind. Completely blind. The tunnel is getting smaller and smaller.

I can't see.

My heart bangs against my chest so loud it could cause an earthquake. This entire tunnel could collapse at any moment and bury me alive.

Was that a hiss?

I distinctly heard a hiss. And scales sliding across the rocks. I get up ready to run. But which direction? Glancing every which way, I think I see snakes. I hear snakes. It feels like they're brushing against my skin, and their wicked tongues are flicking at my arms.

I bat them away.

No, no, these are scratchy roots, not tongues. Scraggly, hairy, hideous roots. I can scarcely draw breath.

Stop!

Stop being afraid.

I am not the white mouse.

Time to use the oil lamp. With shaking hands, I draw it out of my pocket and fumble with the striker. It takes three attempts before the flame at last flickers into being.

Light.

A tiny flicker of golden goodness.

Thank you, God, for light.

I stoop over and breathe. The small flame dances in the darkness, giving me courage. And so, I lift my feet and step forward. Gradually, my racing heart slows. *I can do this.*

Remember the map.

I press forward, certain I must be nearing my destination. The tunnel begins to rise, tilting upward as it approaches the cliffs and the lookout hut. When we girls explored the turret several years ago, we found a trap door in the floor. That is my objective tonight. If Ghost intends to rescue Lady Daneska, surely this would be the route he will use. It is one of the only passages left open, and the entrance is far enough from Stranje House that it would obscure his approach. This is the logical choice.

So far, though, I see no signs of anyone else having traversed the tunnel recently. I turn back and hold up the lantern. My shoes leave a distinct trail of prints in the damp soil, and there are no others aside from mine. Perhaps my hypothesis is wrong. *Good.* I can go back to Stranje House now. Except I can't. Not yet.

There is something...

I sense something in this passageway. A shiver pulses through me. Slowly turning back, I stare into the impenetrable black tunnel before me and listen.

Nothing.

Nothing beyond the slow drip of moisture. Yet a thousand tiny thorny feet tiptoe up my spine—this time I know it is not spiders.

Most assuredly not spiders. I feel something...

No! Not *something.*

Someone.

A presence.

With each uneasy step, I edge closer and closer to a powerful heaviness. Even the spiders seem to be hiding. If there are any adders in this pit with me, they have tucked their scaly tails and burrowed deep into the safety of their nests.

The ceiling slopes ever steeper, forcing me to crouch lower and lower. In places, the walls are slick with moisture, and a constant *drip, drip, drip* accompanies my every step. It means I am drawing very near to the ocean and the lookout tower. My hand trembles and the tiny lantern wobbles, sending shadows slinking into the black chasm before me.

Press forward.

This is the only way I can protect Miss Stranje and the others. And that is what I've sworn to do as Miss Stranje's security advisor. Never mind that this is my job, she and the girls at this school are my friends—my sisters. I love them. I want to keep them safe. I have to protect them.

It is the reason I'm here.

Up ahead the tunnel takes a sharp turn. Rounding the bend, I hold my tiny lantern aloft and squint, peering into the murk. Several meters ahead, it looks as if part of the passageway has collapsed in a mudslide.

I start forward, except a muffled scrape stays my foot. It sounded like...

A shovel?

Instantly, I douse my lamp. Again, the scrape echoes through the winding tunnel. This time it is followed by a soft thud. Definitely not an animal. I edge forward. There's a narrow gap in the mudslide. And light, weak as watered-down mustard, spills from the small opening into the inky darkness around me. Ashen smoke vapors coil and twist through the air carrying with them the unmistakable stink of whale oil burning in a lantern.

A knee-height boulder blocks my path. It is too slippery and muddy to climb atop, so I hold my skirts, carefully stretching my leg above it, almost reaching the other side, and quickly shift my weight, boosting myself up and over the big rock.

It should've been a silent maneuver.

Except it wasn't.

My foot splashes down in a puddle of water and the lantern slips from my hand with a decided *clink*. I failed to anticipate the depth of the puddle. I cringe. Who would've thought the sound of a splash could be so infuriatingly loud? Or that the pesky clatter of my lamp would resound like a church bell.

The scraping shovel stops.

I race past the boulder and press up against the dark side of the tunnel, willing myself to blend into the pitch-black shadows. The man digging moves to the opening, blocking the light, casting the tunnel into a lake blacker than molten tar. He cannot possibly see into this heavy darkness. A moment later he thrusts the smoking lantern through the gap and tries to peer around it. Except it blinds him.

And me.

Even blind, though, I now know who he is. I see him, not with my eyes, but with another part of myself. And I wonder now, in this nerve-rattling moment, whether I have ever seen otherworldly things with my actual eyes. Despite trembling with fear and desperately trying to mash my body into this muddy tunnel wall, I understand now that it is some other part of me that sees spiritual beings.

I sense, rather than see, who is in this tunnel with me.

Ghost.

Ghost in all his vicious glory. If I run, he will catch me. If I try to fight him, he will kill me. I know this as surely as I draw breath.

"Who's there?" he bellows.

I can scarcely breathe. *Please, please, do not see me.* Let me blend in with this mud. I press back as far as possible. If only these damp walls were less solid, and I could meld into them.

"I know you're there." He curses and shoves through the wedge. On my side of the barrier now, stooped to half his height, he squints into the blackness and raises the lantern aloft. "Speak up!"

Mud covered though I am, I know hiding is futile. He is looking the wrong way, but any moment, he will turn back and spot me. It is odd how in a moment of terror time seems to slow to nothing and a thousand possibilities race through one's mind. In one scenario I see myself bravely stepping forward as Lady Jane would do and calmly saying, "*Good evening, my lord. Lovely weather we're having in the tunnel tonight.*" Except that would annoy him. He's not the sort to find anything in life humorous. *A pity.* For I would very much like to say something clever and witty.

Except I am not clever or witty.

I only hope I am fast.

"*Run!*" screams through my mind, louder than any of those other vain imaginings. At that sharp-pitched inner shriek, my white mouse feet leap into the darkness. In a flurry of muddy petticoats, I charge down the tunnel.

He roars.

Or was it a curse?

I don't care. I race to stay alive. Every slogging footfall crashes like thunder in my head. Or is that my heart?

Thump.

Thump.

Thwomp.

He catches me by the waist. My legs flail in the air. Clamped in his iron grip, I am naught but a hapless rag doll. He hauls me back and thrusts me through the opening. If I wasn't smeared with mud before, I am now.

Good. Perhaps if my face is muddy, he won't recognize me.

He shoves the lantern next to me. "You!" He swears at me, burning with rage. Still clamped tight in his grasp, I close my eyes against the flickering light and the inevitable blow that is sure to come. He bellows another string of oaths and finally spits out the source of his ire. "One of

Stranje's brats."

Wait. What? Is it possible he doesn't remember that I am the brat who shot him on Napoleon's ship?

Could it be?

No, that's impossible. He'll remember. There is nothing stupid about this man. I should try to kill him. I'm trained to kill if necessary. Or at least, in theory, I am. I have stabbed Madame Cho's straw dummies at least a hundred times. My dagger is within reach if only I could wriggle my arms just a little.

Except...

I twist to look up at him.

Can I actually stab a living breathing man? Puncture his lung as I've been trained to do from this position? Then when he drops me, can I thrust the blade into his heart?

And end his life?

I had expected to see Ghost infested with demons, hate dripping off him like toxic sweat. Instead, a storm rages around him—a torrent of burning anger and pain. *Pain!* Blood-red wounds whip through his smoking clouds like razor-sharp ribbons. Lightning flashes of confusion and frustration whirl around him.

Demons, yes, they're here, but crawling in the shadows, slinking around the edges of his tempest. They reach in every now and then, snatching their hands back as if his wrath stings even them. He curses Daneska under his breath, "It's her fault I'm in this God-forsaken hole in the middle of the night. *Now, this.*"

He flings me on the ground as if I am a repugnant sack of rotting garbage and shouts at me. "What in the hell are you doing here?"

Frightened mouse–I scoot backward, away from his fury.

"Answer me!" He balls his fist and raises it above my face.

The urge to survive spurs my tongue.

Speak.

Now! Quickly!

My foolish cringing tongue stutters. "I–I thought you *might* be here. Coming for... *her*. For Lady D-Daneska. So, I came to check."

His brows slam together, an obsidian arrow aimed at me. "Alone?" He doesn't wait for an answer. He glances back at the wedge leading to the tunnel as if he expects an army to come marching through.

Yes, alone.

What had I been thinking?

And now I am going to die feeling foolish and childish and... stupid. I swallow, knowing I deserve whatever fate befalls me.

He turns back to me and grabs me by the front of my dress. "Alone?" he repeats in a bone rattling roar, making it clear that if I don't answer he will bash my head against the nearest stone.

"Y-Yes," I blurt. "I thought at this hour I... hadn't planned on finding you. This was supposed to be a-a fact-finding mission. To, uh, to see if the tunnel is passable. Or if anyone had been in it. That sort of thing. Yes, alone." I squeeze my eyes shut, waiting for the blow.

CHAPTER 9

FACT-FINDING GHOST

THE BLOW DOES NOT COME. I peek up at Ghost. He's frowning at me as if I am a two-headed nanny-goat. "A fact-finding mission?"

One second passes.

Two.

Instead of breaking my neck, he jerks me to my feet. "Up," he snarls and gestures with the lantern toward a rough-hewn stone stairway. Seven narrow steep steps ascend to an open trap door. On the fifth step part of the rock flakes off under the sole of my shoe and I lose my balance. With a rude obscenity, he shoves me up from behind. I fly upward through the opening, grate my shin against the top stair, and land in an ungraceful sprawl across the floor of the lookout tower.

Ghost stomps up behind me, lifts me by the collar, and flings me up against the far wall. My head bangs against the stones, I slide into a heap and instinctively curl inward. My hair has fallen loose, so I hide behind the familiar strands.

This is it for me—the end.

Unable to kill. Abandoned daughter. Failed security advisor. Dead.

A dead white mouse.

He sets the lantern on the floor, and in the flickering lantern light, I see my scraped shin. Blood trickles down my tattered white stocking. It looks so very red. Not an ugly red. Nor is it brown like the crusted blood on my other leg. This new rivulet is a deep entrancing hue.

I'm not a mouse.

I'm not.

I'm a girl, a girl with beautiful red blood. Not only that, Mr. Quentin Chadwick kissed me. He called me his brilliant Miss Wyndham. His words may not be any truer than Lady Daneska calling me a useless white mouse. Except I am not entirely useless. Miss Stranje trusts me to help her keep everyone at Stranje House safe.

Not useless.

I lift my chin, *brilliant Miss Wyndham*. I choose to finish my life believing Miss Stranje's assessment and Mr. Chadwick's. Not my mother's or Lady Daneska's.

So, I straighten my skirts and force myself to stand. Since I am about to die, I would like what's left of me to be found as presentable as possible. I brush the dirt off my hands and rake flecks of mud out of my hair.

Ghost retrieves a flintlock pistol from a satchel, primes it, and pulls back the pin. He aims the big ugly barrel at me. "I know you, girl. You're the one who shot me."

He remembers.

I press my back against the wall. "Yes."

He cocks his head. Shocking blue rays burst through the tumult whirling around him. *Why does my answer surprise him?* It's merely the truth. I shot and wounded him. His scowl deepens. "Then you'll die for it."

"I understand." I straighten my sleeve, take a breath, and close my eyes. I don't want to see the shot coming. The pause is too long. I open my eyes and meet his surly gaze. "Go ahead. I'm not afraid to die."

He flinches as if an annoying gnat just buzzed by. "You're either a liar or a fool. Everyone is afraid to die."

"Except I've seen what happens..." *There's no use explaining the things I've seen.* "Never mind. You're right. I am afraid. Mostly of the dying part, not the being *dead* part. So, if you could make it quick, I would be obliged." I ready myself again.

"What's wrong with you?" He pulls back.

I swallow. *Why is he frustrated?* I'm the one who

blundered into this. I'm the one who's about to be shot. He's killed without hesitation before. I've seen him do it. Yet the tempest surrounding him rumbles mysteriously. "Are you daft? Touched in the head?"

"Touched. Quite possibly." I bite my lip momentarily, fighting annoyance that even my murderer is finding fault with me. "But daft? No. I am not daft. Odd, yes, certainly. A misfit by my parents' account. But no, I've never ever been accused of being daft."

He squints at me. The winds inside his stormy countenance churn slower, and he burns with a little less rage.

He's inquisitive! I see sparks of curiosity buzzing around him like bees. He leans in and squints at me. Despite his inquisitiveness, he's as wary as a whipped dog, as wounded as a beaten child.

Anger regains its seat of power. The dark ones surrounding him move in closer. "Daft or not—it makes no difference. You tried to kill me. It's only right I should shoot you."

"*Tried?*" I protest, blinking.

Pride. Wicked pride overwhelms my common sense. And I foolishly snap at him. "If you're going to murder me, at least do it for the right reason. If I had *tried* to kill you, you would be dead."

He scoffs.

This humorless man. This great hulking monster of the first order looks down his nose at me and *scoffs*.

I clamp my lips together to no avail. I cannot hold

back. Gall emboldens me. "You know perfectly well that Miss Stranje teaches us to shoot. That bullet struck your arm. A wound from which I can see you have already re-covered. I assure you, my lord—"

"Don't!" He winces and raises his fist as if to thrash me. It wavers in the air above my head. "Don't *my lord* me. I despise titles."

"Very well," I whisper quietly. "I apologize. Titles mean very little to me anyway."

He lowers his arm, scrutinizing me through a narrowed gaze.

I finish answering but with far less heat and an embar-rassing quiver weakening my voice. "What I meant to say is that if I had wanted to kill you, I would've aimed for your heart."

He sneers as if he doesn't believe me, but a tiny sliver of his wariness falls to the floor. He quickly scoops it up again. "Because you would rather see me hang." He says this as if it is a fact he throws in my face.

Hang?

A hideous image flares into my mind—his neck broken, his head lolled to the side, swollen and discolored, tongue protruding, body twitching.

Revulsion rises in my throat. I swallow against it.

"No!" I shrink back and shake my head. "I wouldn't wish that on anyone. Not you. Not anyone." I press my hand against my souring stomach and stare at him, scarcely able to form the words. "I—I don't want you to hang. I *should,* I suppose. It's only right after all you've done. Except I don't. I can't." I lower my head, gritting my teeth. Why am I so repulsed at the thought? He is our enemy. A murderer. *Aagh! Foolish white mouse.*

"Go ahead and shoot," I mumble. "I deserve to die."

I wait. There's no blast.

I look up confused, baffled as to why he has not pulled the trigger.

"All this innocence," he swears harshly. "It's an act." Red lightning surges through his storming cloak. "Trickery!" he thunders at me. "You're a liar!" Through his teeth, he snarls, "A lying little sneak like all the rest of Emma's brats."

"I wish I was lying," I mumble more to myself than him. "At least I could understand a lie." My frustration lends me just enough strength to speak up. "Look at me. Go ahead, look closely. Am I lying? You deserve to hang for what you've done. And yet the idea of a noose around your neck, squeezing the life out of you, sickens me. It shouldn't. But, God help me, it does."

He bares his teeth and presses closer, close enough that I smell the sweat on his shirt from shoveling dirt. He breathes out such fury that I can taste his bitterness, it bites into my nostrils like the peppery sharp scent of leather oil.

His lips open and close as if he's struggling to find words angry enough. Finally, an insult scrapes across his tongue, "You're no different from Daneska—trying to play me for a fool." He presses the gun against my forehead. "It won't work."

Me?

Like her?

The idea is ludicrous. Daneska must not have explained my white mousiness to him. He thinks me capable of trickery. That's something. Gun or no gun, I stand a little straighter, and tell him, "I have a knife, you know. This close, if I had wanted you dead, I would've already sliced open your neck."

I should have done exactly that.

Miss Stranje would be sorely disappointed if she knew of my inability to kill. Madame Cho would shake her head and require me to stab a dozen more straw dummies, even though it would do no good. Straw is nothing like flesh and blood.

Failure.

Ghost grabs my wrist and twists it until I yelp in pain. "Where?" he growls. "Where is this blade of yours?"

My eyes betray me before I can stop them from stupidly glancing down to my thigh to make sure it's still in its proper place.

He lets go of my wrist and yanks up my leg.

I can't help but gasp.

"Stop." But he does not stop. Anger of my own rears up, and I battle the urge to slap him. Except that would fuel his already blazing temper, so I settle for grumbling at him. "If I *were* like Daneska, I'd have another knife hidden in my sleeve, and I'd use it on you right now while you're mauling my leg."

His fingers find the hilt of my dagger. He jerks it out and tosses it away. The steel blade clatters against the stone floor.

My only weapon.

Gone.

I'm well and truly done for now.

He should be pleased, except he's not. Confusion swirls around him in orange sulphuric ribbons. It adds to his rage. It thrashes him like the whippings he suffered at his father's hand. Demons dance around the room, celebrating his poisonous fury and my upcoming death.

He flinches as if their wicked glee aggravates him. It is almost as if he can hear their snickering and jeering. His eye twitches as he presses the gun harder against my forehead.

Stripped of any defense, I stand at the end of my life clothed only in acceptance.

And now pity—pity for him.

My death will be quick when it comes.

I am at peace.

But he...

He suffers.

The scars on the left side of his face bunch repeatedly each time his jaw flexes. His torment is so palpable it makes my eyes water. Without thinking, I reach toward the burn marks on his cheek. "This is from that night in Calais, isn't it?"

He only frowns in answer.

"We didn't intend for you to get burned. We only meant to free Lord Wyatt." My fingertips lightly brush his cheek. "I'm sorry."

"Sorry?" He snarls and shakes loose from my touch. "What do you know of sorry?"

"More than you think." And suddenly, I understand why I couldn't kill this man. "You and I are much alike."

He laughs—a dry humorless grunt. "We are nothing alike." For a moment, he forgets to press the muzzle of the gun against my forehead and swings it wide as if illustrating the breadth of our differences. "*Nothing* alike."

"You think not?" I stare into his eyes. Eyes that now seem achingly familiar somehow. Can it be that I am old friends with the haunting pain he tries so fiercely to hide? Pain that I recognize from my own mirror? "Weren't you beaten as a child and thrown in a dark place to lick your wounds alone?"

His lips curl but not in humor. "What did my wretched brother tell you? What?!" He lifts the gun as if to beat me with it. Then he glances upward and grimaces as if he sees the creatures slinking across the tattered ceiling above us. "You're lying again. Guessing. You don't know anything about that." He bears down on me again.

I take a deep breath, struggling to still the heart-hammering distress his anger begets inside me. "I know a little something about it." My voice is shaky and solemn, hushed with shame. He leans in to hear. I start to hang my head down. It is my habit to hide, but what is the point of hiding tonight when I am at the end of it all? So, I look back up at him, searching. For what? *I know not.*

Kinship?

The kinship of shared pain.

Am I truly considering telling this stranger, this murderer, this dark-hearted man who is about to kill me, *my secrets?* Secrets I have kept from everyone else.

Why?

Is it because he might be the first person who can truly comprehend? Or is it merely because I am about to die and I want someone, even if it is him, to know the darkness I hide.

He waits.

His eyes dare me to lie. Yet, at the same time, they beseech me to tell the truth.

So, I do. "My parents whipped me with willow branches until my back bled so badly they could no longer tolerate the mess. Finally, they gave up and locked me in the attic, forbidding even the servants from speaking to me when they deposited my water and bread each morning."

His jaw tenses and un-tenses as he grinds through my words. In the end, he shakes his head and roars, "I don't believe you." He presses in so close; it is as if he's hunting for the truth and thinks it must be hidden inside me. "You're lying again. Lying! No one would do that to you."

Shame washes over me. "I have scars to prove it." This time I hang my head despite the gun pointed at my face, despite his closeness, and I whisper, "Go ahead. See for yourself." I clamp my teeth together and face him. "On my back."

If he doesn't find the truth in my gaze, I hope at least he recognizes anguish.

A muffled sound erupts from deep in his throat, not his normal grumble, it sounds more like a drowning man catching his last gasp of air. He hesitates. A minute ticks by—it may as well have been a lifetime. Then he flips me around as if I am nothing but a sack of flour and presses me against the wall. "Don't move," he warns and reaches for the oil lamp. He yanks the yoke of my dress back. The back seam gives way, tearing an inch or two. The lamp sputters as he raises it above us.

I close my eyes and try to concentrate on the thick oil smoke coiling around us. When that fails, and a whimper escapes my lips, I grit my teeth and focus on the night wind rattling the broken shingles, howling through the gaps in the walls. Even the chittering of his blasted demons is preferable to thinking about Ghost staring at the knotted wormlike scars crisscrossing my back. Hideous scars that I have worked very hard to hide from everyone else.

As if he cannot believe the ugliness he sees, he jerks my dress out farther and brings the light closer. So close, I feel the heat of the lamp on my shoulder. He stares too long. Far too long.

Stop, I silently beg. Except I know how it is difficult to look away from such hideousness.

Finally, he lets go and curses.

Unable to move, blinking back tears, my hands remain pressed against the gray stone wall, and I cling to it for strength. One traitorous droplet escapes and burns a path down my cheek. All I can do is stare at the wall.

It seems like a thousand years before he turns me around and shoves me back, as if he finds me as disgusting as my parents did.

Ghost rakes a hand through his thick black hair. "Why?" he asks, his voice hoarse, gravelly, uncertain. "Why would they do that to you?"

I take silent refuge behind the curtain of hair that has fallen loose. I haven't the strength to look anywhere except at the leaves and dirt strewn on the floor. A rat skitters in the darkness behind him. Ghost paces and gestures at me. "I don't understand it. You're not like that she-devil, Tess. Or conniving like Daneska. Look at you—you're not dark like me. You're angelic white and fragile as a china doll."

He paces as he rants. Suddenly he grasps my chin and presses me back, forcing me to face him. It is not disgust I see etched into his features. It is anger and the ever-present confusion that seems to haunt him. "Why? Why did they do it?" he demands and shakes his head. "You're all the things these foolish English prigs love."

"*Love?*" I struggle to say, and he loosens his grip. But saying that word chokes me more than his hand on my neck. "*Love* never figured into the equation." I try to do what Maya taught me and moderate my voice. Except I fail.

Words inch out of me, halting and broken. "They were afraid of me."

"Afraid?" He lets go and sneers. "Afraid of you?"

"Yes," I whisper.

"Of *you*?" His nose wrinkles up as if he might almost laugh. Instead, he shakes his head and lets go of me. "You're naught but a stick of a girl. *Who* would be afraid of you?"

"I'm not a stick," I mumble, resenting his scornful description. "Very well. If you must know, I will tell you who is afraid of me—the people who spawned a heretic who talks to the dead. That's who."

He blinks.

Good. He should be startled. Except all too quickly, mockery quirks up his face, making the scars on his burned cheek curl oddly in this flickering light. "You talk to the dead?"

"No." My shoulders sag.

He waggles the gun at me. At this point, I wish the horrid thing would go off by accident and put an end to this painful interrogation.

Except it doesn't.

He doesn't blow a hole in me or the wall. Instead, he demands an answer. "I'm tired of your lies. Why did they beat you?" He glares ruthlessly at me. His bristling storm boils with impatience, and lightning streaks through his darkness. I've confused him again—I see specks of it darting about him like invisible biting gnats. "Out with it, girl.

What did you do to earn a whipping like that?"

"Very well, I'll tell you. But first, you must tell me why you always assume people are lying?"

His brow wrinkles impatiently, and he sneers as if I am a stupid child. "Because *everyone* lies."

My eyebrows fly up. "But that isn't true, is it? *You* don't."

A flash of pure blue bursts through the gloom around him. Is that surprise he's feeling? Or maybe, pride? I don't know. It vanishes too quickly, and belligerence takes its place. "You can't know that," he quarrels.

"But I do." And I make the mistake of pursuing the point. "I'm curious, though. One would think a man like you, hell-bent on destroying an entire country, would be an accomplished liar. Yet, you are not. *You* don't lie. Why?"

A flash of silver slices through the night between us. Another piece of the mighty Ghost's armor clinks to the floor. He lifts his chin. "Why should *I* lie? I have no need of it." A flair of bright blue swirls through his dark storm and engulfs his being—a rare moment of purity, but all too quickly, the radiant blue light fractures. It disappears in whimpering sparks under the weight of his hatred.

He comes back, storm in full force, and leans over me like a ferocious monster ready to rip me to pieces. "Tell me why they beat you?" The jagged scent of his irritation wraps around my throat and chokes me as surely as would his massive fingers. "Now!"

"There was an—an incident," I wheeze.

His frown narrows. "What incident?"

"Well…" I struggle to catch my breath. "*Several* incidents to be exact." He steps back an inch or two, so I confess more. "They misunderstood. I told you I don't talk to dead people. That is true. But… I do sometimes talk to *other* beings. *Beings* most people can't see." I cringe, expecting him to explode.

"What sort of beings?" he asks, as if it is a perfectly rational question. And there it is again, that intense sunflower spike of curiosity in the air around him.

I would rather not answer that question, so I look away, inspecting our surroundings and the beings that are currently sharing this broken-down antiquity.

"What. Sort. Of. Beings," he demands.

"It's not important. The whippings were my fault." I brush his question away. "I should have learned to keep my foolish mouth shut. Except I was rather young, you see, when I first saw… er… things I shouldn't. And I mistakenly supposed everyone could see them."

I catch my lip and stare at the floor again. I don't like remembering my parents' disgust. It is too painful to recall how they cursed the fact that they'd spawned some sort of wicked deviant.

Ghost waits silently.

"The vicar of our village declared me 'an abomination.' My parents were ashamed, horrified—they didn't know what to do. They argued with each other about throwing me in the river until they decided they might be able to beat the evil out of me."

He mutters something I cannot quite hear.

"Yes, well..." I scuff my slipper against the dirty floor. "It's my fault. I should've learned to keep such things to myself sooner."

He breathes out with a threatening huff of impatience. "What sort of beings?"

I press my lips tight, wishing I could think of some way to avoid the answer.

He shoves his wretched flintlock against my ribs and towers over me, breathing like a lion after a chase. "Tell me!"

I retreat to that place deep inside me where everything is safe and full of strength.

Death is not the end.

You are not a mouse.

I gently press my hand against his chest, and he backs away an inch or two. "The sort of beings you don't believe in."

He studies me intently. His dark eyes peer into mine, searching, hunting—always hunting. Then as if my touch sliced through them, his roiling thunderclouds part ever so slightly, and blood leaks out between us, dripping over my finger, sloshing to the floor.

What have I done?

A wound rips open in his chest and a terrifying stream of blood pours out onto the floor, soiling his boots, splashing over my skirts, pooling around our feet.

My mouth opens. I stare at my reddened palm.

I have killed him.

Horror-struck, I look up into his face. There's no sign of death. No paleness. Not even a grimace of pain. I look at the red deluge around us. Does he not see this river of blood flowing from him?

He is speaking, but I cannot quite make out the words.

Concentrate.

"First," he says sternly and uncocks the pistol, shoving it back in his belt. "You don't know what I believe in." Judging by his robust stance and the forcefulness of his tone—this cannot be *tangible* blood staining my fingers.

Imaginary.

Or is it something else?

I look up at his mouth. He is still talking. "Second, you are probably insane." He nods at this conclusion. "Mad. I've heard about people who hear voices. That must be why they locked you up."

"Ugh!" I wish I hadn't told him. I should have just let him shoot me. "Perhaps, I am mad," I sputter. Then I take a breath.

He may be right.

There is invisible blood dripping from my fingers, which brings my sanity into question. I sigh and with a shake of my head, let my arms fall to my sides. "Heaven knows, I've asked myself that very question a thousand times."

He exhales loudly, with a decided air of irritation, and his thick brows knit together in a heated stare.

I don't care what he thinks of me.

Why should I?

Yet I find myself explaining. "To be fair, though, I take great care to guard against madness. I cling to logic and rational thought as one would cling to a narrow path through a dark forest during a storm. Except it is normally not *my* forest getting hit by the storm. Oh, to be sure, at times, my life is tumultuous. Like now, what with my being captured and all, and you being the most dangerous man in the civilized world apart from Napoleon. Although I daresay, Emperor Napoleon might be a trifle less volatile."

"He might." He continues to stare at me as if I am some sort of demented creature. *Me.* When he is the murderous villain bent on demolishing England.

I don't need to justify myself to Ghost. He has been judged mad as often as I have. Yet here I am, blurting out things I've kept buried forever. I force myself to take a deep breath and proceed in a much calmer voice. "I cannot help seeing what I see. Or that sometimes I know what's hidden inside someone's soul, or—"

"Enough! What *other* beings?"

He grasps me by the sides of my head and holds me not two inches away. If we were lovers, I might think he intends to kiss me. Except that is not love tightening his features. He is losing patience.

"You won't believe me." I squeak, my calm voice

having evaporated.

He tightens his grip, and we are so close I dare not breathe. "Try me," he rasps.

"Demons." I close my eyes. "And on rare occasions, *very* rare occasions, angels. *Hardly ever.* They prefer not to be seen. Although I often feel when they're present."

He lets go and steps back, looking away as if my gaze scalds him. "Demons?"

"Yes," I confess quietly, turning my face to the floor.

His glare returns, piercing and steel-edged even in this dim light. "And do you see one in me now?"

I had always thought I would.

Truthfully, it surprised me not to find several, or perhaps, even a legion swarming inside him. Such is not the case. Nevertheless, I suppose he expects the whole truth. I bite my lip.

"Tell me!" He raises his voice. I can tell he means for it to sound like a harsh demand, except both syllables are weakened by the invisible blood still dripping from his heart.

I stare at the floor. "Inside you? No." I shake my head still wondering what all that invisible blood means.

"Are you lying again?" That is not anger I hear in his voice—it is fear. He's afraid of the answer.

Some oracle deep within me issues a command. *Tell him the truth.*

And so, I do. "Around you, yes—there are several. But I do not see any living inside you." I shrug. "I don't understand why not."

He glances to his left as if he can feel the one leering over his shoulder. He turns, quick as a whip, to check the corner nearby. And yes, that one slinks into the shadows, a friend to the rats and spiders who've been skittering about it all night. Ghost does not seem to notice the one crawling on the ceiling. Nor the one towering right behind him.

"Then it's true. They're real." He stands before me as if broken, this great giant of a man. I have wounded him, yet again. Anguish douses the fire in his eyes. And pain weighs down his shoulders, giving sway to the creatures skulking over him.

His anguish disturbs me more than any demon ever has. It is far more distressing to look upon. I cannot help but reach out to him. He does not take my hand. Instead, he surges forward and grips my shoulders. "Make them go away."

His plea pierces me as surely as a blade. I want to help him. *I do.* Only no one has ever asked me for this kind of help before.

No one.

Ever.

My mouth starts to open, but I don't know what to say. His agony forms a biting gray smoke around us, and his earnestness clutches at my soul.

In answer, I utter the saddest words I have ever spoken. "I don't know how."

"You must." He leans in, peering hard at me, searching desperately. "You do." His breath lands warm on my lips. The murk surrounding him eases, pierced by a faint blue that reminds me of a lake in the early morning.

I wince, closing my eyes, trying to shake off his need, his trust, his misplaced faith.

He shakes me to make me look at him. "You know how to stop them," he insists. "I know you do."

How?

It is a silent whisper, not spoken to him. It is a plea, begging the Almighty for help. A second later, it slips out of my mouth as a soft whisper. "How?"

"I've no idea how you do it. I only know that you *must* know how."

I look up at him and this time it is me pleading. "Why would you think that?"

He straightens and lets go of me. "Because they don't bother you." His words bounce off the stone walls and reverberate around us.

They don't bother you.

The demons around him suddenly freeze like a herd of deer having caught the scent of a hunter—alert, wary.

I blink. For one startling instant, I feel suspended in time, adrift in another dimension. I slide down the cold stone wall until I am crouching on the floor, hugging my knees. He surprises me by sitting on the floor next to me.

He spoke the truth.

They never have bothered me. Not really. Oh, it's bad

enough that I see them. Not *all* of them, of course. There are millions of them. But I've seen enough of them in their many forms, some cloyingly handsome, others so foul it churns my stomach. But he is right, they generally keep their snarling whispery distance. Occasionally, one might spit or screech at me, and plenty of times, they've hissed. I've grown accustomed to it.

I turn to Ghost and study him. What if they constantly whispered their venom in my ear the way they do to him?

When I was younger, during my long sojourns in the attic, some came to mock me or to frighten me. Occasionally, one would puff himself up and make dire predictions about the futility of my puny life. Yet, all along, another voice quietly taught me not to be afraid. Fear, hate, anger— demons feed on these things. They lap at our darker emotions the way thirsty drunkards lick up spilled ale.

If only people understood how tangible emotions are.

I reach out to touch his hand, to offer some meager comfort, but Ghost has threaded both of his through his thick dark curls. He turns to me, his brown eyes filled with bewilderment. "When I'm near you, they are quiet."

CHAPTER 10

THE DREADFUL COST OF BEING NEEDED

WHEN I'M NEAR YOU, *they are quiet.*

I marvel at Ghost's words, as one marvels at sunlight after an endless winter. They warm me as nothing ever has before. The doors of my hiding place swing open. I stop hugging my knees and gape at him.

This man, one of the most feared men in all the world, is asking for my help. Nay, pleading for it. I can hardly fathom it. He does not want to lock me in an attic. He wants my help.

Needs my help.

What's more, owing to my peculiarities, I may, in fact, be capable of helping him. I gawk, even more astonished.

Except... I can think of only one way to help him, and he won't like it. My shoulders sag. He won't like it at all. How can a man so steeped in hate and anger, turn away from his own venom?

"What?" he asks. "What's wrong?"

I bow my head and, searching for more answers, quietly ask, "Do you hear them talking to you?"

"*Them.*" His chest heaves. "Then there *is* more than one."

"Yes." I answer in a hushed voice, studying the ruined fabric of my skirt pulled over my knees. His soul, like my dress, is stained with blood and muddied with grim sludge. How can either one ever come clean?

"I don't hear them." He seems drained of all his strength. "Not exactly. I don't hear them in words, as when you and I speak. Yet, in another sense, I do. Their nattering barges into my mind, provoking and pestering me. It gets so blasted noisy in my head that I can't hear my own thoughts."

He leans forward and grips the sides of his head. "When I try to shut it out my skull pounds like the hammers of hell." He stares across the room as if he is seeing into the past. "And the suggestions they make are beyond the bounds of human imaginings. Unspeakable things—"

I gently lean against his shoulder. "That must be horrid."

He recoils from me. "I don't want your sympathy!" His storm begins to brew again. "Can you make them go away, or not?" He glares at me as if I am his enemy once more. "Well? Can you?"

I swallow. "I–I'm not certain. There may be a way to keep them at a distance, to quiet them. Mind you, you won't like it, and—"

"I knew it!" He whips around and presses closer to me. "I don't care what it takes. I'll pay you."

"Pay me?" I blink, feeling unaccountably insulted.

"Yes. Anything you want."

"I don't want your money."

"What then?"

I swallow.

What do I want?

I stare at him for a moment and then look away. "*Hope*," I whisper, and then I softly add, "And you could give us our Prince Regent back—" Before the words fully escape my lips, a bark far off in the distance drifts in on the breeze.

Tromos.

I stiffen and murmur, "Oh no."

Ghost curses and leaps to his feet. "Those blasted wolves. I should've killed them long ago."

"No! No, don't hurt them." I reach for him. "*Please*. They mean no harm." I try to calm him, but another sound floats in on the night wind. It's far off in the distance, nevertheless I recognize the distinctive Welsh accents. It's Tess calling my name.

His eyes widen, and the air around him boils up into a thundercloud. He yanks the flintlock from his belt.

I jump up beside him and reach out to calm him. "You needn't be alarmed. I'm the only one who knows you're here. She's not looking for you."

More yips drift across the bluffs toward us. This time it's *Phobos*, and then the faint notes of Lady Jane shouting for me.

I groan at their wretched timing and attempt to pacify him. "I've been gone too long. They're searching for me, that's all. And they're well over a mile away. If you leave now, they'll never catch up to you."

"You're coming with me." He grabs my arm and tugs me to his side as he gathers his satchel.

Instead of giving in to fear, I gently place my hand over his heart, as I'd done earlier. Just like before, he flinches and stands there, stunned, as if I have thrust a knife into his chest. He stares down at my hand barely touching him.

"I can't go with you. I won't." I gentle my voice, trying to cushion the harsh things I must say. "If you force me, I will intentionally slow you down. I must. It's my duty."

"Duty be damned." He curses.

"No. You must *choose*. You can shoot me now. But if you do, my friends will hear the shot and come running even faster. Or you can leave me here, now, and escape. I'll not chase you. That much I promise you."

He stares at my hand. The wretched demons are pressing in on him. He cringes. His jaw knots up, and he breathes in ferocious heaves like a cornered bull.

"Go." I ease my hand away and whisper. "Run."

His lips tighten and his face contorts. For a moment, I glimpse the wounded boy inside him, a boy I ache to hold and comfort. That lost boy, *not Ghost*, leans closer and asks, "Meet me here tomorrow night."

My stomach curls into a knot. "Don't ask that of me." I lower my gaze, afraid to look at him. "Please. I can't. You know I can't."

"That's a lie. You snuck out tonight. You have to come back and make these hellish creatures leave me alone." He clamps a hand on my shoulder. "Do it, and I'll tell you where your Prince is."

"I already know where he is." I bow my head and pull away.

"No." He catches my hand in his fist. "You can't possibly know."

"I do." I look up at him and ease my fingers out of his grasp. "I do. There are enough clues that it is down to only a minimal amount of elimination."

"No," he blusters. "You're guessing. You only *think* you know where he is." He paces. "Come to me tomorrow. Help me and I'll tell you exactly where to find him."

I shake my head. "By sundown tomorrow I'll already have his location."

He scowls at me. "You're lying again. I didn't leave any clues. And my men—"

"Left several." I exhale with exasperation. "Listen. Do you hear that?" Lady Jane's faint call drifts in on the night air. "If you leave now, you'll have at least a half hour start."

"I don't care. I'll just shoot them."

"That is precisely what concerns me."

He leans over me and resorts to his menacing growl. "What clues?"

I glance at the doorway to see if I can spot a lantern in the distance, but there is nothing but darkness beyond. "Dozens."

"Name three." He blocks my view and a fiery orange burst of challenge radiates from him.

I cannot hide my agitation, fearing that at any moment one of the wolves will catch my scent and race in this direction. "Very well." I rub my forehead and comply with his demand. "You sent an untrained French sailor to watch Stranje House instead of a seasoned spy—which indicates you primarily have sailors at your disposal, rather than your normal band of Iron Crown... *scoundrels*."

He grunts as if this is meaningless evidence. "Wrong. One of my regulars went with him."

"Yes, that would be the despicable cur who buried that poor sailor alive. Also, your spy carried no kit with him, nor do you have any kit on you, further proof you're encamped nearby. That shirt you're wearing strains at the shoulder seams and does not fit you properly. So, you have either borrowed or stolen it from a nearby farmhouse. That's four clues. Now, will you please go before they catch up to us and someone gets hurt?"

"That someone would be your interfering friends and those mongrel dogs—easily disposed of." He tucks the pistol into his trousers. "Are you going to meet me or not?"

"You threaten my friends and expect me to help you?"

He exhales loudly and his jaw buckles tight. Finally, he utters a grinding, barely audible, "Come." Ghost says that one word not in his customary rumble, but in the same manner another man might request a great favor. It was the closest he would ever come to saying please.

"Very well. I'll do my best to meet you here tomorrow night, but only if you go now."

"Two bells—be here." He leans close and glowers fiercely at me. "And if I arrive and find a garrison of soldiers waiting for me, I'll have left word to put a bullet in Prinny's pea-sized brain."

Only then did I realize Ghost had hold of me again. If his heart hadn't been dripping so much invisible blood down the front of my gown, I might have had the good sense to be afraid. Instead, I stare at his *not-really-there* blood running in rivulets down my chest, soaking my skin, and my own chest begins to ache.

I look up and realize the tears leaking from my eyes are wet and real—they call me back to reason. I dash them away.

"Promise, you'll come," he says, ripping at my soul a

little more.

"I'll try." The words come out wobbly and hesitant.

He lets go of me in a sudden motion and backs away as if touching me has wounded him somehow. I heave in a breath and glance sideways up at him, wincing at the pain I see. "I *will* try."

The lost boy casts me one last desolate glance. "Promise."

And my heart breaks.

CHAPTER 11

WHAT A WOLF KNOWS

HE SEES IT AS CLEARLY as I see the blood dripping from his soul. We both know I'll be here, no matter the cost.

I nod and look away, battling the urge to curl up in the darkest corner and hide from the crushing weight of his misery. If only this crumbling stone tower could give me an escape from his turmoil, and my confusing life.

When I glance back, he is gone, and the last of his demons slinks out into the night, chasing after the lost boy.

I sigh, retrieve my useless dagger, and extinguish the

lantern he left behind. How still this place is without him. The stones have lost all their menace, the ceiling is devoid of dark creeping shapes, and the mice are once again nothing more than quiet little scamps searching for a morsel to eat. Standing in the silence, an overwhelming weariness overtakes me. It is as if some grave illness has drained away all my strength.

I lean against the cold stones, hoping to revive myself, but I cannot stay here. Somehow, I must find the will to move. Slowly, I walk out into the night wishing I had brought a shawl to banish the chill. Stars glimmer like distant fragments of hope in the broad black sky, and clouds race to cover them up. The moon illuminates the silhouette of Stranje House and the trees bending under gusts of wind.

Far in the distance, across the bluff of waving grass, I glimpse the orange pinprick glow of two lanterns. The one farthest away is headed in my direction, the other moves faster and is angling toward Queen's Cape. That one will be Tess, worried that I have jumped from the cliffs after all.

Tired as I am, I break into a stumbling run. If I don't, they will discover I have emerged from the old lookout tower. With each step my legs feel as if they will give out. This weakness isn't from making my way through the secret passages or that horrid tunnel. Instead, it feels as if I have been in fierce combat, wrestling with demonic forces, and I have emerged bruised, aching and nearly beaten.

I swipe at my eyes making certain any remnants of tears are gone. It is only by sheer brutish force of will that my feet continue to crash through the tall grass. Normally, I would tread cautiously through this field at night, wary of adders that might be weaving through the stalks, hunting mice in the dark. Tonight, though, I don't care. Adders are the least of my concerns.

What am I going to tell the others?

With every wobbling footfall, every thud against the soil, a quandary drums through my head.

Duty.

Loyalty.

Sisterhood.

I owe Ghost nothing. He may be a wounded child inside, but he's also a ruthless killer. I owe Miss Stranje and my friends everything. *Everything!* Without them I *have* nothing. Without them I *am* nothing. I run faster and faster.

There is only one choice. I must tell them the truth—that Napoleon and Ghost are holding Prince George here in Britain.

That is what I will do.

The decision to abandon him, to leave him lost and bleeding twists my stomach into a tight acidic knot. I stop running and bend, pressing against my roiling stomach to settle it. The thought should not pain me.

Yet it does.

How can I do this to him?

His wounds may be invisible to everyone else, but I feel them intensely, as if we shared the same beatings as children and the same lashes cut into both our flesh. It is as if we huddled in the same dark corner sobbing for a mother's comforting touch, answered only by a cold empty room.

Silencing an unbidden whimper, I shake my head.

God help me. Ghost is more akin to me than any of my natural brothers and sisters. They never spent their nights locked away in the attic. No, my brothers and sisters sailed merrily away without even sending me so much as a note of farewell. Then again, why should they? They never really knew me. If they had, I'm quite certain they would have looked at me with the same revulsion as did our parents.

Not in a thousand years would any one of them have asked for my help.

Ghost did.

I turn my face up to the stars and silently plead. Isn't there some way to help him without betraying my friends? Surely. If only somehow I could free him from his demons *and* remain loyal to Miss Stranje and my friends.

There has to be a way.

I will find it.

I must!

I bolt forward, running faster and faster with every step. When I am far enough away from the lookout tower I shout, "Here!" Stopping to catch my breath, I cry out louder and wave my arms. "Over here! I'm here!"

Tromos and Phobos hear me long before Tess or Lady Jane. They come galloping through the grass from two different directions and knock me over. Tromos pounces on me and plants her paws on my chest licking my face. Phobos sets up a howl to Tess letting her know that he's found me. Tromos sets to sniffing about me and draws back suddenly as if alarmed. Sniffing me again, a low rumble vibrates in her chest.

I shove Tromos back and sit up. "It's all right, girl." I run my fingers through her thick ruff. "Ghost didn't hurt me."

Phobos butts against me with his nose and cocks his head, ears standing straight up. I dust off my hands and try to get up, but he pushes me down again. "Well, all right. He may have hurt me a little." Tromos has already found the injury on my shin and licks at the drying blood. I push her back and tuck my skirts over the wound.

"I suppose he did scare me a little," I say, striving for a frank but confident tone. Phobos tilts his head the other way, and now Tromos is sniffing at my cheeks and yipping quietly to her mate. "Yes, yes," I admit to my interrogating wolves. "Later he made me cry, but not for the reasons you think. I know he's a very angry man, but he's an incredibly sad lost boy."

I didn't think wolves could roll their eyes, but it looked for all the world as if Phobos just did that very thing. "Well, if you intend to be persnickety about it, I shan't tell you anything more."

Phobos yips and Tromos answers him with a nudge.

"Suffice it to say he has ample reasons," I explain. "Not that I'm excusing him. I'm not. His anger has gone too far. It has eaten into him like a festering disease." I pluck out a stalk of grass and sigh, inclining my head very properly to Phobos. "And now, my dear guardians of the night, may I please stand up?"

They both give me room to get up. I brush off my hands and shake out my skirt. "And you mustn't tell Tess any of this."

Both of them yip excitedly. I whirl around and find Tess running swiftly and silently through the grass. "Tell me what?"

I blink at her, wide-eyed. "You found me."

"To be precise, they found you." She's busy rubbing their necks and praising them. "Where have you been?" she asks me pointedly.

"Researching," I answer without hesitation. "Following a hunch."

"A hunch?" She looks askance at me. "You don't have hunches." She snaps her finger and points at Phobos. He stops pawing at her and stands back. "You make deductions, and you follow clues."

"Yes. That's what I meant. I've been following clues."

Her eyebrow raises skeptically. "In the middle of the night?"

I point at the still dark eastern horizon. "It's barely the middle of the night yet. We've hours before sunrise."

"Go get Jane!" Tess signals the direction. Phobos and Tromos race off, creating two rippling furrows in the grass. We follow in their tracks. "What clues did you find?" she asks me.

I clumsily stumble and clutch at her arm to avoid twisting my ankle. "We need to hurry home, straightway, and rouse Miss Stranje. There is much to tell. Did only you and Lady Jane come out looking for me?"

"Yes." She picks up the pace. "The others were asleep. I woke to find Jane sitting in the window, mooning over that letter that arrived yesterday from Alexander Sinclair."

"That awakened you?" I ask.

"No." She swats at a tuft of grass.

"You had a dream?"

"I'd rather not say."

"I see. How bad was it?"

She breathes out heavily and walks even faster.

"You may as well tell me." Holding my tone in check, more worried and curious than she could possibly know.

She hesitates, stops, and turns to me. "That's the thing. It was more peculiar than bad."

"Peculiar?" I can no longer keep the curiosity out of my voice, so I try levity. "Ahh, so the whole of England wasn't dying of a plague then?"

"That's not funny." Tess frowns and starts walking again. "No. It was nothing like that. I dreamt about Ghost."

"Ghost?" I can't keep the panic from my voice. In the

distance, Lady Jane is running toward us with the wolf dogs bounding playfully at her side. We resume our brisk stride. "What about him?" I ask as nonchalantly as possible.

"Oddest dream I've ever had. He was bleeding. *Profusely*. There was blood everywhere." She gestures widely and then bats a gnat away. "Yet, he wasn't dying. I don't understand it."

A full second passes before I realize I need to close my gaping mouth and catch up to her. Somewhere inside of me, a childlike Seraphina dashes out of her hiding place, arms raised, shouting to the sky, "*I wasn't the only one who saw it!*"

Tess is still talking. "How can a man lose that much blood and not die?"

"I don't know." I shrug noncommittally.

"Do you think your shot wounded him worse than we realized?"

"No." I answer too quickly. "I-I aimed for his arm. I doubt it did much damage."

"That's what I thought." She heaves a sigh. "You should've aimed for his rotten heart. If you had, I wouldn't be left trying to figure out this confounded dream."

"Perhaps he has wounds we don't know about."

"I suppose. Ghost has bled heavily before. There was that time he and Gabriel nearly slashed each other to pieces. And we all witnessed that big puddle of blood on the beach, yet that spy lived."

"Only for a short time." I pluck a seed head from the grass and brave a more pressing question. "Where did you see this happening to Ghost?"

Tess shrugs. "I couldn't tell. It was too dark."

I rake the seed pod through my fingers and shakily ask, "Did you see anyone else there with him?"

There's no time for her to answer. Lady Jane catches up to us in a mad rush. "Sera!" she gasps, and flies into my arms, hugging me so tight I can scarcely breathe. "Thank goodness you're all right. We feared the worst." She takes stock of my face and arms as if checking to make sure all my limbs are properly attached. "Good heavens! What happened to you? You look as if you've been mauled by a bear."

"Yes." Tess frowns. "You do look rather a sight."

I can't help but laugh at Jane's worried expression. "I'll tell you all about it. First, though, we must hurry home and awaken Miss Stranje. I've come across some vitally important information that cannot wait till morning."

"So, you're not hurt?" Lady Jane scans me with her lantern and leans closer. "Wait! Is that blood on your skirts?"

I gape at her. *Is she seeing Ghost's blood, too?*

"There." She grabs my skirt and inspects it closer. "It is blood."

"Oh, that little bit." I breathe in, relieved but also a little disappointed. "That's nothing. I scraped my leg in one of the secret passages. I'll attend to it later. For now, though, it's most urgent that we—"

"Yes, yes. Hurry home."

Home.

CHAPTER 12

FROM TURMOIL TO DISASTER

JANE LOOPS HER ARM through mine and tugs me into a brisk lope toward Stranje House. The wolf dogs remain outside to guard the grounds while we quietly enter through the side door. The three of us are not even half-way down the hall when we hear Tromos and Phobos barking outside. "What are they going on about, now?" Jane sighs.

"That's their warning bark." Tess hurries into the foyer. "Something is amiss. It's coming from the front of the house."

We follow her, and the barking gets louder and louder. Suddenly we hear violent pounding on the door.

Tess stops suddenly. Her lamp drops to the floor and sputters out. "No," she murmurs as if she sees something horrible.

"Tess? What is it?" Lady Jane raises her lantern and illuminates Tess's blanched face. "What's wrong?"

"He..." She points. "It's happening—" Tess's chest heaves as if she can't catch her breath. "It was so long ago... I-I'd thought it must be only a dream."

"With you, it's *never* only a dream." Jane sets her lamp down and hugs Tess, chafing her arms to revive her.

The banging on the door grows louder and more insistent. A man cries out, "Open! Open! Wake up! Please! *Please*. For pity's sake, open the door!" His pleas dissolve into keening.

The sound has me running toward it. Altered, though it is, I recognize that voice.

Mr. Chadwick!

I race to the door, flip the latch, and fling it wide. Quentin Chadwick stumbles into the room and collapses to his knees. Grief rolls off him like a crashing tidal wave that floods the entryway.

"What is it! What's wrong." I hunker down beside him.

"My parents..." He hides his face in his hands.

Miss Stranje dashes out from her room onto the

second-floor landing, brandishing a pistol in her hand, her dressing gown flying wildly about her. "What's ado? What's happened?" Madame Cho bursts out of Daneska's room, her bo-staff in the ready position.

Mr. Chadwick's brown hair is tousled and matted with blood. His nose is swollen, and there's a jagged cut across the bridge—most likely broken. One eye is so puffy I am surprised he can see clearly.

"Oh no!" I cover my mouth, realizing what has transpired.

They beat him.

And worse. Something much worse, because the grief racking his body pounds its fists against me too. I clasp his arm. "I'm so sorry."

"Terrible news." I call up to Miss Stranje. "It's Napoleon. He and his men have taken over Mr. Chadwick's estate. That's where they're holding Prince George."

Quentin squints up at me and despite the lumpy bruises and cuts on his face his expression narrows at me, incredulous, as if I am some sort of monster who callously spewed out these heinous facts.

"H-how did you know?" My hurried explanation momentarily arrests his anguish. But an instant later his features twist again into a mask of pain.

He is so distraught I can scarcely bear it. Tears well up in my eyes. I smooth my hand over his arm. "What horrors you must've faced. I am so sorry."

"Napoleon!?" Miss Stranje demands. She, *who never*

runs on stairs, and roundly scolds anyone who dares such fool-hardy behavior, races down the steps as if the house is on fire. "Tell me!"

Maya and Georgie follow right behind her.

He's so traumatized, I hesitate to say more in front of him. But Miss Stranje needs an explanation, and Quinton is in no condition to give it to her. I have no choice. "Napoleon and Ghost did not sail back to France as we'd thought. That's why Captain Gray couldn't find them." I tilt my head, silently pleading for her to wait until later. But she frowns at me expectantly.

I glance apologetically at Quinton. "That night, um, the night I shot Ghost, they did indeed sail from Brighton past Beachy Head."

"Yes. We knew that much." Her leg is jouncing impatiently. "And."

I take a deep breath and quietly explain. "Ghost and Napoleon were both wounded, and their ship had caught fire during the fight. There must have been more damage than we thought. Instead of crossing the channel and fleeing to France they sailed their crippled ship along the British coast, hunting for an inlet or cove where they could hide and make repairs."

Mr. Chadwick stares straight ahead. Sorrow billowing from him in dark suffocating waves. I scoot closer rubbing his back gently, wishing I knew how to help him. Speaking to him as soothingly as I know how. "Is that what happened, Mr. Chadwick? Napoleon and his men took over your estate and that's where they're holding Prince George?"

He nods.

Lady Jane circles to my side. "Did you see His Royal Highness? Is he still alive?"

Mr. Chadwick stares blankly at my hand, and all he can manage is another choking nod.

"So, that's what they did!" Georgiana thumps the banister and murmurs to herself about it being the obvious solution. "I should've thought of that."

Maya stands off to the side humming soothingly. She must sense Mr. Chadwick's overwhelming distress.

Dark circles ring his eyes and the puffy one is turning purple. That cut on his nose has not been cleaned properly, it's crusted with blood and swollen out of shape. They beat him—the blackguards. Worse than even that, his whole being seems bruised. He slumps over like a man who has lost all hope. "We need to tend his wounds," I address Miss Stranje pointedly.

"Come, Mr. Chadwick. Sit. You've been to hell and back tonight." Miss Stranje takes his arm and between the two of us, we help him to his feet and maneuver him to a chair. "You're with friends now. You must tell us all. What of your parents?" Miss Stranje asks.

"My father—" He blanches and lowers his head in his hands. In choking gasps, he manages to say, "Th-they killed him."

"Good heavens! No! Oh, my—" Miss Stranje seems

unable to speak for a moment. She turns away blinking and takes a deep breath. A second or two later, her back straightens, she rests her hand gently on his shoulder and issues a firm command. "Brandy! Lady Jane, fetch a brandy for Mr. Chadwick."

Turning to Tess, she says sharply, "You must pull yourself together, Miss Aubreyson. I need you to rouse the household. Every last one of them, even the stable lads." Miss Stranje sets her lamp on the side table near Quentin.

It illuminates the rips in his shirt and rope burns on his wrist. I stoop down beside his chair. "How did you manage to escape?"

His head remains bowed. "Captain Grey taught us a method... to manage ropes." He holds out his hands in a manner I recognize. It is the same technique Miss Stranje taught all of us. His shoulders slump even lower. "Tonight, the house was quieter. Ghost didn't come to... to interrogate me as he'd done during the day. The man guarding me fell asleep. There's a window in the library. It no longer latches properly. I..." He gestures as if he jumped.

"You escaped." I urge him to keep talking. "How? Surely there were guards on the grounds."

He looks up. "Kept to the shadows. Didn't take the roads. Stayed in the gullies and behind the hedgerows." He lowers his face into his hands again. "They kept me locked in the library away from my mother. I *ran*. I got out and... I just ran." He sinks even lower, as if running had been a cowardly thing to do.

"Captain Grey trained you well. That is exactly what you should've done. Look here, young man." Miss Stranje's forceful command compels him to look up. "Listen to me. You couldn't possibly have fought them all off. You made a wise decision, the best decision for your mother's safety as well." She stoops down before him and softens her tone. "What do you know of her condition before you left?"

He draws in a deep breath, and his eyes flit anxiously to our headmistress. "They're forcing her to tend Napoleon. I heard her arguing with them. You know how stubborn she can be. And now... now that my father is... is d-dead " He chokes on that dreadful word, then he looks up with a clenched jaw and frustration flashing in his eyes. "Now that they've killed him, I fear she will go too far." Quentin winces before continuing. "I didn't know if I ought to escape. I dare not think what she might attempt when she finds out I have gone, and they can no longer threaten her with my life."

Guilt and torment drag cruel fingers over his features. "I had to chance it, didn't I? I heard Napoleon moving about the house this afternoon. If they no longer need her to nurse him, what might they do to her? Especially with her temper." He covers his face again as if trying to wash away his pain. "Escape seemed the only way I could save her."

"It was." Miss Stranje stands and gives his shoulder a hearty pat, as a gentleman might do to another gentleman.

"You saw an opportunity, and you seized it. Well done."

He is not convinced. Agony floats around him, a tumbling cloud of muddled gray. Never did I think I'd see him so...

Confused.

Beaten.

Lost.

He pushes to his feet and paces in frantic circles. "And now she's there on her own. *Helpless.* We need to do something. We have to rescue her and Prince George. We should muster the local militia! And send word to Captain Grey."

Miss Stranje steps in and blocks his agitated pacing. "Take heart. I already sent a pigeon carrying a message to Captain Grey regarding the spy we found yesterday. Shortly thereafter, I received a reply stating that he and his men will set out for Stranje House in the morning. I had intended to write back and persuade him that immediate action may not be necessary. Fortunately, I held off my reply until Sera could return home and report her findings to me." Miss Stranje pauses and glances sharply in my direction. "As things stand, you may rest assured that Captain Grey and his men should be here by this evening."

She knew I was gone.

I stare, mystified by our headmistress. She lifts one eyebrow in my direction as if to say, "Of course, I knew."

How does she always know?

"This evening?" Quentin rakes through his disheveled

curls. "But that's too long to wait. My mother—she isn't herself. We can't delay on account of Captain Grey. If you lend me a horse, I will ride into town and rouse the militia. In an hour or two they ought to muster—"

"Mr. Chadwick, you know perfectly well our local militia is a band of untrained elderly farmers and shopkeepers." Miss Stranje uses a firm motherly timbre which seems to forestall some of his panic. "I doubt half of their muskets still fire properly. They're certainly no match for Ghost and his men. They would be slaughtered within minutes."

Lady Jane hurries in with a glass of brandy. Miss Stranje takes it and places it in his hands. "Here. Drink this."

He obediently gulps it down. "We cannot stand here and do nothing!"

"No." She takes the empty glass from him. "No, of course not." Her face narrows pensively, and she presses a finger against her bottom lip, thinking. The air around her whirs like a beehive until she raises her finger. "I know just the thing. We shall pen an urgent message to the Bexhill barracks. I'm certain the King's legion stationed there will make all haste to save Prince George and your mother. Will you help us write it? Your signature would lend credence to the matter."

"Yes, certainly, but—"

"Splendid! Lady Jane will assist you. She has a knack for choosing the exact right phrasing to produce quick action. The Bexhill troops ought to be able to march to your estate within a few hours of receiving our message. As for your mother, I have known that great lady all my life. Helpless, she is not. Your mother is as wise as she is brave. I'm quite certain when she discovers you've escaped that she'll know you plan to return with help. You need not fear she'll do anything rash."

He shakes his head. "I am not so certain. If you had seen her, you might think differently." Quentin seems to vacillate between panic and despair until in utter frustration he turns his gaze up at the darkened ceiling, darkened all the more by the thick clouds of his anguish. "After they shot my father, she went into hysterics, screaming and..." He stops and his chest heaves with the telling. "She was not herself. I've never seen her like that. She was torn between fury and despair. My father's death changed her."

It changed him, as well. Anguish pools around him in dark bottomless puddles, and he draws in slow sorrowful breaths.

Miss Stranje signals Lady Jane to lead him up to her study. "Compose a brief letter, Lady Jane, and tell Greaves to have our best rider ready himself to deliver it to the fort."

"I'm our best rider." Tess strides back into the room. "I'll do it."

"You most certainly will not! You may well be our best rider, but I will not have you riding miles and miles in the middle of the night to a barracks packed to the rafters with soldiers. Lord Ravencross would run me through if I were to allow anything so foolhardy."

Tess mumbles her objections, but my attention rivets on Lady Jane who is gently guiding Mr. Chadwick toward the stairs on their way to Miss Stranje's study. I watch in awe at how graciously she coaxes him to the task at hand despite his intense inner turmoil. At the foot of the stairs, he glances back at me for the briefest of moments, as if he questions why I am not accompanying him.

No sooner do I start for the stairs than a stern order rings in my ears.

"Miss Wyndham! A word if you please." Our headmistress's tone halts me mid-step. I turn on my heel and face her.

She is not best pleased.

A field marshal never commanded with more authority than our Miss Stranje. Her unyielding expression rips the imaginary security advisor insignias off my shoulders. Those newly won credentials, imaginary though they may be, now lay in tatters on the floor. I try to gulp down my apprehension, except my mouth is bleached-bone dry.

"My dear girl," she says quietly enough that the others cannot hear. "It is not lost on me that your dress is covered in mud and, in this poor light I cannot tell, but it looks as if some of those stains may be blood." She moves the lantern and checks. "Uh-hmm. In addition to being bruised and wounded, your hair is disheveled and nearly undone. And then there is the fact that you tumbled all too readily to the fact that Napoleon and his men had commandeered the Chadwick estate." She pauses and stares gravely down at me. "I expect a report. Walk with me."

A *report.*

She crooks her finger, summoning Maya to her side as well. "We will need my medical kit. Bring it to my bedroom if you would, please. Oh, and on your way, do please check on the doctor sitting guard with the corpse. I heard him snoring. Thank you for that. Given these new complications, are you certain you administered enough sleeping potion in his wine to keep him asleep until at least midmorning?"

Maya pulls her wrap tighter around her shoulders. "Yes. He should sleep soundly till then and perhaps an hour or two beyond, if—" Before she can finish answering, a loud rap resounds on the door.

Miss Stranje sighs and rubs her forehead. "Tess, do let Lord Ravencross in before he thumps the door down."

"Wait!" Georgie protests. "At this hour, with all that is going on, what if it isn't him?"

Tess ignores Georgie's concerns and hurries toward the door as if heaven waits on the other side.

Miss Stranje sighs. "I seriously doubt Ghost or any of his men would be so polite as to knock."

At the mention of Ghost, I reflexively stiffen. Miss Stranje whips around sharpish, as if that minuscule response professes all the sins I have committed this dreadful night.

The door swings wide and Lord Ravencross strides into the foyer on a chill wind. He grasps Tess as if she has just narrowly escaped death. "You're all right, then?"

She nods and sinks against his broad chest.

He breathes in a momentary sigh of relief and asks Miss Stranje, "What's amiss? In the middle of the night, I thought I heard her calling from the cliffs. I assumed it must be a dream." He turns back to his betrothed and frowns, looking her over again as if making certain she is really alive and well. "Ah, but it wasn't a dream, was it? Here you are, dressed as if you've been out running and it is the middle of the night."

"Early morning," she protests.

"Night," he booms. "Then, to put paid to the matter, your confounded wolves set to with their infernal yipping. You know how everything echoes across the clifftops."

Tess mumbles, "You could try closing your windows at night."

"I tried to get back to sleep, didn't I?" He glares at her and rubs the back of his neck. "Then, what do I hear next, but some fellow howling and pounding at your door as if the world has come to an end. So, I came running as fast as I could."

"Thank you, my lord, for so readily coming to our aid. And for, er, dressing." Miss Stranje's eyebrows lift slightly. "I appreciate your expediency. Although in your hurry, you may have forgotten an item or two of clothing."

He'd donned work trousers, boots, and jammed a

pistol into his waist, but his shirt hung open without a tie to secure it, and he wore no coat.

"Tess, kindly let go of your fiancé and stand a respectful distance. Until you are married, some proprieties must be observed." Miss Stranje sniffed as if guiding us in such matters was a burdensome chore. "And now, my lord, as to *what is amiss*. It is fortunate that you are here. A great deal is wrong, I'm afraid."

Georgiana's foot taps, and like a puppy with an itch, she bursts out with the news. "We know where they're holding the Prince!"

"His Royal Highness the Prince *Regent*," Miss Stranje corrects. "Napoleon and Ghost's men have commandeered the Chadwick estate. It seems they've been hiding there these past weeks, presumably while Napoleon recuperates."

"Here?! That close?" He steps excitedly toward Miss Stranje. "You know what this means—we've no time to waste. We must rescue Prince George!"

"And my mother." Mr. Chadwick rushes back down the stairs. "Exactly my thoughts! And now that you're here—"

"Your mother?" Ravencross frowns, not comprehending.

"Yes. They're holding her prisoner, along with all our servants, forcing her to tend Napoleon. And..." Mr. Chadwick pauses, clamps his lips tight, but then he throws his shoulders back and presses forward, standing face-to-face before Lord Ravencross. "They murdered my father. He tried to warn me away when I was coming to the house and one of Ghost's men shot him in the back."

Lord Ravencross groans. "Cowards!" He shakes his head and places his hand on Quentin's shoulder. "Your father was a good man, Chadwick. Yes, of course, we must rescue your mother."

Miss Stranje clears her throat and explains our plea for assistance from the King's Legion at Bexhill-on-Sea. "If you were to add your signature and seal, my lord, it will strengthen our request."

Ravencross rubs his chin. "Yes, of course, but you do realize Bexhill is several hours away, and time is of the essence."

Miss Stranje sniffs, straightens to her full height, and addresses Lord Ravencross with the same imperious tone she uses to call us to task. "What I realize, my lord, is that we are only seven women and two men. By my reckoning Napoleon commands a crew of at least twenty battle-trained sailors. And that does not even take into consideration the cadre of Iron Crown assassins and henchmen that accompanied Ghost. Apart from calling for troops I don't see what choice we have."

Lord Ravencross's jaw knots, unknots, and knots as he stews. Finally, he raises his chin and steps forward. His countenance shimmers like a knight of old in polished armor, a man ready to die in battle. "I remember your father, Miss Stranje. A brave noble gentleman. Fearless some say.

And I have heard the stories Captain Grey tells of your own heroics. So, you will excuse me for asking, but when has a mere force of thirty or forty men ever stopped you?"

His words seem to knock her backward. She catches her breath and looks away before facing Lord Ravencross, looking as stiff and sharp as any steel blade. "There is much to consider. My young ladies' lives for one." She gestures to us. "Not only that, but the slightest wrong move on our part will surely cost our Prince Regent his life."

He gravely searches each of our faces, hunting for signs of cowardice. Seeing none, he lifts his chin. "Look at them." He gestures at all of us. "Your young women are as brave a troop as ever lived. You've trained them well. What's more..." He glances at all of us. "If we fail to act quickly in this situation, it is just as likely to result in Prince George's death. I would not risk their lives, nor yours, if the future of our country were not teetering in the balance."

Miss Stranje's slippered foot taps with silent frustration against the foyer tile. "I'm keenly aware of that, my lord."

He opens his arms. "Look here, I was there when Tess took a running leap from the dock onto the back of Captain Grey's boat when they sailed for Calais. By all accounts, you and these young ladies went to France and conducted an incredibly daring mission to rescue Lord Wyatt." He looked at all of us proudly. "This lot breached the Iron Crown's fortress in Calais. *Broke into it.* Flew in

SANCTUARY FOR SEERS

on a kite of some sort, and set fire to the place—what's more, you succeeded in saving Lord Wyatt!" He took a step closer. "I ask you, should we be any less daring in trying to save Britain's monarch? Not only that, but Napoleon is within our grasp. *Bonaparte himself!* Think of it, Miss Stranje. You know what capturing him could mean."

"*The war would end,*" Georgie murmurs.

"Exactly." He crosses his arms with finality.

Miss Stranje is not one to be cowed. She stares at Lord Ravencross for far too long. It is as if she's counting her options and sorting through scenarios the way someone else might count the stars. Just then, I catch a glimpse of something, a being I think, shining like sunlight just beyond her shoulder, only then it vanishes from my view.

At last, Miss Stranje exhales. "Very well, my lord, your points are well-taken. We shall devise a way. However, it requires planning, planning for which we have precious little time."

She begins directing us as if she is a symphony conductor. "Lady Jane, you and Mr. Chadwick go quickly and write that plea to Bexhill with all haste. We will require both of you in the strategy room at a quarter past two." She turns to the rest of us. "Madame Cho, we will need you with us as well. Ask Cook to take your place sitting watch over Lady Daneska."

Madame Cho mutters something in Chinese, and then she speaks up. "I am not certain Cook can manage. Lady Daneska has improved since yesterday. She is more

175

recovered than she lets on and woke up several times during my watch. I caught her trying to slip out of bed. You know her penchant for escape."

"*That girl...*" Miss Stranje exhales loudly. Her tone ripples through the air with a trifle more irritation than normal. "Yes, very well. You tell Cook that if Lady Daneska should give her any trouble, she has my permission to take a cleaver to her."

A grim smile flashes across Madam Cho's lips as she glides away, but she quickly dashes it away.

Lord Ravencross gives us a terse nod. "If you will excuse me. I shall collect a few more weapons from my house and rejoin you shortly." He heads for the door and opens it but stops. "It is not only *our* lives at risk tonight." The oil lamps flicker, as his words echo through our foyer. He glances back at us. "You and your young ladies must devise a plan to extract Chadwick's mother and our Prince Regent *before* those soldiers from Bexhill arrive. It is good they're coming in case, *God forbid*, our plan should fail. Trouble is, I know my brother. If he's cornered, Ghost will slaughter as many as he can—maids, cooks, mothers, Prince George, stable lads—*all*. An open attack from soldiers will result in the death of all the hostages."

At that, Lord Ravencross marches out of Stranje House and shuts the door, leaving all of us staring silently into the abyss.

CHAPTER 13

BEHOLD THE MONSTER

"TESS?" MISS STRANJE BREAKS the silence and queries our dreamer of terrible dreams. "Have you had a dream foreseeing any of this?"

Tess turns away from staring at the door and shakes her head. "Only what just happened with Mr. Chadwick."

"That, at least, is one hopeful note in this dreadful opera." Miss Stranje flicks her hand at the rest of us. "Everyone go. Dress for a fully armed night raid. Daggers strapped, weapons at the ready. Meet me in the strategy room in fifteen minutes."

We scurry away to do her bidding, but our stern head-mistress, turned even sterner field marshal, clasps my arm, holding me back. "Well? Out with it."

When she stands this close, I am intensely aware of the unseen strings that knit us together. I can tell she is annoyed with me. Nevertheless, there is only room for the truth between us. A lie would knot and twist our threads of understanding into a prickly tangle. So, I lick my lips which have turned unaccountably dry and tell her the truth. "Ghost was tunneling through the old southeast passageway."

She stares at me, her brown eyes turning darker as she leans closer. "He *was* tunneling? Or he *is* doing so now?"

I try to swallow the dry lump forming in my throat. "Was."

"You should've told me you suspected this." She sniffs with irritation. "I take it you snuck out to investigate. Did you find evidence in the tunnel, or did you actually see the man?"

Not wanting to answer, I look down at the toes of my shoes.

"Hmm. Given your silence, I must assume you saw him. And perhaps..." She rocks forward on her toes. "Sera! Tell me you didn't confront him. You didn't, did you? Surely, not alone."

"No. Of course, not."

"That's a mercy." She almost takes a step to proceed up the stairs. *Almost.* Instead, her attention whips back to me. "You are saying you didn't confront him, but—" She sucks in a sharp breath. "Never say he *caught* you?"

I silently admit the truth with a half shrug and stare more pointedly at the floor.

"He did! Oh, Sera. And you lived to tell." She scoops my arm under hers and practically drags me up the stairs. "What happened? What did he do to you? How did you escape?" She rattles off questions faster than even Georgie could and tugs me up the steps at breakneck speed. Suddenly she stops on the second-floor landing. "Did he hurt you?" She looks me over, surveying my tattered dress for more blood. Finding none, she stiffens. She didn't find a serious injury like the stab wound Ghost dealt Lady Jane when he captured her. Her eyes widen. "Please, tell me he didn't... didn't..." She blanches, and the golden atmosphere around her floods with burgundy fear. "Sera, did he hurt you in another way?"

"No." I shake my head. "Not that."

"Thank God!" Her breath rushes out in a relieved sigh, and she hugs me for one brief moment. "But I don't understand." She gives my shoulders a shake. "*You* shot him. Ghost is the sort of man who does not stop until he gets revenge. How is it you are still alive?"

Ah. Now she has stumbled upon the sticky bit.

Wary of her hawkish scrutiny, I gently extricate myself from her hold and turn away, desperately hoping to avoid telling her this part. Only Miss Stranje is too shrewd, too dogged about the details, to let the matter go. She pulls me close again, and her words rasp against my cheek. "He let you go because he wants something from you, doesn't he?"

I fail to take the step onto the landing, and she catches me. I can't breathe.

"He wants Daneska!" she declares with ringing certainty. "That's it, isn't it? He spared your life in exchange for you bringing Lady Daneska to him." She bustles me down the hall to her bedroom and ushers me to a chair. "Sit."

My shoulders droop in an unladylike slump. If Madam Cho were here, she would rap the back of my chair with her bamboo stick and tell me to sit up straight. But I can't help it. *I want to curl up and hide.* The truth will damn me in Miss Stranje's eyes, and the thought is ripping me to shreds.

At this juncture, I could lie to her. She isn't looking at me. What's more, she's convinced she has struck upon the correct answer. I might get away with it. Except my stomach sickens at the thought. How can I deceive her? This woman has been kinder to me than anyone else on Earth.

She closes the door and wheels around. "How does he expect this exchange to take place?"

My hair has fallen across my face, and I glance up through the strands.

"Go ahead. You can tell me." She leans down and tucks my hair back with the tenderness of a mother to her child. "When and where are you supposed to take her?"

My heart is breaking. I know that love cannot survive

in the poisonous mud of lies. I will lose her if I lie, but I will lose her, too, if I speak the truth.

She stands, hands on her hips, waiting. "Come now, Sera, you *must* tell me. How can we proceed if you don't?"

In answer, I sink farther until my shoulders hunch under the weight of decision. Yet there is really only one possible choice. Even if I must face her damnation and live out my life locked in an attic, I will not—I cannot—lie to her.

Hot tears burn the corners of my eyes as I struggle to find a way to tell her.

"Sera, what is it?" She stoops down in front of me, her voice crooning, and concern softening her features. "What's wrong?"

I grip my folded hands into a tight knot on my lap. "It is not Lady Daneska that he wants."

"No?" She blinks. "What then?"

At this point, I am too weary, too broken, to do anything except confess. "He has a notion that I might be able to..."

"To?"

I try to swallow but my mouth is drier than ever. It is hopeless. "To rid him of the demons that harass him."

"Demons?" She draws back, staring at me as if I have just yanked off my mask and revealed that I am indeed a monster.

The clock on her mantel ticks.

My life is over at five minutes before two.

Her head tilts as if she's trying to make sense of a terrifying puzzle. "By demons, you don't mean simple unsavory character traits, do you?"

I shake my head.

"You mean the real sort."

I nod.

Barely.

"Ah, I see." She sits back on her haunches. "Then it's true."

I jolt to attention. "What's true?"

"You are able to see into spiritual realms." She says this as if it is an everyday thing, like it is nothing more than a comment on the color of my hair.

I squint at her. "You knew?"

She shrugs and gets up to retrieve a basin of water from her bureau. "I have long suspected as much." She sets it on the floor beside her. "Come, let us roll down your stockings. If we are to be ready for the raid, I must tend to your cuts and scrapes."

"But... but you never said anything."

"Of course not." She dips a cloth in her basin and sets to work wiping the crusted blood from my leg. "I assumed, if my theory was correct, that you would discuss it with me when you felt comfortable doing so. A gift of that sort is extremely personal."

A gift?

Gift. I love her for saying that more than I thought humanly possible. "Then... you don't think me a monster?

An abomination?"

"No. Quite the opposite, my dear girl. Quite the opposite. Your mother's letters intrigued me. The idea that you might possess such a rare gift is largely the reason I allowed you to be a student here at Stranje House."

I must've fallen asleep or hit my head in the tunnels. Surely, the words I hear her speaking cannot be real.

She turns down the hosiery on my other leg. "Oh dear, I'm afraid there will be no mending these stockings. They're torn beyond repair."

The door opens and Maya comes in carrying the medical bag.

I whisper to Miss Stranje, "He made me promise I would try, except I can't do it."

"Can't do what?" Maya asks in a soothing cadence.

Miss Stranje finishes washing my leg and wrings out the rag, turning the water rose pink. "She can't rid Ghost of his demons."

Maya and Miss Stranje exchange glances. Maya exhales loudly and turns to me. "So, you do *see things*."

All this time and both of them suspected.

My cheeks flood with heat.

"She does." Miss Stranje answers matter-of-factly, then she turns a quizzical look on me. "Are you quite sure you can't help him? It might be the answer to our problems. If you were to do it, perhaps he would come to his senses and stop trying to destroy England."

Maya hands her a clean rag. "Yes, that would be—"

"No!" I'm astonished at both of them. I draw back and shake my head. "No, I can't. What's more, I doubt it even works that way. If I were *somehow* able to send them away, it's his intense anger and hatred that invites them. He wouldn't suddenly turn into a docile lamb. More importantly, I am *not* an exorcist."

"Quite right," Maya says too cheerfully. "I doubt an army of priests could banish the evil surrounding that man." The air about Maya vibrates like yellow flowers in a breeze. She covers her mouth, no doubt hiding her mirth. How in the world she can find something humorous in the midst of this horrid night is beyond me.

Miss Stranje wraps a clean bandage around the scrape on my shin. "Yes, but Seraphina, you have something I doubt many priests have. I've observed you when you think no one is looking. At times you appear deeply entranced in conversation with some invisible being. *Praying,* I assumed. And if that is true, it would mean you have the sort of relationship with the Almighty..." She pauses and ties a knot in the bandage. "Well, I should think if anyone could free Lucien from his demons, it would be you."

I sit back, my posture straight enough to please even Madame Cho. "How?" I smack my hands against the seat of the chair. "It's impossible. I haven't the vaguest idea how one would go about doing such a thing."

She pokes at the wound on my other leg with a pair of tweezers. "What have I taught you girls to do when you don't know how to accomplish a task?"

"Ouch." I wince as she pulls out a splinter.

Maya answers spontaneously, as if we are in the middle of a class lecture. "We are to consult an expert." She sets a neatly folded bandage beside Miss Stranje.

"Just so." Miss Stranje continues her rather painful investigation of my puncture wound. "Sera, unless I miss my guess, *and I rarely do*, you have a relationship with the Supreme Authority on such matters. I suggest you ask Him." She taps whatever it is she extracted from my leg into the basin and points at a jar of ointment. "We'll need salve on this leg. I don't know what she gouged it on, but it is already festering."

"Oh, I nearly forgot—" I recall what else I needed to warn her about. "Bats have infested our east wall on the lower level. I cut my leg trying to jump past their droppings."

"Ewh. Bats." Maya purses her lips, and the two of them glance at one another, silently communicating their concerns. "Should we try the powdered charcoal to absorb the infection?" Maya immediately sorts through the numerous vials in the medical bag.

"Yes, and also the drawing compound." Miss Stranje holds out her hand for the items. "If we survive this night, I'll instruct Greaves to have the bats smoked out. We can't allow them to breed in the passageways."

"*If* we survive?" Maya's hand trembles slightly as she hands our forthright headmistress the jar. "*If*? Are you that uncertain about this raid on Ghost and Napoleon?"

Miss Stranje doesn't respond. Silently she applies the powdered charcoal, smears a thick layer of a castor oil unguent over it, then quickly wraps my calf. "That's done. Now both of you hurry and change into suitable clothing. *Quickly*. Move along. Meet me in the war room in five minutes."

"War room. She only calls it the strategy room when she anticipates a battle." Maya loops her arm through mine as we hurry to the dormitorium. "And apparently it does not bode well for our chances of survival."

I tighten my hold on her. "Let us hope a sound strategy will prevail."

"Yes," she says in a lilting cheery tone, but her yellow lion flower bloom wilts under a gray shroud. She sighs. "I wish Lord Kinsworth were already here. I would like to bid him farewell before dying."

"Maya!" I scold. "You mustn't be fatalistic."

Just then Georgie rushes out of the dormitorium toward us. She grasps Maya's arms and turns her around. "Think of it, Maya! Later today Lord Wyatt and Lord Kinsworth will arrive." Her sparkling grin seems to brighten the entire hallway. She spins away. "I'll go on ahead and set up the maps." She waggles her palm and calls out in a singsong voice, "Today, Maya, Today!" She's halfway down the hall before either of us can respond.

"Yes. I will be so happy to see him." But Maya's broad smile fades and she mumbles to Georgie's retreating backside. "*If* we survive,"

In heavy silence, we swiftly change into dark blue blousy pantaloons and loose-fitting, tunic-like overdresses of the same dark color. Maya finishes first and turns to me to help secure my ties. "Ghost does not deserve your help. You know this, do you not?"

I straighten my pantaloons, kicking out one leg to make certain I can move unencumbered. "The man is wounded, Maya, deeply wounded. And in much the same manner as I am. Do I not deserve mercy?"

"You are nothing like him. Nothing! Not in the least. If you could hear the dreadful sounds his soul makes—"

"Sounds?" I tilt my head trying to grasp her meaning.

"Never mind!" She huffs and bends to lace up her half boots. "He is evil. You may trust me on this."

I wince. Wishing it weren't so. I know she is mostly right, and yet... "Not entirely. He's not evil through and through." I reach into my wardrobe to find my boots. "No one is. He and I are more alike than you might think."

She straightens, fists on her hips. "Seraphina Wyndham! Why are you playing these sad songs for him?" Sparks of her irritation shower over me. "You are too soft! For pity's sake, guard your heart."

"I cannot help it," I admit in barely more than a whisper, and stoop to tie my boots.

"Hmmm," she mews at me. "Yes, I know. I'm not angry at you. It's him. Ghost and Napoleon. They're the cause of this horrid predicament we're in." Then she sighs and her ire drifts away. "That soft heart of yours—I suppose it is the reason I love you so much." She tucks back some of my fallen hair. "We must hurry. Let me pin your hair up for you."

I clutch her hand for a moment. "I don't mind if I die tonight. Truly, I don't. But you—"

"Me?" She stops me from saying more and bristles. "I fully intend to live to a ripe old age and give Lord Kinsworth a great many children. Which means you, my dear Sera, must promise not to do anything foolish in this war Ravencross and Miss Stranje are undertaking. Swear it! For if you should die, I shall be quite vexed with you."

I lift my palm. "Nothing foolish."

Risky.

Dangerous.

These options remain open.

I will do what I must to protect the only family I have left.

CHAPTER 14

WARS AND RUMORS OF WARS

OIL LAMPS ARE ABLAZE when we enter the strategy room. Smoke coils and floats in snake-like wisps about the ceiling. Weapons that must belong to Lord Ravencross sit in a heap upon the threadbare sofa, everyone is gathered around our big worktable spread with maps. Maya joins them, but I stand back watching.

Mr. Chadwick is pointing to a rough sketched outline of his house and the roads leading to it. "My mother's rooms are here." He pauses to look up at me, squinting, as if he does not recognize me with my hair tucked back in a severe bun and wearing these dark fighting clothes. My entrance distracts him for only a moment. He takes a breath and turns his attention back to the drawing. "But, if Napoleon's men have taken over all the bedrooms, I've no idea where they might be holding her. Prince George is being kept in one of these two upper rooms. Either here, or over here. They kept me tied up in the library below, and I heard a lot of tramping about above me in that direction. And I'm quite certain I overheard His Royal Highness shouting demands from there."

"How do you know? Anyone might've been shouting demands." Lord Ravencross rubs the stubble on his chin. "Could've been Ghost or Napoleon himself."

"I suppose." Quinton rubs the stubble on his jaw carefully avoiding the cuts and bruises. "Except I heard a distinctly British accent, and whoever did the shouting employed the royal 'we' in his cry for sustenance. At the time, I suspected Napoleon might be in this other room here. I recognized Mother's footsteps coming and going in that direction, and since they made her tend Napoleon's wounds, it seemed the natural conclusion."

"Yes. Yes, that makes sense." Lord Ravencross takes an even broader stance and leans studiously over the map. "So, we ought to make our approach through the cornfields on this side. If we stay low and keep to the shadows behind this wall, we can enter the house from the kitchen entrance and if there's a back stairway—"

"Begging your pardon, my lord," Lady Jane interrupts

with an impressively gentle tone. "Don't you suppose that by now Ghost will have discovered Mr. Chadwick has made his escape?"

Lord Ravencross purses his lips and heaves a deep breath. "Most likely."

"I agree," Lady Jane nods. "And if that is the case, surely, he and his men will take the reasonable course and evacuate the premises with their hostages in tow. Particularly if Napoleon is recovered enough to be walking about the house as Mr. Chadwick observed yesterday."

"Yes. Of course!" Georgie pipes up. "They'll make a run for it."

"A logical conclusion." Mr. Chadwick leans in and smacks his palms on the table. "Then we must hurry! They could be on the run this very minute. My mother..." He stops and clamps his lips together, as if he's afraid to speculate as to her fate under these conditions.

But Lady Jane raises her palms, calming their enthusiasm. "If they are indeed planning to leave, we might have better luck ambushing them as they make their exodus." As the others lean in to listen, Jane continues serenely laying out her plan. "They've had enough time to make essential repairs on their ship, and if they plan to retreat to France, they will make their escape by sea." She sweeps her hand over the map near the Chadwick estate. "The question is where did they dock their ship? Mr. Chadwick, do you have any idea where they might have concealed Napoleon's sloop?"

Quentin brightens under Jane's attentive gaze. Some of his courageous purple halo bursts back into being. Seeing it, I experience an uncomfortable twinge in my solar plexus. Lady Jane is both beautiful and charming, graceful and clever. Whereas tonight, I feel like a lump of cold porridge. If jealousy does indeed taint one's atmosphere with sour green as I have seen it do to others, I'm afraid at the moment I may look a bit like an unripe apple.

"Indeed, I do." Quinton sets his house drawing aside and bends over our map of the coast. He taps his finger on a small inlet. "Here! This is our dock. It has not seen much use over the years, and it isn't wide enough for a full galleon. But at high tide, a sloop such as the one you described belonging to Napoleon, could glide in and out quite handily. Notice the way the cove loops back behind these cliffs, making it nigh impossible from the open sea to spot a ship docked within it."

"Small wonder we couldn't find them." Miss Stranje rubs her chin considering the location. "That cove is the ideal place to hide a ship. Well, done. Lady Jane." She bestows this rare snippet of praise on her brilliant protégé and points to the shoreline on the map. "Given the steepness of those cliffs, we would do best to make our approach from the beach. If we can climb up those cliffs silently, keeping to the shadows to avoid lookouts from the ship raising an alarm, then we can lie in wait along the path. That will give us the advantage of surprise. We'll have to make our approach without lanterns and hope the moon lights our way. If all goes well, we might just be able to rescue our Prince Regent *and* seize Napoleon."

Lord Ravencross shoves back from the table. His brows are pinched, his lips pressed in a tight line, and a storm cloud brews around him. My breath catches. In this flickering light his mannerisms startle me—they are so similar to his brother's.

"What's amiss?" Tess asks him quietly and touches his elbow.

He gestures at the map. "On the face of it, this seems like a sound plan. Logical. Except my br—*that is to say*, Ghost..." He nearly chokes on his brother's nickname. "...is not logical. Lucian is never one to run from a fight—*any* fight. Especially not one he stands even the faintest chance of winning. What's worse, if he thinks he can inflict damage, he will do it."

"That is how black his heart is," Maya whispers and glances across the table at me.

Mr. Chadwick blanches. "My lord, are you saying that rather than put out to sea, Ghost will stay holed up in our manor just for the opportunity to fight and kill as many of us as he can? What of the hostages? Would he willfully murder them too?"

Lord Ravencross does not look directly at Mr. Chadwick. Instead, he stares into the darkness of the shadows. "Prince George is a bartering chip. He might take him with them when he sets sail after defeating us." Lord Ravencross lowers his head gravely. "But yes, I believe he would do just as you say, even if it means fighting to his death. I wish it wasn't so." He grips the edge of the table with both hands and bows his head. "But sadly, anger and revenge rule Lucien's every waking thought." Regret distorts Lord Ravencross's strong features. "Our best chance is to sneak into the house somehow and extricate the prisoners without anyone knowing."

Georgie leans over the drawing of the house. "That will be exceedingly difficult. Although... if Tess were to climb up the wall to this balcony." She glances up at Tess. "We all know she's quite adept with scaling walls."

Tess and Lord Ravencross exchange guilty looks with one another. Instead of blushing, Tess casts an annoyed look at Georgie. "Get on with it."

"Tess could lower a rope, and two or three of us could climb up and rescue the Prince Regent." Georgie turns to Mr. Chadwick. "Is it possible they have your mother sleeping in the kitchen? If so, you might sneak in through the mud door, and—"

"His mother will be held under guard," Lady Jane reminds her. "Aside from that, how do you propose to get the wounded Prince down that rope?"

"Hmm." Georgie's brow pinches up in consternation. "What if we use a harness like the one we made to use with Lord Wyatt? Remember?"

"Of course, I remember," Jane snaps. "Only it won't work because the Prince Regent weighs close to—"

Miss Stranje clears her throat and glances sideways at

me. Ideas are whirling about her head, spinning and weaving, tiny orbs of light far more luminous than our flickering oil lamps. She's summoning me without words. These impish lights of hers twirl like a dance in my direction, crooking their nonexistent fingers at me.

I move to the table and slip in between Georgie and Madam Cho. Quiet as the white mouse I am, I make my stale bread offering. "I may know of a way."

The room goes still.

Even the lamps seem to stop spitting and flickering. Their smoky tails uncoil and drift lower in slow expectant strands.

I swallow. "He trusts me."

"What!?" Quentin exclaims. "He *trusts* you—that monster? He doesn't trust anyone." He shakes his head. "No, no, you must be mistaken."

Georgie tugs on my arm as if to shake some sense into me. "He's right, Sera. You're the one who shot Ghost. He can't possibly—"

Miss Stranje silences Georgie with a wave of her hand. "Go on, Miss Wyndham, tell us more. What is it you're suggesting?"

I struggle to ignore Georgie's grip on my arm, the turmoil flashing around Mr. Chadwick, and the butterflies frantically beating their wings against my stomach. "We might use Lady Daneska as a distraction to lure him away from the manor house."

Miss Stranje's hawk eyes narrow on me as if she's

hunting for gaps in my plan and weighing it against what I told her about my dealings with Ghost.

Lady Jane sketches intently on a scrap of paper, each scratch of the graphite stick makes my throat feel drier and drier. Without looking at me she asks, "How, exactly, would we use Lady Daneska as a distraction?"

Details. She wants details, and I have not yet worked out the particulars. I press my hand against my fluttering stomach. The confounded butterflies seem to have morphed into frantic bats. "We—that is to say, I—I would approach Mr. Chadwick's house with Lady Daneska in tow. If we stand far enough from the entrance and call out for him, it should draw Ghost and his men out to the front grounds. That would allow several of you to slip in through the back entrance and climb onto the balcony. I will do my best to occupy him long enough for you to rescue Prince George, Mr. Chadwick's mother, and as many of the servants as possible."

Quentin's mouth gapes open as if I am suggesting something outrageous.

Lord Ravencross steps back, raking through his dark hair. "Won't work. Ghost will never fall for it. He'll suspect a trap and shoot you. You'll be dead, we'll lose our prisoner, and all for naught."

"Exactly!" Quentin bellows, and the air explodes around him in colors I do not understand. "Whether he trusts you—*an assertion I cannot fathom*—his men won't care! They shot down my father without a second thought." He smacks his hand against the table and heaves in a breath. "It's too great a risk. You can't go. I—I forbid it!"

"Mr. Chadwick." Miss Stranje employs her stern teacher's voice to summon him down from the boughs. "Unless, unbeknownst to me, you and Miss Wyndham are engaged, I'm afraid you are overstepping your bounds."

With a red-faced grimace, Quentin rubs the back of his neck. In a less demanding tone he says, "I—we have an understanding. And regardless of that. I can't stand by and allow those barbarians to murder another person I care about."

"Ghost won't let them shoot me," I protest quietly.

"You think not?" Lord Ravencross scoffs. "Why? Because you're a female? I assure you he doesn't give two figs about such distinctions. And, as Miss Fitzwilliam pointed out, you fired the shot that wounded him aboard Napoleon's ship. With one bullet Ghost will have both his revenge *and* free his paramour."

"You don't understand." Frustration pushes my voice too high. "He *won't* shoot me. He won't! I know it because this very night he had ample opportunity to kill me. Yet, he didn't. He let me go."

Gasps echo around the table. Madame Cho raps my arm as if I have sinned.

Quentin gapes at me as if I am a stranger. "*This* night?" The air around him pales and shrinks.

"Ghost let you go?" Lord Ravencross shakes his head as if such a thing is impossible. "Why?"

I slowly lower the hand I had clapped over my too-hasty mouth and hesitantly try to answer. "Th-there isn't time to go into the reasons why." Unplacated, they still gawk at me. I gulp and try again. "Miss Stranje thinks he spared me because he wants me to bring Lady Daneska to him in exchange for my life."

"A logical deduction." Lady Jane studies me through a turquoise haze of suspicion.

"Yes." I nod discreetly and quietly explain, "And that is why I think we might consider using Lady Da—"

"Wait!" Quentin points at Miss Stranje but keeps staring fixedly on me. "Miss Stranje *thinks* that is the reason?" His head tilts as he struggles to calculate this troubling equation. Except he can't solve for the unknown variable because I'm hiding the critical factors. "*She thinks,*" he repeats, his woundedness squeezing each syllable. "Which means that is not the real reason."

I catch a shallow breath. If only he wasn't so perceptive. The hurt on his face makes me wince. I want to bury my face in my hands, only that would be childish and cowardly. So, I do my best to answer, except I cannot force it out much louder than a whisper. "Yes. I... I have something else he wants." I look down, afraid to meet his gaze. "I am very sorry, Mr. Chadwick, but I cannot tell you what it is. All I can tell you is that it is something Ghost wants even more than Lady Daneska."

"More than his she-witch?" Lord Ravencross demands skeptically.

I battle the urge to run away and hide from the force of their distrust. It comes at me like a rolling wave that threatens to drown me. Maya and Miss Stranje may understand about demons and such, but the rest of them will not. I cannot let them prod me into exposing my secrets.

If this wave drowns me, so be it.

I straighten my back and take a deep breath. "Yes. But I believe if we offer to bring Lady Daneska to him it might serve as bait enough for our purposes."

Lady Jane plunks the graphite down and rubs at her forehead. She turns to Miss Stranje. "I take it you know what this *something else* is. And pardon my bluntness, but are you absolutely certain it is a powerful enough enticement to keep him from murdering Sera?"

Miss Stranje and Maya exchange covert glances. "Under these circumstances, yes, I believe it is."

"Circumstances. Hmm." Lady Jane turns to me. "Very well then. Sera, your plan has potential, but I would like to amend it somewhat."

I shrink back and offer the table to her.

She adjusts one of the oil lamps and pulls Mr. Chadwick's drawing back to the center. "Napoleon will demand his security be given highest priority, and Ghost is nothing if not thorough. We know from dealing with him in the past that he sets up multiple strategies within every plan and has alternate stratagems for every contingency. That means the house and grounds will be guarded from all sides. Even if you were to lure Ghost and a dozen of his men out to the front drive, slipping in through the back would still prove impossible." Lady Jane glances around the table to see if anyone disagrees with her.

No one does. Madame Cho murmurs in agreement. Georgie sighs. "Like when he set up two bombs at the launch of the *Mary Isabella*."

"Precisely."

"And aimed his rifle at the Admiral if the bombs failed." Tess huffs and puts both hands on her hips.

None of us will ever forget that day. My shoulders slump. What made me so foolish as to think he would so easily leave himself vulnerable?

"Cheer up, Sera. Your plan offers us a workable solution." Lady Jane beams at me. "We need only to alter it somewhat and apply a two-pronged strategy. First, you must change back into the soiled dress you wore earlier with the addition of a dark hooded cloak. You will then ride with all speed to Chadwick manor, behaving as if you snuck out of Stranje House to bring Ghost an urgent message. Be sure to cower and glance around as if fearing you might've been followed. I'll leave you to compose the note. However, it must offer him *both* enticements. Promise to bring him Lady Daneska and give him the other incentive you hold over him. Make it clear that you are offering *both* in exchange for Prince George. Instruct him in the note to meet you at a destination some distance away from the Chadwick estate." Lady Jane leans over the map. "Let's see... some place remote enough that he'd risk venturing there."

I choke out a whispery suggestion. "Would the old lookout tower serve?"

Lady Jane slants a reproachful glance in my direction. "Hmm, yes. That should do." I can tell she has guessed that's where I encountered him earlier. She marks an X on its location. "The old lookout tower is far enough away from the Chadwick estate to occupy Ghost sufficiently. If he protests that the rendezvous is too close to Stranje House, you can tell him that Lady Daneska is still weak and feverish, and that the tower is the farthest you would be able to transport her."

I nod in agreement.

Jane reaches across Madame Cho to grasp my hand. "Sera, you must be brave. If one of his sentries captures you before you arrive at the house, don't resist. Beg to be taken to Ghost. If what you say is true, he will agree to the exchange and release you."

"No. No." Quentin breathes as if he's running uphill. "This is far too dangerous!" He shakes his head and leans over the table pleading with me. "Ghost's men are un-thinking brutes. They could murder you before you even have a chance to hand a sentry the note or ask to be taken to Ghost." He turns to Miss Stranje. "Don't let her do this. It's too much to ask of her."

"Trust us, Mr. Chadwick." Lady Jane rushes to explain, "Sera will approach them acting the part of a helpless in-nocent. It will be child's play for her to convince the guards she has slipped away from Stranje House with an urgent message for Ghost. I assure you—Miss Wyndham has been well trained to play these deceptive sorts of games. We all have."

Deceptive games.

His expression pains me. His face twists into a mask of confusion. From the looks of it, he doesn't know whether to keep fighting to protect me, or whether to believe that I am a master of deception, the kind of woman he would never be able to trust.

I'm not sure which I am, either.

I do know this—he is right not to trust me. Not because I am skilled at deception, but because I keep too many secrets.

I clear my throat and without looking at him explain, "This assignment will require very little deception. For the most part I will simply be telling him the truth. We *are* willing to trade Lady Daneska for His Royal Highness the Prince Regent." I finally summon the courage to face Quentin Chadwick squarely. "Think what this could mean for Britain—for all of us. We have been given the rare opportunity to capture Napoleon and end this wretched war. For that reason and for all the innocent captives trapped in your house, we *must* take this risk."

"Just so," Lady Jane murmurs.

And for the second time that night I declare with complete sincerity, "I assure you, I am not afraid to die."

Quentin Chadwick groans. "No, I can see that." He

leans forward, looking at me as if I am the only person in the room, melting my resolve with the sorrow I see writ in his eyes, and he says, "I, on the other hand, am terrified of losing you."

Terrified?

He does not blush. My own cheeks, however, fill with so much heat it is as if they've suddenly caught fire. I look away.

Miss Stranje clears her throat. "Thus far, this is the only plan that offers us any hope for rescuing the hostages alive." She holds out her palm to Lady Jane. "Pray continue explaining the rest of your proposal."

"You call this *hope?*" Lord Ravencross crosses his arms imperiously. "How can you think so? My brother will never surrender Prince George to us. He'll devise some sort of trickery or—"

"Of course, not." Lady Jane cuts in. "Even if Ghost *were* to agree, Napoleon would never allow such an uneven exchange. This is where the second part of our strategy comes into play."

He uncrosses his arms and tilts his head attentively. We all lean closer to listen.

"Sera," Jane taps the table in my direction. "You must let it slip that Mr. Chadwick came here to Stranje House and that Miss Stranje sent a messenger to Bexhill summoning the Kings legion to rescue His Royal Highness. If Ghost agrees to the exchange, he and two or three of his men will travel to the old tower in order to retrieve Lady

Daneska from you."

When Lord Ravencross begins to object, she forestalls him with a raised finger. "I doubt he will bring His Royal Highness. Ghost's intention will be to take Lady Daneska and whatever else Sera has promised him. With Ghost occupied elsewhere, Napoleon will assume command and oversee their removal to the ship. Ghost may be willing to die fighting an entire legion, but Napoleon is not. Then, as Miss Stranje suggested, the rest of us will have entered the cove from the beach and climbed up the cliff trails to lie in wait for them. This gives us our best chance at rescuing His Royal Highness and capturing Napoleon."

Lord Ravencross leans across the map. "Trouble is, if we are here." He jabs his finger on Mr. Chadwick's cove. "And this little one—" he gestures at me and taps the map where the old tower stands on the edge of our cliffs. "—is over here. It will be painfully easy for Ghost and his men to overpower her and escape with Lady Daneska. We can't just let him go—not after all he has done."

"That is a conundrum. However..." Lady Jane takes a deep breath and presses her fingertips together. "We must face facts, my lord, we are outnumbered. *Grossly* outnumbered. It all boils down to a matter of priorities. If, by some wild throw of the dice, we succeed in rescuing Prince George and capturing Napoleon, we shall have achieved two vitally important, nearly impossible, victories—"

"I'll go to the old tower and wait there." Quentin interrupts enthusiastically. "That way I can protect Miss

Wyndham and stop Ghost from escaping."

Miss Stranje shakes her head. "No, Mr. Chadwick. I'm sorry, but that will not do. We need every man possible with us on those cliffs. Not only that, but no one here knows those trails down your dock as well as you do."

"But she—

"*She* is a soldier in this battle. As are you." Miss Stranje's voice turns to molten iron. "I warned you of the perils before you signed on. I have no doubt that Miss Wyndham will do her part. The question is, are you willing to do yours?"

He sucks in a sharp breath.

Trapped.

His countenance bursts into red flames.

Trapped and angry.

"Yes," he says, and though he barely moves his mouth, that lone word reverberates through the room like the aftershock of a cannon.

For the first time in our acquaintance, Mr. Chadwick looks dangerous. Truly dangerous. He lowers his warm inquisitive eyes and hardens them into cold steady steel. The smooth muscles of his jaw bunch into knots. My breath catches and, despite a sudden rush of heat coursing through me, I shiver.

I catch my bottom lip in my teeth and tuck a wayward lock of my hair behind my ear. I am not altogether certain what he meant by that thunderous response. His mouth said one thing, but his visage seems to say he intends to do precisely as he thinks best.

Nor do I know what to make of the tendrils shooting out from him, cannon-blast-like arms reaching out and winding around me as if they are fiery shields meant to keep me warm and safe.

Miss Stranje, too, seems startled by his intensity. She swallows and frowns briefly before turning to me. With all the harshness gone from her voice, she says, "Sera, my dear, you may go now and change into the gown you wore earlier. Hurry now, time is getting away from us." She then fluffs out the skirts of her fighting dress and crooks a finger at Tess. "Would you be so kind as to assist her in choosing a proper mount." One brow wings up as if they share a secret. "A horse that will get her to the Chadwick estate as soon as possible."

Tess issues a soldierly nod and heads for the door, but she glances sideways at me as she passes by. "I'll saddle Ajax for you."

"Wait." I hurry after her. "Ajax? But he is so tall and—"

She turns sharply and stomps her foot. "Daisy dawdles too much. You may as well walk if you insist on riding that absurd little pony. Ajax is a hundred times faster, and he's not so tall that you can't handle him." She spins around and marches out the door. "Don't fret. I'll talk to him—he'll mind you."

With a sinking feeling in my stomach, I watch her go. I'm not like Tess. I have no command over horses. Or animals of any kind. It is more the other way around—they behave as if *they* own me. No doubt, when Ajax decides to jump over an obstacle rather than go around it, I will end up thrown in a ditch.

Maya gives me a quick hug, and murmurs by my ear. "Be wary of Ghost. He's not your friend, no matter what you may feel toward him."

"All right. But you and the others are in more danger than I am. I'm concerned that all of you must fight a battle on the side of a cliff." I shake my head. "The very thought has me quaking."

"We'll manage." Georgie sidles up and loops her arm through Maya's. "We've all been in skirmishes before. As for me, attending Lord Castlereagh's ball was far more daunting."

She's putting a brave face on it for my sake. I try to smile. "If you say so. But do be careful. No needless risks—"

"Always." Georgie grins.

"Do not be concerned for us." Maya gives me a playful nudge. "We have our ways." She waggles her fingers, pretending she's mesmerizing me, as if I didn't notice the calming overtones in her voice.

Georgie laughs, and they join the others around the arsenal of weapons, discussing which firearm will suit who best.

Miss Stranje steps into the emptiness they left. "You must go quickly now and change out of those fighting clothes. You'll find ink and parchment in my office for writing your note." She reaches for my hand and leans her forehead against mine. "And Sera," she says, ever so quietly, "thank you."

Startled, I ask, "For what?"

She pats my hand, then lets go. "For being willing to do this—to face him alone."

I nod, unable to speak. It isn't her words squeezing my heart. Rather, it's the way she patted my hand, as if I am precious to her. Holding back tears, I hurry out into the hallway and catch my breath.

Tess is already leaving through the side door, setting out for the stable. I head in the other direction until I hear footsteps running after me. Bright sparkling strands of light wing through the darkness, chasing me, wrapping around my waist.

"Sera, wait!" Before Quentin even called my name, my feet slowed to a halt.

I stand in the dark hallway unmoving, afraid to turn around.

What fresh pain will I see on his face?

He catches up to me, and before I know what is happening Quentin pulls me into his arms and hugs me so tight, I can feel his heart hammering against mine, galloping as if he'd just run here from the cliffs. The prickly beard stubble on his jaw brushes against my temple as he bends down to whisper in my ear. "Don't die. Promise me you won't die."

Can anyone promise such a thing?

When I don't answer he holds me tighter. "You can't,"

he whispers. "You're worth a hundred Prince Regents to me, a thousand Napoleons. I'd rather England burn to the ground than lose you."

I shake my head. "You don't mean that."

"I do!" He says too loudly. Then his voice melts into a mournful caress. "I love you, Seraphina Wyndham. I love you."

Impossible. I press my face into the hollow of his neck and shake my head. "You can't mean that. You hardly know me."

"I do." He pulls back and lifts my chin. I open my eyes, blinking at the earnestness in his face. "You're not like other women. I knew that from the moment we first met. You... you're... you're like a prism, Sera. I've never seen the like. You refract the world in such fascinating ways—seeing things no one else sees."

I shrink back at his words.

Seeing things?

Does he know? He can't know about all that. He wouldn't be standing here holding me like this if he did.

He doesn't.

But if not *that*, what does he mean?

He leans closer, and I cannot escape his intensity. The air around him, though we are in a dark hall, begins to glow with light. "You're like a diamond," he says, breathing the words into the air between us. "In a world filled with lifeless stones."

His words flow over me running their fingers through

my mind, smoothing long forgotten wounds. He closes his eyes briefly as if he's in pain. "I can't bear to be parted from you. Promise me you'll be careful around Ghost and those murderous swine working for him. Promise you'll stay alive."

His warmth coils around us and for the first time in my life I feel, if not understood, appreciated and respected. And something more...

What is this feeling?

Protected?

Cared for?

I'm not entirely certain. My eyes fill with water. I do know this, whether I live or die today, I shall store this moment in the deepest trenches of my heart forever. So for his sake, for the kindness and goodness he has shown me, and for the hope he needs going into this terrible battle, I decide to tell a lie.

It is difficult though, and my voice cracks and stumbles in the trying. "I promise."

Blissful gold floods the air around him. He cups my cheek and pulls me even closer. His mouth covers mine, gently at first, but then it quickly turns deeper and more desperate as we drown in the heavy wine of a goodbye kiss.

I pull away and he moans.

"I must go." Edging away, knowing we may never see each other again in this life, I memorize his features even though they are wrenched with sorrow. "Be well." I whisper and tear away from him, racing for the stairs.

CHAPTER 15

SOLDIER, SAILOR, MONSTER, MAIDEN

TESS HANGS A LANTERN on a hook in the stable. She pats Ajax's neck and whispers in his ear—something in her native Welsh no doubt. Then she pats his backside, and my steed takes off into the night with me bouncing like a rag doll on his back.

I am not afraid of getting lost or of Ghost killing me. Well, I admit to being somewhat leery of that last bit. That is to say, I don't relish the idea of getting shot or stabbed. As for getting lost, *that* would be nigh impossible. I had a look at the map. The way to Mr. Chadwick's estate is simply a matter of making seven turns correctly. That does not trouble me. On the other hand, riding a horse like this one—now *that* has me quaking with fear.

Ajax is much too tall for my comfort. Although Tess is right, Daisy would've ignored my nudging and stopped to dawdle so often that it might've taken two days for us to arrive at the Chadwick estate. This horse likes to run, and he bolts forward at the slightest shift in my seat. I'm riding astride because Tess insists it is infinitely more practical. "You learned to swim," she reminded me before boosting me into the saddle. "Riding astride is much easier."

She's wrong about that. I'm hunched over, hanging on for dear life, and praying. Praying prodigiously. "Please, please, please, God, don't let this horse throw me into a ravine, or leap over a hedgerow at such a great height that I cannot hold on. I'm begging you..."

Thus, did I murmur most of the way there.

Our sixth turn takes us into a broad wooded area that borders the Chadwick estate. Ajax slows his pace and stops suddenly, shying and jerking his head about as if he senses danger. "Walk on," I whisper and thump him with my heels.

Moonlight drips sparingly into this thick stand of silver birch and alders, so we must pick our way slowly. Ajax's head is raised, and his ears stand straight up. "It's nothing, boy. Those rustling sounds are probably just mice scampering through the leaves." I lean close to his neck, patting him, and murmuring soothing platitudes I do not feel. But at the sudden movement of a deer darting out from behind a nearby bush. I sit bolt upright, and he rears lightly.

Breathe.

I command myself and press a hand to my chest. Only then, the shrill *kew-wick kew-wick* of an owl undoes me. I jump like a startled rabbit. Ajax skitters sideways, and my leg snags on a holly branch. I move my leg, and he lurches forward.

"Whoa! Slow down." I fight to stay seated and regain control. "Calm down, boy. It's only an owl hunting her dinner."

Just an owl. Ajax answers with an indignant snort. He doesn't believe me, but at least he settles back into a walk, and I rub my leg where the thorns pricked through my skirts.

Finally, we emerge from the trees and make our seventh turn at the end of a hedgerow, which puts us within sight of the house. A gentle breeze has temporarily chased an opening in the storm clouds. Moonlight washes over the Chadwick's long gravel drive, gilding the shrubbery and decorative urns with gleaming silver.

I allow my hood to fall so that anyone who might be watching from the house will notice my hair. I want them to know it is only a harmless girl invading their lair. A few minutes later, I yank it up again, and glance over my shoulder, following Lady Jane's instructions to behave as if I'm frightened that I might have been followed.

Ajax must sense the danger ahead, or else he is picking

up subtle clues from my nervousness. I nudge him forward, even though his withers flinch and he whinnies as if I'm forcing him to walk into a fire. He's so noisy that if Ghost's lookouts haven't spotted us yet, they certainly will now. I pat his neck. "I know, boy, I know. But this is where we must go."

He tosses his head and sidesteps, fighting me. I wish I had Tess's gift with animals, but I do not. The best I can do is pat his neck and try to console him. "Shhh. Calm down. It's going to be all right."

He settles, somewhat, but I still feel wariness humming through him. Does he sense that my words are mere mollifications invented to calm him down? Are horses that perceptive?

Movement to our right snares my attention. A man leaps out from the shadows and jerks the reins from my hands.

A startled scream escapes before I can clamp my lips around it.

Ajax rears. It is all I can do to clutch the saddle's pommel and hang on. This is it. Jane warned me to expect capture.

Stop panicking.

Act!

Breathe. Think.

I can almost hear Miss Stranje's calming voice telling me, "You have trained for this." So borrowing her firmness, I order my quivering joints to steady themselves.

Ajax makes several noble attempts to stomp the intruder. "Please, sir," I rasp, still fighting to keep from flying out of the saddle. "You must help me."

"*Arrêt!*" he commands my horse and jerks viciously on the reins. My noble steed decides against having his mouth jerked to pieces and resorts to snorting angrily and expressing his displeasure by high-stepping sideways.

I continue leaning over Ajax's neck, clinging to the saddle, playing the part of a frightened girl. Which, by the by, requires no artifice at all. Mere seconds ago, I'd been quite certain this stubborn horse would toss me through the air and crack open my skull on the gravel drive. "Please!" I plead. "I need to speak with Ghost. It is most urgent, *s'il vous plaît.*"

It is not lost on me that the man has drawn and cocked his pistol. The barrel glints threateningly in the moonlight. It is unclear whether he intends to shoot me or put a bullet in my obstinate horse.

"Shhh," I whisper to Ajax. "Settle down." I try to apply a similarly soothing tone to my captor, although a decided quiver in my voice betrays me. "Please, sir, *c'est très* important. I must speak with him." How I wish I had Maya's gift of persuading others with her voice, or Lady Jane's bold commanding manner. Instead, even to my own ears I sound like a pitiful child.

The man does not shoot me, at least not immediately. He silently secures Ajax's reins to a tree branch while staring unwaveringly at me from under the dark brim of his hat. His suspicious gaze cuts through the night like gleaming knives.

I must do something.

"Please, if you will not take me to him, I've brought a note. You must deliver it to him." But when I reach inside my cape to retrieve the missive, he raises his pistol.

"Stop," he roars with a thick French accent.

Immediately, I hold my arms wide. My French is only passable. Nevertheless, I try again to explain that I carry a message for Ghost, but that it would be best if I could speak with him in person. "C'est impératif."

"He will not like it." His English is better than I expected. With a one-armed swoop around my waist, he yanks me from the saddle and jams the pistol barrel into my breast. I dare not take a breath, nor can I swallow the lump of fear choking me. The sharp tang of rum assails me when he speaks. "What can a sparrow like you have to do with one such as him?"

"More than you need to know." A tall dark figure steps out from the shadows behind my captor.

Ghost.

The guard stiffens and loosens his grip slightly. He withdraws his pistol.

"Let the sparrow fly." Ghost growls.

I exhale with relief.

It is all I can do to keep from rushing into Ghost's arms. Except I can't. I dare not even take a step. The instant the sentry lets go of me, my knees crumple. My legs have turned to water. Perhaps it is from being unaccustomed to riding so far or so vigorously. Or maybe I am simply too frightened to stand.

I reach out for help.

Ghost catches me before I fall. "Stay with her horse," he orders the guard and props me up. "Walk," he says gruffly, but continues to support me with an arm around my shoulder. With each tentative step, the jelly in my legs begins to firm up.

"You're lucky Jacques didn't shoot you. What in the blazes possessed you to come here alone?"

Ghost is treating me as if I am a foolish child. That will not do for my mission tonight. "What makes you think I came alone?" I say, jutting my chin upward, hoping to provoke him, and unsettle his annoying confidence.

Except it doesn't work. He stops walking and stares down at me wearing a most peculiar expression. Surprising sparks of amber flash in the dark cloud surrounding him. I gape in open-mouthed wonder.

Is that...? Can it be...?

It is!

I never ever expected to see anything even remotely resembling humor in his vicinity. "Oh!" I blink and lower my eyes afraid he will see something in me that he shouldn't. I should not feel a fondness for this man. It is wrongheaded. And foolhardy. A complete disaster in the making. I grit my teeth and face him with as much severity as I can manage. "You think me silly and that I should have guessed you would post watchmen at every approach."

He emits a self-satisfied, "*Hmph.*"

It dawns on me how very thorough he must have been. "In that stand of birch trees—the owl I heard, that was one of your men signaling, wasn't it?"

He doesn't answer. Instead, he tugs me back into a brisk walk, filling the air with his forcefulness. He is taking me deeper into the trees rather than toward the house. "Where are we going?"

No answer.

I need to break the silence between us and somehow diminish this hold he has over me. "Very well, you know I came here alone. But I did it for a very good reason. I—I came to make a trade."

He stops again and, this time, exhales as if I just said the stupidest thing in all of history. This time he does not emit any sparks of humor. I'll admit, I am disappointed. At least if he thinks me a fool he could have the good grace to find it humorous. Instead, he is all hard sharp edges again. He must've already guessed what I intend to trade.

I swallow and take a different approach. "Aren't you the least bit curious how I found you?"

"Let me guess, the Chadwick whelp went running straight to Stranje House." Ghost clasps my arm, and we are walking again.

This is not going at all how Lady Jane planned. She made it sound so simple. Let it slip that the troops are coming from Bexhill. Instead, I say, "He looked awful. You tortured him."

"I interrogated him. Useless prat. A pity I didn't kill him when I had the chance."

"Why must you say such things?"

"Because I mean them."

"Cruel," I mumble, stumbling along beside him.

"War is cruel."

"There's a difference between killing in battle and murder."

"Is there? And you would know this because...?"

"Everyone knows the difference. It's common decency. In battle one must kill or be killed. It is different if one's foe is tied to a chair and helpless."

He only grumbles in response.

"And even worse, I overheard Quentin telling Miss Stranje your men shot his father in the back."

"Quentin?"

"Mr. Chadwick," I say, even though I know he is questioning my familiar use of Quentin's Christian name—a slip on my part—but I pretend otherwise. "Your man murdered an unarmed man. Shot down him like a dog. And..." I bite my lip.

"And?"

"And Mr. Chadwick was so incensed he insisted they call out the militia. But Miss Stranje was frightened and instead of the militia she sent a rider to Bexhill begging the King's legion to come."

Ghost's storm clouds flash with blood-red lightning. Only it's not the soldiers he's furious about, it's me. He slams me against a tree.

"What game are you playing at?" Teeth bared; he presses in until his face is inches from mine. All that biting rage—I can't breathe.

He thunders, "Emma Stranje is never frightened! Never!" It is more than anger twisting his features. I've wounded him somehow. "Not *that* woman." He gives me another shove and lets me sag down the rough bark of the elm. "You're lying." He squints at me, as if I am gutter slime.

I squeeze my eyes shut, cringing at how stupidly I'd soiled the trust between us. Arrogant of me. I know full well I'm no good at deception. I shouldn't have tried even so small a prevarication. I hate lies as much as he does.

"I misspoke." I bow my head, focusing on the decaying leaves beneath my feet, too upset with myself to face him. "You're right. She wasn't frightened." I recall the exact details of Miss Stranje's face during the interchange between her and Mr. Chadwick. "Not frightened. She was... a more appropriate word might be concerned. She explained to Mr. Chadwick that the militia is a band of untrained farmers and shopkeepers with only a half dozen guns between them. And that you and your men would butcher the lot of them."

"Practical," he snarled.

"Yes, practical. Prudent. So, she sent for the King's

legion instead. But when I heard it, I..." I wrap my arms around myself, overcome by a sudden chill. "The truth is I am the one who was frightened." I catch my lip and look up at him. "I knew you wouldn't run when the soldiers surrounded the house. You wouldn't, would you?"

He doesn't say anything, but the way his chin lifts and the steely set of his jaw is answer enough.

I close my eyes against his harshness. "So many people will die." I swallow and dare to peek up at him again. "I thought... I thought if I came to you, I might be able to stop it all from happening." I push away from the tree and stand up. "No one needs to die. You told me you would trade Prince George if I would rid you of—"

"I remember what I said!" He grits his teeth and steps back clenching his fists.

"Please." Dead leaves crunch under my boots as I reach out to him, pleading. "I'll try to do it, if only you will give me Prince George."

Why is he hesitating?

The air surrounding him thickens, turning blacker and more viscous than even the gloom of the woods around us. I hold out my hand, beckoning him out of darkness threatening to swallow him. "I'll do what you asked of me. I'll do it *now*, if you'll release the Prince Regent to me."

He rubs his forehead. "You told me you didn't know how."

"I thought about it, and I think there is a way." I touch his shoulder, but he pulls away as if my touch stings him.

"Please. I'll even bring Lady Daneska to you if you'll just let me take Prince George. I know Lady Daneska means something to you. You went to all that trouble to dig out the collapsed tunnel so you could sneak her out of Stranje House. It will be my turn to stand watch soon. Even though she's still sick and weak, I can sneak her out through the secret passages and bring her to you near the tunnel where I found you earlier."

He wheels on me, towering over me like a menacing bear. "Did it never occur to you I was trying to get into Stranje House so I could cut that self-serving wench's throat before she tells Emma or Grey anything I'd rather they didn't know?"

"No! No, that isn't true." I shake my head, edging away from him and nearly losing my balance. I grasp his sleeve to keep from falling. "You wouldn't do that. You wouldn't! You love her."

"Love?" He glares at me as if I am an ignorant child. And for the first time since seeing him again his tormentors appear. Like shadows hidden within shadows, they darken and materialize into our world, polluting these peaceful woods with the poisonous stench of death.

He leans close and says through his teeth, "I would cut that baggage's throat without a second thought. Just as I will cut yours as soon as I figure out what your game is."

I can't bear to look at him, nor do I want to see the hateful beings sneaking around behind him, so I look up at the moonlight trickling through the leaves. "I don't believe you."

"No?" He pulls out his dagger. "Then believe this."

He brandishes the wickedly curved blade in front of my face. Innocent moonbeams twirl along the steel edge—an edge that I have witnessed performing the very act he now threatens to do to Lady Daneska and me.

His anger wearies me to the bone. What a pitiful waste of his life! Why must he spend it on hate and vengeance?

I don't care that my eyes are watering. I will not stave off this grief.

Instead, I speak to him with a boldness borne of the heartache for what he could be. "I thought you wanted my help?" I stand straighter, ignoring his wretched knife, and I push closer to him, pointing at his chest. "Instead, you invite them to come hiss their venom in your ears." I jut my chin in the direction of the nearest fiend leering over Ghost's shoulder.

"I invited no one." Ghost's eyes wince into tight slits. The shadowy hoard must already be murmuring their spite at him.

"Didn't you? Then why are they here? Your anger is an irresistible siren song for them. You may as well have whistled for your demon hounds."

He grabs my arm as if I am his anchor to this world. "Well then, girl, do something! Send them away."

"Is that how you think this works?" I tilt my head at him, incredulous. "I am not their master."

"I thought you said..." His words trail off as I glance

down at his hand clutching my arm. He sees it, too, that he's holding on to me, not as a captor, but as one clinging to me in desperation. He gives me a gruff shake and tightens his hold into a harsh fist. His roughness does not ease the sorrow I feel for him.

Whether or not I asked for heavenly help in that moment, I cannot be certain. Such interactions occur faster than a blink and generally without words—fleeting images and bursts of meaningful colors make such requests much more fervently.

Whether by gift or request, warmth and strength flood my being, bathing me in fearless understanding. And I know *they* are here too—the others—the unseen ones who move in the light.

I am not alone.

"Let go of me." The air of command in my voice startles even me. Ghost's fingers fly open as if my flesh has burned him.

I step around him and approach the gathering swarm. They shrink together, conferring with one another, scheming, seething at my interference. It is not me who speaks, instead a far greater force speaks through me and issues a simple command. "Leave him."

Two words.

Yet those words gust through these woods like a whirlwind blasting through the trees, bowing their branches. The shadowy hounds of hell stumble backward, howling and shrieking. With frustrated snarls, they vanish into the void.

Ghost stares at me, open-mouthed. He doesn't gasp, but his shock trembles in the air between us like a startled bird, uncertain which direction to fly. He retreats into the shadows and roars, "What *are* you?"

His question stings. I've heard it too many times before, aimed at me like a ruthless spear.

An accusation.

A curse.

Only now, for the first time in my life, I know the answer.

What am I?

"Loved." That lone word passes over my lips softer than a whisper, yet with a certainty that stirs the leaves around us and sets them rustling again.

Until this moment, I'd never fully comprehended the serenity hidden deep within me. No matter how troubled I felt, or how lonely, or how frightened, I could always run to that place deep in my heart and find shelter.

My hiding place.

And I was never alone there.

I finally understand. It's true that I may not be loved by my parents or any of my family, but there is a being infinitely greater than any of them, and that being loves me boundlessly.

I know this without so much as even a quiver of doubt.

Here, in these dark woods, pestered by demons and shaken by a murderer, peace rushes through me with so much power it feels as if it might burst out in rays through my fingertips. How can I *not* smile? I turn back to Ghost, unable to disguise my joy.

He does not smile in return.

No, he sags against a giant elm as if I have thrust a blade into his heart.

CHAPTER 16

RIVER OF REGRET

IT IS NOT MY JOY wounding Ghost, but rather it is his own shame scorching his soul. Agony swirls around him. I wish I couldn't see it, but the rot filling the air around him is unmistakable—a river of regret so caustic it stings my nostrils.

In the face of his pain, my joy recedes, but the peace I'd felt remains, wrapped around me like a protective shield.

"You—" He stares at me sideways, as if it is too painful to look at me straight on. His arms hang limp at his sides.

"You made them go." His words are half bewilderment, half declaration, as if saying them aloud might assure him it really happened.

I nod, quietly, sadly, wishing I didn't have to warn him. "They'll be back."

Despite being a powerful man, the wounded boy flinches as if I am whipping him anew. "But you made them leave."

"Yes..." I reach for his hand and gently lift it along with the razor-sharp dagger he still grips in his fist. "Demons are like starving dogs who feast off your anger. Your hatred beckons them. They smell it wafting through the air just as vultures catch the scent of a carcass."

I gently pry the carved handle out of his fingers. And he stares with rapt attention at my hand wielding his fearsome pirate's dagger.

"If you want them to leave you alone..." I place his dagger across my palm and offer it back to him. "Put away your knife. Sheath your vengeance."

He takes it from me and stares at the two-edged blade, a blade that has torn through too much flesh and ended too many lives. A breeze tousles his curls, and ripples through my cape. I stand before him patiently awaiting his decision.

"Impossible." His gaze finds its way to me. Those eyes— so wounded. Yet so recklessly fixed on his path.

I want to scream at him. *No, no, choose a different way.*

"It's not," I plead.

He jams the dagger back in its sheath.

Now, it is my heart pierced by him. I had foolishly hoped he would cast away the venom poisoning his soul. I bow my head to hide the sorrow crumpling my features.

No! I will not hide it.

I stomp my foot against the grass and leaves beneath us and glare up at him. "Why? Why must you be so set on ruining England? Can you not see how it is destroying you?"

He leans close, and despite the sulphuric tears searing their way down my cheeks, he spouts his nonsense. "Because sometimes, little one, you must burn down a thing before it can be purified of its filth."

And so, we stare at one another. Me, heaving with frustration. Him, chilling the air around us with icy determination. I swipe at my cheeks. "Very well. I did my part. I rid you of your demons for the time being. Will you honor your promise and bring me Prince George?"

He backs up and inhales furiously. "That pompous little toad. What I will gladly do is hand you Prinny's head on a platter."

"That wasn't our agreement."

He heaves like a bull ready to charge. "Napoleon won't—"

"Of course, Napoleon won't like it. Did you expect anything less? Is he not still recovering from his wounds? You are in charge of all this, are you not? The watchmen in the woods, the spies on our beach—these are all your doing not his."

His answer is an irritated glare.

I list out the facts on my palm. "*You* are his protector. *You* are the only reason he has not been captured. You can do as you see fit." *There*. That was convincing. I smile as if I have won the point. "If you were to decide, I daresay, you could bring the Prince Regent to me *now*, this very minute."

That stubborn look tells me he is not going to do anything of the kind. "Tell me," he scoffs. "Did you really think you could haul that fat prig all the way back to Stranje House on that little bay you rode in on?"

"Ajax is not little." I cross my arms.

"He's not big enough. You've seen Prinny. It would take a shire plow horse to carry him, much less the two of you."

"I—I could walk and lead the way."

"Pfft," he says and crosses his arms. "Don't be daft."

"I am *not* daft." I lift my chin. He says nothing, so I concede a little. "Well, perhaps, I did not think through the details of transporting him properly. In my defense, this has been an exceedingly difficult night."

"Hmph." He sneers at me. "And you are making it all the more difficult."

I kick at a small mound of leaves, and they don't even have the good grace to scatter. I straighten my shoulders and try to sound as stern as Miss Stranje. "Very well then, I'll offer you a compromise. There must be a suitable horse in the barns on this estate. You bring Prince George to the old lookout tower, and I will bring you Lady Daneska. I'll meet you there in two hours." I turn to march back through the woods to where I left my horse, except he grabs my arm and spins me around.

His lips are pressed tight, yet I can tell he wants to say something. I see it in his eyes.

I tilt my head studying him. "What?"

"You," he begins but shakes his head. "You are exasperating, and reckless beyond comprehension, but... you're not like other women."

I look away, not sure why his comment makes heat rush to my cheeks. It isn't exactly a compliment. Maybe it is the way he holds my arm as if I'm made of velvet and his thumb cannot help but unconsciously smooth up and down.

"What I mean is..." He blinks and grimaces as if losing a fierce inner battle. Then I notice a rose tint blooming in the air around us. My breath catches. Does he mean to kiss me? No, that can't be.

"I—I have to go," I say raggedly. "They'll think something is amiss if I'm not there when it is time for me to sit with Lady Daneska."

Except he doesn't let me go. "I wish—"

A hundred endings to his sentence run through my mind. And I don't know whether I should pull away or stay there waiting impatiently. Wretched curiosity moves my lips. "You wish...?"

"Never mind." Ghost yanks his hands away. "Just go."

He has banished me, yet I am unable to move.

Why must he be so confusing?

Frowning, I ask, "What is it?"

"Nothing of consequence. Go!" He turns and walks away.

The darkness of these woods nearly swallows him before I hear him say, "I'll meet you at the tower."

At least, I *think* that's what he said.

⁞  

Alone now, I retrace my steps through the trees, struggling to decipher Ghost. What did he want to say? There were clues. I know there must've been. Why couldn't I read them? Usually, I'm the first to solve Miss Stranje's test ciphers. But Ghost is impossible to decipher.

Still baffled, I retrieve my horse from the grumbling mean-eyed sentry. Instead of helping me climb onto the saddle, that brute stands there, arms crossed, leering at me like a sneering troll.

Climbing up is no small feat on my part. Ajax is so tall, I can barely reach the saddle. In order to hoist myself up into the stirrup and get my leg over the saddle, my skirts ride up shamefully high. I'm sure Tess would've accomplished this far more expertly. And if that man smirked at her, as he is doing to me, she would rap him smartly with her riding crop. I, on the other hand, duck my head in a clumsy struggle to get situated atop Ajax, who decides at that inopportune moment to be contrary.

That despicable churl slaps my unruly horse's rump. Ajax bolts forward, and I am left flailing like a caught fish in a mad attempt to keep hold of the reins. That awful man laughs at me with such loud disdain that it resounds over and over in my ears as I ride back to Stranje House.

Two hours.

He will meet me in two hours. Ajax trots at a bone jarring pace, but a half hour has already passed, and we are not yet home. Wind whips my hair loose, and I flick a bug away from my face. As soon as I get to Stranje House, I will need to wake Lady Daneska, dress her properly, and feed her some broth so she has the strength to walk. If she is too weak to walk...

Hhmm, if she can't walk, we will have to ride. Perhaps Daisy will do for that short a trip. For now, though, I must go faster, so I risk nudging Ajax with my heels and he breaks into a brisk bouncy canter. Twenty minutes later, I slide off his back and hand him off to the stable boy.

The house is quiet. Except for our few servants, who must have returned to their beds, everyone is gone. According to Lady Jane's plan, Miss Stranje and the others should be on their way to Mr. Chadwick's cove where Napoleon's ship is hidden. To prepare for the rendezvous with Ghost, I dash up the remaining stairs and stride down the hallway. But I find the door to Lady Daneska's sick room standing open and slow my steps.

As instructed, our cook, Magda, is on guard inside. Cook is not a dainty woman. Over six feet in height, she's built like a Nordic giantess and probably weighs twenty stone. Her snow-white hair glimmers in the flickering lamplight. Ordinarily, her heavy black eyebrows are set in an alert but perpetual glower.

Not today.

Today, she is sprawled in a chair, legs stretched out, arms flung wide, snoring louder than a rattling mail coach. As Miss Stranje suggested, Magda did indeed bring a cleaver with her. I would not have thought such measures would be necessary. Now, though, I wonder. Cook's Viking-worthy weapon has slipped from her grasp. The chunky axe-like head rests on the floor with the wooden handle poised near her dangling fingers. If she were not snoring so loud, I might've thought her dead.

And...

Lady Daneska's bed does not look right.

Lady Jane once warned me not to underestimate our former classmate. "Daneska learned to scheme before she left her nurse's teat. And she probably bit that off on her way out." Since then, I've learned the hard way that Jane was right.

Truly. Wraiths and demons need not lure Lady Daneska into evil. To the contrary, I suspect she could teach them a thing or two about cunning and corruption.

The oil lamp is turned down so low, it is naught but a glowing ember, scarcely enough light to distinguish whether that lump on the mattress is our treacherous patient or, as I suspect, merely bedding wadded up to approximate the shape of our devious prisoner.

"Aaaghh!"

I cannot help but groan. I am tired beyond reason, and after that jaw-rattling gallop, every muscle in my body feels as if it has been beaten with a stick. Atop that, Britain's future dangles by a dangerously thin thread. And now, if Lady Daneska is on the loose—

I yank back the covers.

God help us all!

CHAPTER 17

A TWO-PRONGED STRATEGY

Miss Emma Stranje
Two hours earlier; descending the cliffs of Stranje House

MY YOUNG LADIES STORM down these cliffs as if they were born at Stranje House. I press my lips tight in a futile attempt to quash the pride welling up in my chest. This is not the proper time to wax sentimental, yet I cannot help it. They've become remarkable women. Even our brilliant new student, Georgiana, impresses me with the confidence she has developed.

And there is Lady Jane... she glides down these

treacherous paths with the poise and elegance of a queen treading the halls of Buckingham Palace. When I think of how she dazzled the patronesses in London with her strategic prowess, my heart swells.

Some time ago, I had thought perhaps Lady Jane might be the one to take my place at Stranje House. Now, however, if we should survive this mission, and if by some miracle we are able to rescue His Royal Highness the Prince Regent, I expect she and Mr. Sinclair will marry and produce a handful of little masterminds.

Tess, on the other hand, has little use for the machinations and politics of high society. I watch as she effortlessly maneuvers over boulders and bounds over crevices and narrow places where the path has fallen away. She glances back at Lord Ravencross, who despite his injured leg, is doing his best to keep up with her.

"Watch your step," she cautions, and points out a crumbled drop-off.

"Mind yours," he grumps. "And stop skipping around as if you're immortal. One slip of the foot and—"

Tess ignores him and sets off again, intentionally performing another daring leap.

I chuckle quietly. He'll have his hands full with our Tess. I don't have favorites. I love each and every one of them as if they were my very own daughters. Tess, though, seems to lighten my heart most often. It is ironic that a girl who endures such agonizing dreams should be the one who fills me with the most mirth.

Mr. Chadwick jars me out of my ruminations. "Do you suppose Miss Wyndham has reached my estate by now?"

He walks directly behind me, ostensibly so that I might guide him down these cliffs. He seems sure-footed enough to me. And after his display earlier, I suspect he insisted upon taking the rearmost position, so he would be able to turn around and race back to rescue Seraphina should he suddenly deem it necessary.

"Not yet." I retrieve the small watch from my pocket and dust off the clock face. "By my reckoning, she should arrive there a quarter hour from now." I show him the time and put it away. "You must not dwell on it, Mr. Chadwick. Miss Wyndham is an extremely capable young lady."

"Capable, yes." He hesitates. "In matters of perception she is unequaled. But in other ways, she…" Quinton Chadwick pauses, and I am tempted to turn around, only I shan't like seeing the worry on his face. Worry that mirrors my own.

I lengthen my stride, even so, his words still land softly on my shoulder despite my attempt to outpace him. "In other ways, Miss Wyndham seems extraordinarily fragile." He says this with such tenderness that all at once it overwhelms me with both joy and sadness.

Stop it, I want to shout. *You mustn't indulge in such emotions*—they will drown you. I know firsthand the stabbing pain of watching someone you love ride away on a mission from which he might never return.

I want to warn him of the dangers of falling in love

when one is engaged in our business—the business of war and death. Only Mr. Chadwick does not stop talking even when clambering over a boulder. When my foot slips on loose gravel, he catches me from falling without so much as a pause in his conversation.

"Miss Wyndham is so slender and delicate—almost childlike." His wistful sigh is so loud I hear it even over the ocean crashing against the shore.

"I should have gone with her." He flings a stone far out into the sea, and there is that steely tone again. The tone that tells me he intends to protect her at all costs. "I can't bear the thought of her facing that monster on her own."

I wish I could tell him not to worry. Except I can't. That would be callous and hypocritical of me. I, too, have been galloping beside her in my mind, ticking off the mileposts, and envisioning her inevitable confrontation with Ghost.

Again and again, I have asked myself how I dared to send such an innocent as Sera into the lion's den?

How?

Why?

I pick my way slowly and carefully over a pile of crumbled sandstone. The sea laps rhythmically far below us as we take one blind step in the dark after another. Yet, in that slowed motion, while teetering between the stars and earth, clarity arrives. Pieces slide into place. And I realize exactly why I risked sending my fragile tender-hearted Seraphina on such a critical and treacherous mission.

I come to an abrupt halt on the trail, stunned by the answer.

Sera was the only one who could carry out that mission.

Our weapons are only made of iron and steel. She wields something much stronger. Despite her ethereal appearance and quiet nature there's a stillness inside Sera— an unwavering power of some kind that keeps her from bending in the storm. I felt it from the first moment I met her.

Whipping around, I clutch Mr. Chadwick's arm. "You are right. Ghost *is* a monster. A terrifying monster. But, my dear Mr. Chadwick, if you truly love Miss Wyndham, you must understand this about her—in her short life, Sera has faced a great many monsters." I watch as he blinks and struggles to form a dozen questions that I will not answer. "*And* she has defeated every one of them."

Without waiting for his response, I resume my descent. "Now come along. If we are to do our part, we must arrive at your cove well before the tide comes in."

We are not more than a hundred yards from the bottom, when I come up to Maya stopped in the middle of the trail. She rests one hand on the cliff wall for balance and appears to be listening intently. She glances up at me, alarm widening her eyes.

"What is it?"

She seizes my forearm. "Did you hear that?"

I listen. Halfway down the cliffs like this, the waves sound thunderous, especially at night. They crash against the shore, and the roar bounces off the cliff walls. But living beside the sea, one learns to discern subtle distinctions in wave patterns. "Yes, I hear it. The tide is beginning to shift. It will be coming in soon."

"No! Listen *between* the waves." She tugs on my arm and pulls me closer. "There. That! Did you hear it?" Her face brightens.

Between the waves?

Perplexing.

I listen more attentively for a moment and shake my head. "No, I–"

"There!" She bounces up on her toes. "I heard it again. It *is* them! They have come." Her delight fairly lights up the darkness. She hugs me abruptly and dashes off.

"Careful," I call after her. Maya is graceful, but portions of these trails are known to collapse unexpectedly. Heedless of my warning, she scampers off, bounding like a deer on her way down to the shore, yet looking every inch a princess despite wearing our dark blue fighting garb.

They have come.

That can only mean one thing. I try again, endeavoring to listen between the waves. This time, I catch snippets of the same faint music Maya heard. The rhythmic slap, slap, slap, of a steam-driven paddle striking the water.

Captain Grey–my Ethan!

My foolish heart wants to race down behind Maya. Instead, I stand locked in place. How did he know to come? How does he always seem to know when I need him most?

I want to weep and shout hurrah all at the same time. Except I find I am unable to do either. Instead, I stare out into the dark, straining to catch sight of them, wondering if their arrival might simply be wishful thinking on our part.

"What happened?" Mr. Chadwick leans in beside me. "What is it? What's wrong?"

I close my eyes, listening to the excruciatingly faint rhythm of the *Mary Isabella*. "Nothing *wrong*," I murmur. "If we are hearing correctly, something is *right*. Maya believes she heard Mr. Sinclair's steamship sailing in our direction. It could be that Captain Grey and the others—"

"Are headed our way!" He leans in beside me to listen. "Can it really be?"

"Hush." I whisper. Except my own heart is beating so fast I can scarcely hear at all. "If you listen carefully, I believe you'll hear the *Mary Isabella* churning toward us."

Wonder of wonders, Ethan might be nearly here.

But then again, is it wonderful?

That part of my mind that I cannot turn off, starts digging down into scenarios, possibilities, consequences. Captain Grey's arrival might well prove even more tragic, mightn't it? We are embarking on a mission that is bound to end in bloodshed. What if my Ethan is sailing toward his death?

My stomach twists into a Gordian knot.

Like a gentle wind, my father's training voice breezes through me, calling me to task. My father, the spymaster.

My mentor, and the main mast by which I have always sailed. Oh, how I wish he were still here to guide me. Thankfully, he trained me well enough that I know what he would say as well as I know the sound of my own breath.

Emma, my dear girl, you've examined the options.

You've chosen the wisest course.

Now, for pity's sake, stop pondering it to death.

Oh, Papa, it's the *death* part I can't quite let go of—not mine, but his, Ethan Grey.

I can still see Ethan, fifteen years younger, not yet a captain, standing beside my father. He admired my father as much as I did. Papa was training him to take his place in the foreign office, consequently Ethan took it upon himself to oversee *my* training as well.

"Yes, Emma," he would say, with that wicked grin of his quirking up one side of his mouth, and a roguish dimple that made everything he said sound wry and suggestive. "Do stop your incessant pondering."

Humph.

Inevitably, I would cross my arms and glare severely at him. Now, though, I wish I hadn't scowled so often at his teasing. Thank goodness Captain Grey is still alive, but he is called upon to do Lord Castlereagh's covert work so often—one never knows if he will live to see tomorrow. I would prefer he remembers me wearing a kinder, gentler expression.

I will strive to do better. To frown less and smile sweetly. Perhaps *sweetly* would be doing it up too brown.

And now that I think on it, I doubt I possess that sort of kinder, gentler nature.

"I hear it! I do! He's on his way here *now*." Mr. Chadwick slips past me, straining to see. "I can scarce believe it."

"Neither can I." I practice easing my severe expression. "It is a most fortunate turn of events."

"Fortunate? It's the first good news we've had all night, that's what it is!" Young Chadwick fails to notice my feeble attempt at pleasantness, nor does he stop and listen. Instead, he edges past me and shouts, "Thank God!" He then dashes off as if the cliffs have caught fire.

I stand in young Chadwick's wake wondering if he is right. Which, I suppose, is far too much like pondering.

But is it good news?

Or is a tragedy about to tear my world to pieces?

I rub my throbbing forehead in a failed attempt to banish my painfully persistent pondering. With a deep sigh, I turn my face up to the stars warring above us.

God help us all.

Then all at once I am running.

Running!

I am rather fleet of foot for a woman my age, even if I do say so myself. I slide across a pile of crumbled rock, leap over a crevice in the path, bang my shin on a protruding root, still I keep dashing down the slope. In no time at all, I close in on Mr. Chadwick. We're almost to the beach. And Ethan is only minutes away.

Unless, instead of the beach, they steer for the dock hidden inside our cave. That would put them a quarter mile the other way.

That will not do!

"Signal them!" I shout. "Maya, light your lantern! Let them know we're here." The same thought must've occurred to her. Mere seconds after my shout, a thin beam of light shoots out over the waves. And then another from the side. Georgie has climbed up onto the boulders that jut out into the water, and despite the sea spray, she's waving her lamp back and forth. By the time I reach the shore, I can see the *Mary Isabella* in the distance, and she's sailing straight for the beach.

"Georgie! Back up, before you get soaked to the bone." I bark orders at her.

But inside, I am singing Captain Grey's name, *Ethan, Ethan.* And my heart flutters like the trilling thrush flying overhead. If anyone were privy to my thoughts, no doubt they would scold me for behaving like a foolish schoolgirl. So, naturally, I keep nonsensical sentiments such as those well-guarded and stowed away under lock and key.

I clutch my skirts with tight fists and tromp across the sand until I stand mere inches from the edge of the waves. Wind chaffs mist and salt air against my face, yet still I stand blinking and straining to see into this starless night, waiting for the first glimpse of him. *Ethan.*

Lady Jane glides quietly over the sand and stops next to me. Shoulder to shoulder, we stand and watch as the steamship paddles ever closer. Despite her poise and silence, she is uneasy. Jane has telltale signs. Oh, they are subtle to be sure, but if one listens closely to her breathing, her moods become obvious.

"What's troubling you?" I ask.

Other than the fact that we are heading into a skirmish that will undoubtedly test each one of us to our utmost limits and may end in utter devastation.

Aside from that, what troubles you?

Her only answer is another agitated breath. So, I try again. "What's amiss, Lady Jane?"

"Ahem." She clears her throat as if she is about to address a magistrate. "As you know, Alexander is..." She stops and clears her throat again. "What I mean to say is that Mr. Sinclair is not trained for combat of this sort. I think it would be prudent to have him remain aboard the ship. Perhaps we ought to ask him to sail the *Mary Isabella* into the caves and see to it that she is docked properly. Yes, I think that would be best."

I turn and stare at her. She continues to keep her eyes fixed on the ocean. Surely, she doesn't expect me to agree with her. "When it comes to combat, Lady Jane, I could say the same of you."

There it is—a telltale sniff of irritation. "My readiness is a different matter entirely," she snaps. "And it's not true. I brought the crossbow. Surely Madame Cho told you I've become rather proficient with it of late."

The ruddy thing is strapped to her back. So, yes, of

course I know she brought it.

Proficient?

Accuracy is one thing when one is aiming at straw dummies, quite another when one's arrow must pierce a living moving person. I took her rabbit hunting, and twice I saw her miss intentionally. If a rabbit is too hard for her to kill, how will she use it on a man tonight?

I refrain from rehearsing any of that. Now is not the time. "Yes, Madame Cho did tell me. Indeed, the crossbow is an excellent choice of weapon for you."

"I have daggers, too." She traces her fingers over the sheaths strapped to her sides. "I'm getting quite good with them. I fought with Lady Daneska in Brighton, remember."

How can I ever forget? You came away with a bleeding arm, and I remember all too vividly the massive scar you now carry from Ghost's blade.

Instead of saying any of that, I nod briskly. "You will be magnificent. Of that, I am certain." I pat her arm, praying that her magnificence will be death-defying, and that this darkness is hiding the slight quiver I bite down on momentarily. "As for Mr. Sinclair, you mustn't underestimate him. He handled himself quite well when that bomb landed on his ship."

"He did not! He chose to save his ruddy ship," she says indignantly and stamps her boot against the sand. "*His ship!* He could've died. Or been maimed for life. His beautiful mind lost to us forever. As it was, the man limped for weeks."

"I think he dealt with a deadly situation quite admirably." I wrap my arm around her. "Aside from that, you know perfectly well that I am not the one who will decide who goes with us and who does not. It is up to Captain Grey to decide which of his men will accompany us into the fight."

There is that heavy breath again. "He would listen to you. You know he would. I've seen the way he looks at you. The man thinks you walk on water."

"Ha!" I nearly choke. "You are mistaken there, my dear." The *Mary Isabella* churns ever closer, and I can see him now, standing at the helm. Maya's lantern illuminates the crew. He *is* looking at me.

He is!

Only I am no saint. I prefer to think he is looking at a woman he is quite fond of, a woman he can't wait to gather in his arms and kiss—not a saint who walks on water.

"See!" Jane says smugly.

"I assure you Captain Gray is fully aware of my flaws. More importantly, I would never presume to advise him on matters concerning his men."

She wheels on me and clutches my forearm in a very un-Jane-like attitude. "But if he should ask your opinion..." There is begging in her eyes. And fear. Wretched gut twisting fear that I understand all too well. "Please."

I place my hand on her cheek. "Lady Jane, listen to me carefully." I pause, commanding my own wayward overly protective heart to take heed. "People will tell you hate is the opposite of love. That isn't true. Fear is love's greatest enemy. Fear is a vicious weed that strangles love. Our fear clamps an iron shackle around our loved one's leg. Do you understand?"

I know that heavy exasperated sigh of hers—she wishes she didn't understand.

"My dear girl, courage is not a virtue we must cultivate merely for ourselves. The harshest test comes when we must exercise courage in regard to those we love."

Lady Jane squeezes her eyes shut under the crushing weight of my words. I am sorry for that, but both of us must be careful not to poison our loved ones with fear.

I turn and watch the men we love sail toward their destiny. Be it life or death.

Lady Jane stands beside me with her lips pressed tight, drawing short tense breaths. I can feel the mixture of frustration, fear, and resolve churning through her as furiously as the *Mary Isabella*'s paddles slapping the water. Softly, I dare to counsel her one last time. "You know as well as I do, that Alexander Sinclair would not allow you to fight this battle without him. Do not allow your fear to hobble the man you love."

🙰 🙰

The closer the *Mary Isabella* gets, the wilder my pulse races. The moon sails out from behind the clouds for a moment, silhouetting Captain Ethan Grey and his men as they stand on the deck. They look like magnificent titans gliding over the sea.

Mr. Sinclair releases a blast of steam, cutting the engine as they run up on the sand. Captain Grey gestures to Mr. Digby, who splashes out in the waves to help guide the ship onto the beach. We all stand at the water's edge, eagerly waiting. Georgie dashes down the rocks to join us. Lord Ravencross wades out to help secure the raft.

"Hold!" Captain Grey shouts and raises his arm, stopping everyone in their tracks.

He jumps down and wades ashore, his expression stern and fixed as he wades toward me. Ethan grasps both of my hands in his. His fingers are cold, but they warm me through and through. He studies me briefly and begins analyzing. It is his way. "What's happening, Emma. Your signal lamps surprised me, and now I see you're dressed for an assault. Given the hour, circumstances must be dire."

Relief overwhelms me, temporarily robbing me of speech. All I can do is nod.

"You've found them haven't you." He peers at me intently. "Ghost and Napoleon. Where?"

"Not I, it was Miss Wyndham and Mr. Chadwick." I quickly relay the details. Ethan scarcely breathes during the telling, absently rubbing his thumb over my hand as he listens. The instant I finish explaining, he lets go, and my fingers twitch at having been so abruptly abandoned.

"You escaped." Captain Grey nods at Quinton Chadwick, who lingers at my side, and claps the young man on the shoulder. "Well done."

Ethan begins issuing orders, but he remains near enough that I steal the opportunity to relish the strength and assurance of his voice. "We will take the *Mary Isabella*," he says to all of us. "Sinclair modified his steam engine, so she's even faster now. She'll get us there in half the time. If we anchor on the shore before entering the cove, Bonaparte will never hear us coming."

Unable resist pondering, I look up at him and ask, "Then you do think our plan is sound?"

His lips curve in the briefest of smiles, or perhaps it is just the fickle moonlight playing tricks because his wry grin is gone when he leans closer. "Emma," he says in my ear. "It's the best—nay, it is the *only plan* we have. We will have to make do."

He calls to his men on the *Mary Isabella*. "Wyatt, Kinsworth, come and help the ladies board the ship."

I cross my arms, grumbling. "I don't want to *make do*," I mutter through my teeth. "I want to succeed. We *must* succeed." I cannot suppress an exasperated *ponderous* huff.

To which Ethan sniffs patiently and glances up at the storm clouds.

Then I remember another of my father's sayings. "But I suppose, success is measured—"

"One obstacle at a time." Ethan completes the sentence and winks at me. "Now let's get aboard and go rescue our Prince Regent."

"You mean, His Royal Highness, the Pri—aaih!"

Ethan whisks me up and wades out into the waves.

CHAPTER 18

CALM BEFORE THE STORM

Miss Stranje aboard the Mary Isabella

VERY FEW THINGS ARE as restful as sailing aboard a steamship at night. The rhythm of the paddles turning and the sea lifting and falling soothes the soul. I glance around at the daughters of my heart, my young protégés. How foolish that their parents were not able to see their worth. What remarkable women they are! I cannot help but be pleased at the way they look at their young gentlemen with such open-handed love. Not one of them is calculating his annual income or considering his standing in the peerage.

Look at them standing arm in arm with these men, heading into a battle in which we are sure to be outnumbered, and yet they stand facing the dark night like warrior women of old. My breath trembles as I tamp down an overwhelming flood of pride, fear, and a hundred other emotions that threaten to undo me.

Ethan wraps his arm around my shoulders briefly. "Courage, Em. The battle belongs to—"

The Lord.

"Yes, yes, I know." I cross my arms.

He cocks up one side of his mouth. "That's my stubborn little Viking."

"I am *not* a Viking."

"Oh, begging your pardon. My stubborn little *pirate*."

"I'm not little, and I'm not a pirate either." I shove out of his embrace. "And isn't it time you explained our plan to your men?"

Unruffled, the man dimples up at me again. "I was giving them a few minutes to commune with their, uh... *their friends*." He gestures at the couples standing together about the ship—all *communing* a trifle too intensely. All except for Mr. Digby, who appears to be taking a nap atop a crate of supplies, and Madame Cho and Mr. Chadwick, both of whom sit staring glumly out at the sea.

I bristle as if all the sighs and mooncalf stares aboard ship irritate me. "You'd best get on with it, lest they get too *lost* in their *communing*."

"Aye, aye, my Warrior Queen." He salutes me.

Naturally, I huff at him, ignoring my previous vow to not scowl at his teasing. After all, we are heading into a battle for our lives, he'll be more comfortable if I don't change just yet. He might find improvements in my character unsettling.

Captain Grey calls his men together. Lightning flashes on the horizon, and the moon disappears again as they gather in a circle. As soon as he finishes explaining, his men begin offering suggestions and quizzing Mr. Chadwick as to the approach along the cliffs in the cove. Alexander Sinclair remains quiet during most of the strategizing until there is a pause and his American twang cuts brightly through the windy air. "I brought along a dozen or so of Miss Fitzwilliam's Greek firebombs. I've been tinkering with the design and hoped we might have a chance to test them. I don't know if they'll come in handy or not, but if you light the end and throw them quickly, they ought to light up the night like the fourth of July."

One and all looked at him blankly.

"Americans celebrate their independence with displays of fireworks," I explain.

Alexander scratches at the back of his neck. "Yes, well, it might not be like fireworks exactly—a small explosion and some fire."

"Splendid!" Lord Ravencross claps him on the back. "I'll put three or four in my pack."

I opt to do the same, and so does Georgie.

Lord Wyatt presses forward. "There's something I

don't quite understand. Do you mean to say you sent little Miss Wyndham alone to distract Ghost?" Lord Wyatt glances directly at me as if I've run mad. "*Ghost?*" he says, as if I missed the name.

Georgie springs to my defense. "Sera is stronger than you think. And it was our only viable plan."

"Sera possesses some rather unique skills." Maya employs that soothing voice of hers so effectively that even I relax as she speaks. "She assures us she can manage meeting with Ghost, and I believe her."

"She's a clever one to be sure." Lord Wyatt sounds somewhat placated. "And it's extremely helpful that she has lured Ghost elsewhere during this battle. There's no arguing that."

"Aye," Lord Ravencross agrees. "During a fight, it is as if the man is possessed by a demon. And I say that as his brother."

A *demon*—I suspect that may be truer than he realizes. Maya glances in my direction, but neither of us attempts to explain. It is not our place.

"True enough." Lord Wyatt rubs the back of his neck. "When I think back on my time in Calais, when Ghost held me captive—he seemed to lack even a shred of humanity. I cannot fathom how such a wisp of a girl can possibly manage a beast like Ghost."

Mr. Chadwick groans beside me. "Exactly! That's the very reason I wanted to stay back and protect her."

Captain Grey sighs heavily and rubs his forehead

before turning to Mr. Chadwick. "Lad, do you know why Napoleon is the best general ever to stand on a battlefield? What is it that even his greatest opponent, General Wellington, says of him?"

Quentin Chadwick swallows as if he understands what is coming next. I smile at how nobly he faces his commanding officer and takes his medicine. "Yes, Captain. Wellington says that Bonaparte is single-minded on the battlefield. He gives his entire attention to the fight at hand and determines the best way to achieve victory."

"Right. Single-minded. He thinks only of what must be done to win. Do you think you are single-minded tonight?"

"No, Captain," he answers without flinching. "I am not. I cannot stop thinking of what Ghost might do to Miss Wyndham. It's tearing me to pieces inside."

"I see." Captain Grey sets his jaw. And for a moment I am afraid he might be angry with the young man. Instead, my Ethan rubs his chin thoughtfully and asks, "How fast can you run, Chadwick?"

"Depends on my reason for running."

"If it were to go to her aid?"

"Like the wind, sir. Like the wind."

"Very well. After you guide us to the cliffs and point out the vantage positions, you may run. Run back to her. But listen to me—mind you, do not charge in there like a bull. Approach with stealth. And don't interfere unless you see it's a matter of life or death. Your presence would very likely explode the situation, making it worse. When provoked, Ghost is a warrior that would make Goliath quake in his boots."

Quinton Chadwick nods obediently, but I see the fire in his eyes and the fist he clenches at his side. I daresay, for Sera, he would take on Goliath.

CHAPTER 19

DOWN TO KNIVES

Emma Stranje and the others approach the enemy.

A RISING WIND BLOWS mist and salty sea spray against our faces as the *Mary Isabella* thumps and thuds over increasingly choppy waves. My heart seems to rise to breathless heights, then plummets into a bottomless pit every time the ship surges up and crashes into the sea.

Captain Grey flexes and unflexes his jaw. "It's starting to rain."

He's not saying what's really troubling him. He's

thinking the same thing I am. We're headed into trouble enough, and those paths along the cliffs are getting muddier and more slippery by the minute. They may even wash out in places, making our dangerous task all the more treacherous.

"Never mind, Ethan." I tug his sleeve. "It's only a light mist." I manage this morsel of optimism with a cheerfulness I don't feel.

He peers skeptically over his shoulder and down his nose at me. A nose that I still find handsome, even though it has been broken one too many times. Rain trails down his cheeks and fine droplets stick to his eyelashes, making an eloquent argument.

I shrug. "We're almost there."

Mr. Chadwick stands on the bow, leaning forward on one leg, straining to see through the *mist*. "There." He points. "That's the place! Turn! Turn sharp."

Alexander Sinclair spins the wheel and banks the *Mary Isabella* suddenly. At the same time, an oncoming wave crashes against our port side and the ship tips precariously. Saltwater splashes over the deck. I slide into Captain Grey who seems to keep his footing effortlessly.

"Steady on!" shouts Mr. Chadwick, hanging nearly sideways on the headrail to keep from tumbling into the sea.

"I'm trying," Alexander shouts, fighting with the wheel. "A little warning would've helped. I'm not a ruddy magician."

"Aren't you?" Lady Jane grips his coat with both hands, struggling to keep her balance. "And here I thought you— Oo-aah!" The ship rights itself, sending Jane sliding the other way while still clinging on to him.

This earns a crooked smirk from Mr. Sinclair. Water washes back into the sea, and he shouts over the wind, "Ladies and gentlemen, please move to the bow so the next wave, which is due to hit our stern any minute, won't sink us."

Georgie tugs Lord Wyatt forward in a mad dash for the bow. "Hurry, we've got to counteract the impact."

"Do we?" I note the mischievous glint in Lord Wyatt's eyes. "What if, instead of breaking over us, the wave rolls under the ship? Won't moving forward sink us?"

Georgie freezes in her tracks and mimics the sea's undulation with her hands. "Oh no! It could." She whips around squinting into the darkened sky behind us and points. "I can't see the next wave. Is that—"

A wave thunders over our stern, drowning out the rest of her words. She falls against Lord Wyatt, who catches her with one arm while simultaneously brushing water off his overcoat. "Imagine that, Mr. Sinclair timed it correctly."

Alexander snorts. Captain Grey shakes his head. "Don't encourage him, Sinclair. If you do, he'll persist in making jokes throughout the entire raid."

True enough.

Lord Wyatt is Captain Grey's nephew, but Sebastian is the closest thing to a son I will ever have. The lad cannot resist teasing, and the more troubling a situation the more he jests. I love him for his bravado in the face of death, but too much rides on this mission. We need to muster every ounce of concentration.

In grave silence, we steam toward the shore, drag the *Mary Isabella* aground, and quietly secure her.

We are now in the enemy's lair. Like mice scampering from a prowling cat, we race across the open beach. Then keeping to the deep shadows at the base of the cliffs, Mr. Chadwick guides us toward the cove. At the point where the cliffs jut out and curve back to form the small bay, we hunker down behind a rocky spur overlooking our quarry.

"There it is," Ethan frowns at Napoleon's ship docked on the far side of the cove and shakes his head. "Searched the entire French coast for that blasted ship."

"You've found it now." I grasp his arm, not really for balance, but because touching him makes me feel safer.

"*You* found it. Chadwick and Sera—your students," he says, and the pride in his voice sends a warm shiver through me.

"Chadwick is yours," I whisper, just as the young man in question wedges up beside us.

Mr. Chadwick points to the trail leading down from the bluffs. "They're not quite as steep as your cliffs at Stranje House. It's difficult to see in this rain, but there are only two S curves winding up from the beach. Our house stands about two hundred yards beyond that middle crest."

Ethan pulls out his spy glass, scans the bluff, then turns, and aims it at the ship. A rumbling noise comes from his chest. *I know that sound*—it means it isn't good news.

"There's more crew aboard than I'd expected. I count five, no make that six lanterns, and twice as many men." Ethan wipes moisture out of his eyes and adjusts the focus. "Blast this rain! The water level is rising faster here because of the storm. The spars are all in place on the masts. As soon as they rig the sails, they could put out to sea. His men are rolling canvas even now." Captain Grey retracts the scope with a curt snap. "I'd lay odds Napoleon is already aboard."

I let go of Ethan's arm.

Then we're trapped. We've no choice but to go on that ship.

Our main advantage, *our only advantage*, was taking them by stealth and surprise. That advantage just sank beneath the dark waters of this bay.

As if we were still crashing over the waves, my stomach plummets and my fists tighten into white knuckled knots. I glare at Napoleon's ship, tilting and swaying, its dark masts stirring the dark clouds like blackened skeletal fingers.

Lord Kinsworth dashes rain out of his eyes. "Surely, they won't risk setting sail in weather like this?"

"I'd make a run for it. Wouldn't you if you thought the King's legion was coming for you?" Captain Grey hands his telescope to Mr. Digby and mumbles, "Storms aren't the worst thing, at least there's wind."

Another advantage in Napoleon's favor.

Digby surveys the cliffs. "I count three, maybe four lamps heading down the path. It's a sure bet that he's loading up." He lowers the scope. "We're caught in the middle, Capt'n."

Alexander Sinclair leans over the wet rocks, rubbing his chin. He's staring, not at the ship but at the narrow inlet to the bay. I recognize that look. He's brewing an idea. "What is it, Mr. Sinclair?" I demand. "I can hear you ruminating from here."

He edges closer and crouches down beside me and Ethan. "Seems to me we ought to try to disable Bonaparte's ship and trap them here on the island."

His idea offers a glimmer of hope. "How?" I ask.

"We could bring the *Mary Isabella* around and blockade them at the mouth of the cove? We could hold them here until the troops arrive."

Lady Jane leans over his shoulder. "Using the ballista?" She's asking about the harpoon gun we rigged several months ago to fire arrows laden with Georgiana's Greek Fire grenades.

"Exactly." His face lights up. "We'll fire on the emperor's fancy ship and set it ablaze."

"It could work." I nudge Ethan.

Ethan nods thoughtfully, but his brow pinches together. "I didn't notice harpoon bombs aboard. You can't have brought many?"

"Well..." Alexander glances apologetically at Ethan. "Half dozen." But he hurries to add, "It ought to be enough, Captain. I've been working on that Congreve switch—that's why I brought them along. I wanted a chance to test it."

Six isn't nearly enough.

And it's a test.

My shoulders droop.

Ethan winces too and rubs his jaw. "Only six?"

Alexander edges closer. "Six ought to do enough damage to keep her here. Trust me, even in this rain that oil mixture will stick and burn. And with those changes to the trigger switch, the bombs ought to explode better than ever."

"Six." Ethan sighs heavily. "I suppose there's a chance."

I pull my pack around and cautiously remove the fire-bombs he'd given me earlier. "Here. Take these. If all else fails, you can hurl them at the ship."

Georgie jumps up excitedly. "Yes! Take mine too!"

Lord Wyatt grabs her and pulls her back into a crouch. "Quietly, my love. Quietly."

"Very well, Mr. Sinclair." Captain Grey clasps Alexander's shoulder. "It's worth a try. Aim for the hull first. The rest of us will be aboard searching for Prince George. Try to leave the deck free for our escape."

"Will do." Alexander salutes.

"But if that ship breaks free..." Ethan's grip on

Alexander tightens. "If it looks like she'll get out of the cove—fire on it with everything you've got. Do you hear me, Sinclair? Burn it down."

"But, Captain, even if you're still aboard?"

"Sink her! We can't let Napoleon escape."

"I understand." Alexander nods grimly. "One small worm in the soup, though. I can't steer the *Mary Isabella*, load, and fire at the same time. I'll need someone to man the—

"Bomb Harpoon. I'll do it." Lady Jane yanks off her crossbow and shoves it into Maya's arms. "Here. You're much better with this thing than I am, anyway."

"Shooting at targets, perhaps. But a human being?" Maya clutches the bow at arm's length and looks as if she's about to tip over. "I could never—"

"Well, I could." Georgie takes the weapon from her and straps it across her back. Then she leans in close to Maya. "If you can't... um..." She hesitates, blinking for a minute, grimaces, and I watch as the reality of what we must do arrests her. But Georgiana quickly unbuckles her lips and finishes her question. "If you can't kill anyone Maya, why did you come?"

"I will help in other ways." Maya smiles serenely and pats the pouch strapped to her waist. "I brought bandages and tinctures."

Lord Kinsworth takes a deep breath and rests his arm around her shoulders. "*And* hopefully you will stay out of harm's way."

Too late for that.

Maya knows the truth of it, but she smiles innocently. "Oh, yes. That too."

And there goes my heart again. *Falling. Airless.*

Lady Jane unties two of her sheathed daggers and thrusts them at Tess. Tess purses her lips and shakes her head. "You might need them. And I'm already armed with five."

"Don't worry. I kept one back." Lady Jane pats the remaining dagger still strapped to her thigh. "Take them. It increases your odds."

Odds.

I frown at Napoleon's sloop of war, manned with too many sailors and armed with cannons on every side. *Our odds are...*

Not good.

Captain Grey clears his throat. "Get going Sinclair. You'll also need a man to help you shove off." He gestures to Quinton Chadwick. "You've shown us the way here, now go help Sinclair get the *Mary Isabella* back into the water. Then you can make your run back to the old tower."

"Thank you, Captain." Mr. Chadwick draws a quick short breath. "One request. It's my mother, sir. She's..." He squints up toward the cliffs. "If someone could—"

"I'll see to your mother." Lord Ravencross says solemnly. "Upon my life."

With that, I watch the three of them disappear into the shadows. This may be the last I see of her. *Lady Jane.*

My clever brilliant Jane—so many things I wanted to teach her before I...

Before leaving her.

Before leaving all of them.

I survey their faces as they gather around Ethan. A lump rises in my throat—a lump so jagged and tight I can scarcely breathe. I clamp my jaw, fighting to swallow it down, struggling to remember my father's voice. *One obstacle at a time, Emma. One at a time.*

As if he can feel my torment, Ethan glances in my direction.

He knows me too well.

For a split second, his expression softens. He drops his guard just long enough to show me that he, too, shares my concern for these students of ours, these proteges, who we've come to care about so dearly.

He turns away, resumes the mantle of Captain, and addresses the troops. "The rest of us will board the ship. But we can't allow those men up there to see us and raise the alarm. They must be silenced." It is a command but also a gruesome request—*who can manage this brutal task?*

"Consider it done." Lord Ravencross answers solemnly. Digby nods. And Tess is already evaluating a route up the cliffs.

"Tess." I touch her elbow, and she whips her attention to me, wildly alert. "Afterward, find a way into the house. We need to protect any hostages left behind."

"Yes. Just so." Captain Grey agrees and signals them to

go. Tess bounds off like a deer, except she isn't headed for the path. She clambers up the cliffs at an angle, scaling them at an uncanny pace.

"That girl..." I mumble, watching her movements in amazement.

"Is very clever." Madame Cho stands next to me, a wraith in her dark fighting dress, hardly distinguishable from the shadows around us. "She will mount that incline with ease and position herself above the trail. That way she can attack from above, giving her the advantage."

I nod my approval. "You've trained her well, Xingyu."

Lord Ravencross is not as pleased. He glances up at his fiancée and grumbles. With his bad leg it is impossible for him to follow her. He and Mr. Digby must duck down and race across the beach toward the path.

Tess scampers up those wet rocky bluffs as sure-footed as a cat. And just as graceful. It's as if I'm watching a beautiful yet frighteningly dangerous ballet. My breath catches when she makes a daring leap across a precipice. Seeing that, I doubt that *anyone* could have followed her.

Captain Grey gathers us in a circle around him. "As soon as they've made certain we won't be spotted from above, we'll head for the ship." He glances over his shoulder at our target. "We've only two objectives—find Prince George and capture Napoleon. Anyone who gets in your way, you must... disable." He looks hard at each of us, making sure we understand the cost. "These men are merciless. It is kill or be killed. Do you understand?"

We murmur our assent. Everyone but Maya. After he assigns groups of us to different parts of the ship, we hunker down to wait. Ethan trains his spyglass on the ship, studying the sailors' movements.

I am not good at waiting.

I turn and grasp Maya's arm, leaning close enough that the others can't hear. "Tend the wounded, but you must also promise me this—you know better than anyone how to move without being seen—promise you'll do that." I clamp my lips together to keep from saying anything more.

And stay alive.

"And you," she says, as if she heard my unspoken words. Then Maya presses her forehead against mine. "Fight with the strength of a thousand tigers." I recognize that melodic cadence, she's using her voice on me. Except this time, it is as if her words vibrate, pulsing through me like warm water, rushing into my shivering muscles and cold bones, making them feel flushed and lively.

Startled, I lurch back.

At my astonishment, her eyes brighten. With a knowing half smile, she slips away and crouches beside Lord Kinsworth.

"Now!" Captain Grey signals, and we swiftly advance toward the ship. Madame Cho brings up the rear, her sword at the ready.

We are only fifty yards from the ship when a shower of mud and pebbles tumble down on us. I glance up just in time to see a body crashing down from the cliffs. It lands

SANCTUARY FOR SEERS

with a thud at Georgie's feet.

A sailor, face up—with a knife lodged in his throat.

Lord Wyatt clamps his hand over Georgie's mouth to muffle her scream. He wraps his arms around her and hastily guides her past the body. With a shuddering breath, she glances back at the dead man. "I'm all right," she whispers. "It startled me. That's all."

"Uh-huh." Sebastian tugs her along.

"Truly, I am."

"Shhh."

Has our Georgiana truly grown that brave? She showed tremendous courage in Calais. But she did that for Sebastian's sake. It's still dark here. Perhaps she didn't recognize the knife handle or see all the blood. I stoop down to retrieve Tess's dagger and wipe the blade off on a tuft of grass. I'll return it to Tess if we survive this foray into hell. For now, though, it may prove useful.

Hurrying past, I glance up at the bluffs, letting rain wash the stench of death from my nostrils. I can't see Tess or Lord Ravencross, but neither do I see any more pinpricks of light, no more lanterns weaving down to the shore. How many bodies, I wonder, are lying on those dark trails?

I shake my head and run to catch up to the others. Rain beats down on us relentlessly, but we push on to the dock and Napoleon's ship. Crouching low, we scurry up the gangway. The wooden planks creak beneath our feet, and my chest tightens at the sound of men on the ship shouting back and forth, loading supplies. I grip the handle of my dagger, knuckles taut, tensing for what is sure to come.

At the side of the ship Ethan slowly edges up and peers up over the gunwale to plan our move onto deck. He turns and slides back down. "It's now or never," he whispers. "Three men just went below deck. There are still two on the far side of the mainmast setting a boom. They'll be rolling and tying the sail next. Now's our best chance."

Thunder cracks through the sky, muffling the sound of our approach as we climb over the railing and sneak aboard. Waves beat against the hull, rocking the ship in an unsteady pattern, and rain has turned the deck into a veritable ice-skating rink. I slip and skid like a newborn calf in a mad dash down the side of the deck. Breathless, we hide behind a stack of water barrels and wooden crates laden with cabbages, turnips, and potatoes. No doubt stolen from the Chadwick estate.

Oil lamps flicker in the wind and rain, casting eerie shadows across the deck. The ship is in uncommon disarray, with ropes in heaps, sails strewn haphazardly, and supply crates lying about unsecured, sitting out in the rain. Clearly, they're in a rush to depart. Even so, I am surprised Napoleon would allow such sloppiness. It makes me question whether he is aboard after all. Or if he is, is he still too wounded to care?

Captain Grey motions for us to split up. Georgie, Wyatt, and Kinsworth head toward the bow. A sudden gust of heavy rain obscures their race across the deck. Maya must be with them, *she must*, but I can't see her.

We duck down when two sailors tromp up the ladder from the galley, the very place we need to go. Despite the tossing ship, the sailors walk across the deck without a misstep and join the other men working by the foremast. We are just about to make our move when two of them stand.

The older of the two points up at the foremast crosstrees and barks an order. The younger sailor squints against the pouring rain and curses at his assignment. Nevertheless, he obediently slings a rolled sail across his back, loops the ropes through his arm, and scampers up the shrouds faster than a spider climbing its web. He mounts the second set of shrouds and scuttles out onto the crosstrees. When he stands to unsling his sail, a jagged streak of lightning illuminates the sky. I think I see an arrow whizzing toward him.

It happens so fast. Just a flash.

Georgie's arrow?

I'm not even certain I saw it.

Another wave smashes into the ship tipping her precariously. I grab a crate of turnips sliding toward me and glance up just in time to see the sailor arch as if he's been slugged. He cries out and falls from the mast into the sea. The other sailors on deck rush to the gunwale shouting their companion's name. One hollers for a rope, the other two climb over the side.

Ethan tugs me to my feet. While the men are busy, the

three of us race for the open hatch to the galley. If Napoleon is aboard, he's sure to be down there in the captain's quarters. Hopefully, that's where he's holding Prince George.

Madame Cho is close behind me as we whisker down the ladder-like steps, silent as mice.

As we descend below deck, the air grows colder and thicker, and the sharp oily smell of fresh tar and oakum makes my nose itch. We quickly duck behind the hatch stairs and crouch down to assess our surroundings. Ethan silently taps his finger against the galley floor. I can almost hear him weighing our options, determining the best way to breach that extravagantly carved mahogany door to the captain's quarters.

Muffled laughter bursts through the air coming from the midshipmen's room across the galley. Ethan puts a finger to his lips calling for absolute silence. We exchange questioning glances.

Which way should we attack first, the captain's chambers, or the midshipmen's room?

Just then, a sailor steps down on the stairs directly above our heads. We edge back into the deeper shadows beneath the ladder, pressing our backs against the cold damp hull, not breathing. He thumps down the steps lugging a box and mutters, *"Alors c'est là qu'ils sont."* So, that's where they are, he says in French, and adds a string of grumpy curses.

At the sound of his grousing a hush falls over the men

in the midshipman's room. He plunks down the box with a grunt, dusts off his hands, and stomps to the midshipmen's room. Yanking the door open, he scolds the men at the table roundly but in an unexpectedly hushed tone. As near as I can tell, he must be the boatswain.

My French is not perfect, and sailors have a language of their own, but I believe he is saying, "An injured quartermaster doesn't give you worthless sluggards leave to sit on your diseased arses drinking, lest you want to be tied to the mast and flogged." He adds a few more colorful words that I can't translate and glances back across the galley at the captain's closed door. "Small wonder you haven't awakened the Emperor. You'd be hung on the yardarm then." He leans on the table and complains, "Pierrick, that clumsy fool, has fallen from the mast, and now we are short another man."

"You worry too much." One of the men shows him a bottle. "His Imperial Highness gave us this bottle himself. And not just any wine," the fellow boasts and his companions vigorously agree. "This is fine wine from the big house. Come. You must try some." Another sailor entices him by holding out a tankard. "Just one," he insists. "After working so hard."

The boatswain grumbles unconvincingly, curses the storm for making his job harder and finally relents. Reaching for the tankard, he kicks the door shut behind him.

I gesture at the captain's quarters.

Napoleon must be inside.

Ethan nods and rises, ready to spring into action. I pull out my over-and-under pistol and quietly cock the hammer, hoping that the flash pans remained dry enough to ignite the fuses.

Tiptoeing from our hiding place, we move out into the open and make a mad dash for the captain's quarters. We stop beside it and press against the wall, trying not to breathe too loudly. Ethan leans over and listens at the door. A quick shake of his head tells us he didn't hear any movement.

Sleeping. Just as the boatswain said. I've heard that Napoleon is known for taking short naps at odd hours and then waking completely revived as if from a full night's sleep. *Perfect.* We will catch him unaware.

Ethan reaches for the doorknob.

Suddenly, we hear footsteps coming down the galley hall—multiple boots moving fast. More than one man. Two of them round the corner of the midshipmen's room.

"*Oyé!*" The first man sees us.

This is no sailor. By the look of him, he's one of Ghost's henchmen. He produces a dagger so fast I scarcely have time to shift my position. His companion draws a single-barrel flintlock pistol.

That sound—cocking the hammer. Small, though it is, that lone click ignites my senses and sets me ablaze. I ready my stance and take aim.

"Emma!" Ethan dives and knocks me aside and my shot goes wild. The henchman's shot explodes around us like a blast from hell and sets my head to ringing.

There's smoke—so much wretched smoke.

Ethan lies atop me, protecting me needlessly. "Are you all right?" he asks.

"Yes. Get up."

The midshipmen's door flies open. I hear chairs overturn as sailors spring into the fray shouting and cursing in French. *Too many men in this small space. Too much smoke.* On my left, Madame Cho's sword whirs through the air and connects with someone. The man's scream adds to the chaos. "Je suis tué!" *I am killed,* he bellows.

"Get up, Ethan. Get up! Xingyu is fighting by herself. I need to help."

Why isn't he standing up?

He rolls to the side. Still half on me.

I squint up through the clearing smoke, pointing my gun at whoever approaches us next, struggling to see where to place my shot—*my last shot.*

A lantern swings crazily as the boat rocks transforming the white smoke into a fiery orange. It dissipates just enough for me to see the man with the dagger materialize before me. I squeeze the trigger, and the blast deafens me again.

My target staggers backward. A big man like that won't stay down for long, not unless my bullet found his heart. Once again, we are blanketed in smoke. And since there's no time to reload, I'm down to knives.

I shove Ethan's shoulder trying to wriggle out from

under him, but my fingers are met with warm liquid.

Rainwater?

No. Too warm. Too thick.

Like a wicked thief, come to steal all the joy from my life, the reason Ethan isn't moving sneaks into my consciousness. "Ethan?" I shake him. "Ethan?" I gasp, terror threatening to suffocate me.

No sound.

Not even a groan.

My hands are covered in his blood.

It can't be true. All this wretched smoke, I can't see clearly. I lean closer, staring frantically into his face. "Ethan? Dear God, please don't do this. *Please.* Ethan, wake up!"

The only man I have ever loved does not move. His eyes, usually so full of mischief even at times like this, have rolled back in his head. Only the whites show, cruelly altering the face I love so dearly into a grotesque empty mask.

"Ethaaan!" I cry one last time, and even I hear the despair strangling my voice. If he had one ounce of life left in his veins he would answer. *My Ethan would answer.*

"No." I mumble. Shaking my head, I let go of his blood-soaked coat, and he thumps against the wall.

Dead.

"Murderers!" I screech like a banshee and scramble to my feet. "You've killed him!"

"*Une femme?*" asks a man obscured in the haze around

us. *A woman?* He manages to sound baffled and lecherous all at the same time.

I spin in that direction, and my blade silences the blackguard. He drops to the floor. And somewhere in the distance, there's an explosion. It could be another gunshot, or maybe it's Alexander bombing the ship. It doesn't matter. Ethan is dead.

I'm going to kill Napoleon's murdering hoard.

Every last one of them.

"Xingyu!" I shout for Madame Cho, needing to know where she is lest I swing my blade too wide and nick her.

"Emma!" she answers, and I recognize the familiar *clang* of her sword followed by someone's guttural cry. It's coming from the galley walkway beside the midshipmen's room.

"Ethan is dead." I roar through gritted teeth.

Her answer is a war cry.

I've only heard that cry once before—in the battle when my father died. And just as I did that terrible day, I raise my sword and wield it with a numb fury that only grief can produce. I slash through assassins and sailors with mindless vengeance until the door to the captain's room flings open.

"*Arrêt!*" Napoleon stands in the opening. He points his sword at me. As if that feeble gesture is supposed to make me stop.

Hardly. Instead, I whirl and meet his blade with a boneshaking crack. He jerks back, as if the blow dumbfounds him.

Eyes wide, he swiftly makes a counter thrust. Except his sword is too long, too bulky for a close fight like this. I meet his saber and knock his blade away once more.

"You are a woman." He makes this observation, not as if he is surprised, but as if I've committed a sin for holding a sword.

I gauge his stance, calculating my next move. He feigns an attack hoping to catch me open if I move to parry.

I don't.

Instead, I advance.

Only he manages to dodge my blade and attempts a quick side thrust. So, I slash down. He's faster than I expected. Instead of cutting off his arm, our blades clang together. I knock his blade aside.

Instead of pulling back, I flick my sword in a circular motion and nick his upper arm.

"*Mon Dieu!*" He retreats, circling. Focusing. Hunting my weaknesses.

He lunges.

I parry his attack. But with a quick turn, Bonaparte jerks aside and springs forward in a clever attempt to spear my ribs.

I dodge.

Too late.

His saber slices through the fabric and slashes through the skin on my ribs. The sting of it turns into a scorching burn. A burn that provokes me to fight with even more speed and force.

I knock his sword aside and make a swift advance. Our swords clash again and again. Parry. Riposte. Parry. Riposte.

I hear footsteps running in our direction.

More men.

I roar, furious at being outnumbered. The fire in me burns even hotter. He tries it again—to spear me in the ribs. My weakness, he thinks. But I see it coming and strike his saber so hard he nearly loses his grip. He fumbles to recover, and I drive him back, attacking over and over until he is against the wall.

Pinned.

I vaguely hear someone call my name.

Someone familiar.

Only it sounds far, far away, a thousand miles from this hell in which I'm trapped.

Napoleon attempts a remise—a frantic counterattack.

A mistake.

This time I lock his sword against mine and press his arm up against the wall. He pushes back, remarkably strong for a man recovering from a wound. Stronger than me.

Except I have the advantage of a second blade in my other hand. I press the dagger point up under his chin. "*Tu es mort.*" I murmur. *You are dead.*

His imperial blood trickles onto my hand, but I don't look. Instead, I fix my gaze on his arrogant face. Watching him squirm, holding him in checkmate. This pompous man is responsible for millions of deaths. *Millions.* I slam his arm back harder. He's the reason my Ethan lies dead on this godforsaken ship.

I will watch this murderous tyrant die.

Napoleon drops his sword. "*Je cède*," he says through clenched teeth, careful not to move his jaw.

"No!" I grind out the words. "Fight, you coward. Fight."

He opens his hands in defeat.

"You can't surrender." I push the small blade harder, drawing more blood. "I won't let you."

Someone approaches me from behind. "Stay back!" I warn without turning. "Stay back, or I'll kill him."

"Emma."

I know that voice.

"Emma. It's me, Sebastian." Lord Wyatt kicks Napoleon's sword aside and stands next to me. "Bonaparte has surrendered to you, Em. The forecastle is on fire. It's spreading fast. We have to get off the ship."

"No." I shake my head. "No. He should die for what he's done." I push the knife deeper into Napoleon's jaw. He winces, and the sticky trickle turns into a stream.

I flinch when Sebastian gently lays his hand on my shoulder. "You've captured him, Emma. He'll stand trial for his crimes."

I struggle to hear him over the fiery war drums throbbing through my veins, blinding me to anything but death.

"But... Prince George?"

"It's all right. He's alive and safe. We found him tied up in the hold." Sebastian wraps his fingers around mine on the dagger handle and gently eases it away.

I shake my head. "I can't leave the ship. I can't. Ethan is..."

"I know." There's sadness in his voice. "I know."

"I won't leave him, Seb."

"Of course not. Lord Kinsworth is carrying him out now. Maya is with him."

Maya is with him?

I blink, as if trying to awaken out of a stupor. "Where's Xingyu?"

"I am here, Emma." At the sound of Madame Cho's voice, a cool wind surges through me, and I sink back releasing Napoleon. But, instead of relaxing, my insides begin to tremble—a tight nauseating quiver at first, then it turns to uncontrollable shaking.

Madame Cho yanks a blanket from the captain's bed and wraps it around my shoulders. "Come. Let us leave this ship before it becomes a funeral pyre."

Lord Wyatt and Georgiana take charge of Napoleon. Binding his hands and marching him up the galley steps at the point of a sword. I stumble after them, numbly letting Xingyu guide me, careful not to look back at the carnage in the galley, afraid I might see my Ethan's blood spilled there against the wall.

CHAPTER 20

A LADY IN HIDING

Seraphina, upon entering Lady Daneska's sickroom.

TURNING UP THE LANTERN, I shake Magda's shoulder. "Cook! Cook! Wake up! Where is Lady Daneska?"

She snuffles, drools, and mutters incoherently, but doesn't rouse. Her breath smells of alcohol and... something else. I pull up one of her eyelids and am met with the unseeing stare of an opiate delirium. Her pupils are the size of pinpricks. Even when I hold the lamp near her face, there is no change.

Drugged!

I groan. Again.

On the bed table sits the small bottle containing a tincture of opium, the laudanum we used to ease Lady Daneska's pain. I hold it up to the light to see how much is missing and evaluate whether Magda has been dealt a killing dose.

It had been half full when I last saw it, and now there's scarcely a drop or two in the bottom. I set the nearly empty bottle down with a hard *plunk* and examine Cook's teacup. Only the dregs are left. She ingested a substantial amount.

Another weary groan passes my lips. *This horrid night!* It feels as if I'm trapped in Dante's Inferno.

Fortunately, Cook is a hale and hearty woman. She should wake up from the stupor in a day or two. We all know Magda likes to tip a bottle into her tea. Given the late hour in which she'd been summoned to sit vigil in the sickroom it is quite likely she would've done so. Daneska would've administered the drops after Magda dozed off. Then, when Cook roused, still groggy, and gulped down the remainder of her alcohol laden tea the poor woman would've failed to taste the laudanum.

Daneska would then be free to slip away, except she would not have done so clad only in her nightgown. I dash to the wardrobe and find Daneska's clothing gone. So, she dressed and made her escape, but how long ago?

Impossible to tell.

I lean over the banister and call for our servants. "Greaves! Peggy! Philip!"

They stumble out from wherever they'd been resting and gather beneath me in the stairwell. Greaves carries a lantern with him, and despite his humped back he lifts the heavy old oil lamp and squints up at me. "What is it, Miss?"

"Lady Daneska has escaped! We must each take a floor and hunt for her. I will search here on the third floor. It is unlikely that she would go up to the attic as her objective would be to leave the house without being seen. Greaves, if you would please search the second floor. Peggy, the ground floor. Don't neglect the secret passageways. She knows them all very well. Philip, take a lantern and check the grounds around the house. If any of you see *anything* out of place, *any* clue or indication of where she might've gone, summon me immediately." I grip the banister and lean out to shout my final command. "Hurry! She may have left her bedroom only a short time ago."

"Miss!" Peggy calls up to me, straining to see through the dim light. "After Miss Stranje and the others left the house earlier, I couldna get back to sleep on account of me joints aching sumptin' fierce. Point is, I heard nary a soul coming nor going, save when you came back a few minutes ago."

I groan, yet again. "That means Lady Daneska may still be in the house!" *And most likely inside the secret passages on this floor.*

"Hurry! Find her! Lives depend upon it." I snag the oil lamp from the sickroom, and race down the hall to the nearest passage entrance which happens to be in Miss Stranje's bedroom. Like the rest of us, Lady Daneska memorized every passage in the house. This is where she would come. I kneel down and creak open the narrow squat panel. Taking a deep breath, I plunge into the cramped space.

I do not relish combat in close quarters. Hopefully Daneska is still fairly ill. That ought to give me a slight advantage. I'm all too conscious of the weighty dagger strapped to my thigh. It is a killing blade. Madame Cho has trained me well, and I should be at ease with it by now. But I'm not. It is a worrisome burden. *To save myself, even if I were to gain the advantage over Daneska, would I actually be able to stab her?*

Doubtful.

The thought of plunging my dagger into her chest makes me cringe. I couldn't bring myself to kill Ghost when I had the perfect opportunity. If I couldn't do so to him, our mortal enemy, how could I do it to Lady Daneska—she who was once one of us.

Then what will I do when I find her? How can I subdue her?

Reason with her?

Ha! As if that would do any good. Knock her over the head, or...

Or what?

The answer arrives like a cooling breeze. I need only tell Lady Daneska the truth, that Ghost is waiting for her at the old lookout tower. *Simple and uncomplicated.* Now, to find her. Time is ticking by all too fast, and I am due to meet him at the end of the hour.

I lift the lantern, scouring the narrow dingy passageway for signs of her being here, *anything*, plaster bumped out of place, dislodged spiderwebs, or...

There!

A footprint in the dust.

I hurry to inspect it. She's wearing boots. How very sensible of her, given the debris strewn in these passages. But where did she find walking boots? I distinctly remember she wore fancy heeled shoes aboard Napoleon's ship, no doubt to give her added height. Yet this imprint is unmistakably from a walking boot. Although, it does look slightly larger than I remember her foot being. In any case, this dust has been freshly disturbed—it must be her!

Farther down, glinting in my lamplight there appears to be a piece of cloth or lace snagged on a nail. I tug it free and examine the exquisite fragment of tatted lace. It is the very same lace that adorned Lady Daneska's dress. She definitely came this way and in a roaring great hurry, else she would not have snagged her gown.

I follow the clues until I come upon one of the small exits that we'd blocked off. She has torn aside the slats barricading the opening. I shove the hatch open, and a burst of cool air slaps against my face. The storm is picking up. I crawl out and nearly collide with Philip, our footman.

"Stars above! It's you, Miss Wyndham." He exhales

heavily and lowers a rock he holds in his hand. "I heard noises and thought..." The rock drops from his fingers. "Here, let me help you up."

"You thought I was Lady Daneska." I brush dirt off my skirts.

"Aye. But now that you're here, come and look at some footprints I ran across." He guides me to a path several paces southeast. "At first I thought they might be left by any of you young ladies, but then I noticed something odd."

"Odd?"

"It looks like a shuffling gait if you know what I mean? And it seems to me, knowing the grounds as well as all of you do, you'd have avoided this soggy part of the path. Ah, here they are." He points at a set of indentations in the mud. "See for yourself."

I stoop down and raise my lantern, inspecting the size and shape. They look to be the same as the walking boot prints I'd found in the passageway. I stand and brush off my skirt. "Excellent work, Philip! These are definitely hers. And you're right! This print shows that she's dragging her left foot. Her injuries must be causing her pain and slowing her down."

Lifting the lantern high, I scan the area, hoping for a clue as to which way she might be headed. Seeing nothing, I tap my foot in frustration. "Philip, if you were running away, fleeing for your life, what direction would you take?"

"Oh, that's easy, miss. I'd head for the trees over there.

Next, I'd sneak alongside the hedgerows up to the main road. If I felt like chancing it, I'd try'n beg a ride on a farm wagon headed to market. Elsewise, I'd hoof it, keeping to the woods and bushes. Either way, I'd get m'self to London fast as fast can be. I've heard London is full of hiding-holes—plenty of places to lie low—in the rookeries, the docks, and such-like."

"Yes. A sensible plan." I clutch the thin cotton fabric of my dress to keep it from billowing in the gusts of wind, and stare at that uninviting section of woods, trying to think like Lady Daneska. She isn't the sort to lie low and hide, and I cannot for the life of me picture her living in the squalor of the rookeries or docks. London, though, *would* appeal to her. She would have accomplices there, allowing her to hide in more plush parts of Town. Although, it's highly unlikely she would consider walking the entire way.

"Did you check the stable, Philip? Are any horses missing?"

"I went there first, miss. All the horses are accounted for, Daisy, the coaching teams, Miss Stranje's Penelope, Ajax, and—"

Before he lists every single horse in our stable, I interrupt. "Where are Phobos and Tromos? Surely, they would raise a fuss if Lady Daneska entered their territory."

"Before she left, Miss Aubreyson put them in their compound with the pups. She said it was... he pauses and glances at me with worry written all over his prim proper features. "... in case she didn't come back by morning." Philip shakes his head. "Those wolves have a mind of their own, and she told me she didn't want us to have to coax them into the pen using Sunday's ham."

She knew she might not return.

Philip's words are a harsh reminder of the gravity of our mission. Tess and the others are risking their lives. Meanwhile, I have lost our only bargaining chip. It is imperative that I detain Ghost for as long as possible.

"Come along, then. We must search that copse of trees for any sign of Lady Daneska." Before starting for the thicket, I once again brush my fingers over the dagger sheathed to my leg. "Oh, and Philip, you'd best retrieve that rock you were carrying earlier. You may yet have a need for it."

Miss Stranje insists on keeping a certain portion of her estate *Au Natural.* She maintains that this naturalized area provides the perfect deterrent to overly inquisitive visitors, and in addition, "It creates a lovely home for owls and rabbits."

Yes, but that means it is also a home for snakes, rats, and other vermin. Decaying leaves swirl in the wind as Philip and I scramble over fallen branches and trudge through dense underbrush. Most of it is scrub oak, but there are also poisonous yew and monkshood, which is difficult to avoid in the dark. We clamber over a fallen tree and find ourselves trapped amongst prickly bushes.

I lean back from a sharp pointed spike of holly and

ask, "Without a scythe, I don't see how Lady Daneska could've gone any farther, do you?"

Philip stands right behind me. "I don't see how a young lady like her could've come even as far as this." Something slithers beneath the leaves off to our right. Philip yips, jumps sideways, and tosses his rock into the brush. "She isn't here, miss."

"Agreed. There's no sign *anyone* has been in here for a good long while." By my reckoning, three quarters of an hour have passed since I found her missing.

She's gone! I've lost her.

I've failed.

There must be another way to detain Ghost. But if I am to meet him at the appointed time, I must hurry.

We fight our way out of the thicket much faster than we did going in. As soon as we reach the clearing, I charge Phillip to keep looking. "Check the outbuildings—chicken coops, the pigeon house, anywhere she might be hiding. And, Philip, find another rock in case you run into her. She's dangerous. Don't underestimate her. After that, please ask Peggy to look in on Magda. Lady Daneska dosed her rather heavily with laudanum."

"Good heavens. She dosed Cook?"

"Yes." I stride toward the cliffs.

Philip follows close on my heels. "And you, miss, where will you be?"

"I must run to a..." I bite my lip.

A failed rendezvous.

With the most dangerous man in England.

And he'll be angrier than ever when I arrive empty-handed. I have lost Lady Daneska, our lure. If only I'd come home sooner, ridden faster, maybe I would've caught her. Now who knows what mischief she will get up to. What if Ghost rushes back to Mr. Chadwick's estate? My stomach clenches at the thought. Sweat prickles on my neck. If he sees what Miss Stranje and the others are doing, he'll turn into an enraged lion and kill everyone in sight.

"I must go."

Quickly!

And contrive a way to keep Ghost in the tower.

At all costs.

I dash forward, breaking into a run, and shout over my shoulder. "Find Lady Daneska! I'm counting on you."

CHAPTER 21

RUNNING TO GHOST

RACING ACROSS THE BLUFFS I wonder at this endless night. The dark ought to be fading at least a little by now. Dawn is only a few hours away, yet there is not even a faint gray on the horizon. Instead, the storm that has been brewing since yesterday has gathered a blanket of clouds and blackened the sky. Wind swirls its fingers through the tall grass as I run toward the old tower. The closer I get the slower are my footfalls.

His men will be with him, and he will be annoyed with me for not bringing Lady Daneska. To show his authority he'll need to punish me for failing him.

Will it be a death blow?

Or mere bruises?

My shoulders sag, yet I run, one foot sailing out in front of the other. If I were truly a white mouse, I would not dare to show my face. But I need to detain him as long as possible. Miss Stranje and my friends, my sisters, will be fighting for their lives and for England. Come bruises or death blows, I cannot fail them.

With every thudding step I draw closer. From here, I can see the faint orange glow of a lantern through one of the small openings in the stone turret.

He is already there.

A crack of thunder masks the loud pounding of my heart. I shuffle to a stop and try to catch my breath. A brief flicker of heat lightning outlines the silhouette of his horse standing off to the side.

Swallowing the dry lump in my throat, I take a few steps more and my fingers touch the cool stones of the tower, steadying me as I go around the doorway. The door itself has long since rotted and fallen away. I step over dislodged stones and broken timbers until I am well inside. My head hangs heavy, and I can only look at the floor, yet I feel his presence looming before me.

"Where's Daneska?" His voice rumbles low and steady, coiling around me with a surprisingly soothing effect, yet I can't bring myself to face him.

"I have failed you. I'm sorry, my lord. She—"

"Don't!" he warns. "I told you not to do that—I hate titles." He does not sound furious. Annoyed, but not furious. Blinking against the lamplight I risk looking up at him. He is alone.

He came alone.

That is good for me, I need not die tonight. But it is not good, not good at all for Miss Stranje and the others. More of Napoleon's men will be there to fight on those cliffs.

He stares at me for too long, and I stand speechless under his scrutiny. A thousand thoughts race through my mind. This is likely the last time I will ever see him—the one man who truly knows me. That should not matter. What does my being understood count for in a world being torn apart by war?

Nothing.

Less than nothing.

He stands too close. He need only to reach out, and my neck would be within his grasp—easily snapped. I dare to look up and my breath catches. He does not look as angry as he ordinarily does. Where is his storm cloud? Why is it not rumbling and flashing around him like a volcano about to erupt?

There are no dark companions sulking in the corners.

No wraiths.

Just him. I have rarely seen him without his fiendish stalkers, not in the light. Yet even without the demons and his raging storm, Ghost seems to fill the tower with his presence. He is a giant of a man, to be sure, but it's more than just his size. Ghost pulses with strength. The very air around him crackles with power. Seeing him now, I can guess why his father beat him. Even as a boy Lucien must've easily overshadowed others. A petty father, an envious father might have felt threatened by such a son and foolishly tried to beat it out of him.

Ghost stares down at me as if he is waiting patiently. How unlike him. Perhaps he didn't understand me. I open out my empty arms. "Lady Daneska escaped."

He should strike me now. That is what Ghost would do—a swift backhand to my face. I flinch as if he is going to do it.

Instead, he tilts his head, studying me with an intensity that makes heat flood into my cheeks. Far too calmly he asks, "When? How did she get away?" Ghost's voice, when he isn't thundering with fury, is low and earthy. It hums through the ancient turret, flowing over the stones as if they are old friends.

My lips open to speak, only I cannot stop gaping at the changes in his face, even his scar seems to have faded. He is waiting for an answer, and I am standing here like a dumbstruck fool. I swallow. "I—uh—while I was with you. It looks as if she drugged Magda, our cook, who was supposed to be on watch duty—"

A sudden snort of laughter draws our attention to the doorway.

I gulp back my surprise. "Daneska!"

She must've been hiding on the far side of the turret. Not that it matters now. She holds an old flintlock pistol in her hand. *Miss Stranje's extra gun*—the pistol she keeps loaded in her bedchamber. And it is pointed at me.

"I didn't drug your precious cook. No." Lady Daneska smirks as she steps across the threshold. "*Zthat* dose should have killed *ze auld...*" Having slurred her words, she grimaces, wipes a hand across her eyes, and squints at us as if she's having trouble focusing. "... *staraya vorona!*" she blurts, then frowns. She shakes her head and seems to regain her composure. "Old crow." She shakes the gun at me. "That's it, she's an ugly old crow. A crow who should be dead. As should you, my annoying little mouse."

"You're not well, Lady Daneska. You should not be out of bed." I do my best to sound calm even though I know that gun has a skittish trigger. In her condition her finger could slip and—

"What did you expect, *ma petite souris?*" Lady Daneska smiles crookedly. "Did you think I would lie there like a helpless infant and wait to be interrogated? Tortured? Did you really think I would let them mount my head on a spike at London Tower?"

She forces a sardonic titter at a pitch that makes my ears wince and whips her attention to Ghost. "I'm too pretty for that, don't you think?"

Ghost sighs heavily. "Put the gun away, Daneska."

She doesn't.

Instead, she points it at him. "And you! Are you so

dunderheaded that you didn't realize this was a trap?"

"I see no trap," he booms.

"He's right, Lady Daneska. There is no trap." I hold out my hand to her. "I was supposed to bring you to him. That's all."

She winces and clutches her wounded side, but her mouth quickly morphs into her customary. "Ahh, I see." She nods as if this placates her, except the next instant her pretense of a smile turns into a vicious scowl. "*You* think I am *stupid*. You think I did not overhear your plans. Have you forgotten the priest hole above the planning room?"

I sink back. "You overheard us?"

"Of course, I heard." She whips her attention back to him. "This isn't a trap for you. *Idiote*! It is a trap for Napoleon. You left the Emperor defenseless. And all because of this worthless little mouse." She aims her gun at me again, then swings it back to Ghost. "Fool! How could you let her lure you here? Miss Stranje and the others are at this very moment attacking Napoleon and your men in an attempt to free their fat prince."

"What of it?" he exhales. "A handful of girls against my men—they can't possibly succeed."

"You can't be sure. Not when it comes to them. Emma Stranje's brats are not just girls. They don't spend their days learning how to pour tea. What possessed you to leave Bonaparte and come here?" She tilts her head and narrows her eyes in warning. "Don't you dare pretend it was for me. We both know you'd just as soon I was dead than alive."

"That isn't true." I hold out my hand in protest. "He—
"

"Shut up!" she screams and grimaces in pain. Ghost lurches forward and reaches for her pistol. But Daneska jerks back and raises it to his face, backing away. "Answer me! What hold does she have over you? This... *this spineless wretch.*" She spits. "Of all Emma's brats—she's the weakest, most irritating of them all, why her?"

He doesn't answer except with a glower that has me shaking.

But Daneska doesn't shake.

Even ill she stands her ground. "*Well?*" she shouts into the rising fury that is Ghost. "What is it? Why is she not dead at your feet for having tricked you? Why didn't you cut her throat just for being..." she waggles the gun at me again. "*Her.*"

In answer, Ghost edges back and reaches for the pistol tucked in his belt.

"Don't," she warns him. "I no longer trust you." He rumbles angrily and lifts his hands to placate her.

Lady Daneska looks pale and flushed all at the same time. I swallow and strive for a steady tone despite the fear trying to overtake me. "My lady, you've been out of bed too long. Your fever is returning."

"How very kind of you to *care.*" She makes a singsong mockery of the words. "You!" Her tongue turns it into a venomous screech. "This is all because of you. You've been an irritation since the day we met. Always everyone's little favorite. Poor pitiful sweet, Sera," she snarls. "Enough! Past time for you to die." She takes aim.

"No!" Ghost jerks me behind him. Daneska is a practiced marksman, so she instinctively follows her target, and she squeezes the trigger.

CHAPTER 22

THE LANGUAGE OF DEATH

LADY DANESKA PULLS THE TRIGGER.

The hammer clicks, a soft ping compared to the blast that follows—a deafening explosion pulses through me and seems to shake the stones. Something knocks me sideways.

Ghost ramming into me?

The bullet?

I don't know. My ears ring as if I'm trapped in a bell tower. A cloud of gunpowder smoke envelopes us. Acidic. Sulphuric. It stings my eyes and burns my throat. I cough trying to catch my breath.

"Sera?" Ghost reaches for me.

I clasp his arm. "Here."

The sour white smoke eddies around us in caustic puffs that soon drift apart. Blinking, squinting, the first thing I see is Daneska's blue silk gown splattered with...

Is that blood?

I follow her riveted gaze as she gloats at the havoc she has wreaked and realize it is blood and *whose* it is.

Ghost!

I scream. Blood pours out of him front and back. *Not imaginary this time. All too real.* "You shot him!"

He glances down and clutches his stomach as if he only now realizes he's wounded. His eyes widen. He holds out his open hands, staring at them as if he can't understand why they've suddenly turned red.

"Traitor." Daneska flippantly tosses the smoking pistol to the floor the way a spoiled child discards a toy. "You deserve to die." She raises her chin proudly, watching blood spurt out of his wound in rhythmic gushes. And now I see that, even though she intended to shoot me, she's just as pleased to have put a bullet through him.

Backing away, Daneska pauses in the open doorway and wrinkles her nose like she smells something detestable. "You were useless to me anyway." She sniffs at us and scurries away into the night.

Ghost stumbles forward, as if he intends to go after her, except he teeters and collapses into my arms. Ghost is a giant of a man. I brace myself so as not to topple over and do my best to ease him to the floor without jarring him too much. As soon as he is down, I notice his wound gushes even more. I need to stop the blood somehow.

But instead of being useful, I start to shake. "You should've let her shoot me," I moan. I could cope with dying. But this—

I stare helplessly at the gaping hole she blew through him. "Why did you have to save me? Why?" Frantic to stop the bleeding, I press my hands over the wound. "There's too much blood—too much! What do I do?"

I'm trying not to cry.

Struggling to be brave.

He stares at me, his mouth opening and closing, as if he wants to say something but doesn't know how. "No use..." He exhales loudly. "I'm dying."

"No! No." I shake my head, my jaw set firmly and continue to press my hands over the opening even though blood oozes up through my fingers. "Don't say that. You survived wounds like this before." I yank the cloak from my shoulders and try to pack it into the gaping wound, but the cloth quickly saturates.

"Sera." His lips press together, and I can see he's giving up.

"No! You can't die. Not because of me." I dash away burning tears, except all that does is smear his blood across my cheek. "*Please*. Please, don't die."

But I know he's right. Those vile hounds of hell are gathering in the shadows of the tower, crowing with glee, bouncing with eagerness. They've come to take their bounty.

Wraiths slink ever closer, crawling up the walls, jittering with excitement. I shake my head at them.

I know he's done vile things. Horrible things. Yet in some deeper sense, this man is the only true kin I've ever had. And he saved my life. That should count for something. "No. Stay back!"

They pause, cocking their heads, gauging whether I mean it or not. The leader bares his teeth at me and snarls defiantly. And then the horde recommence their ghastly onslaught.

Ghost clutches my arm and says, "Ask him to forgive me."

Him?

"Who?" I bend over him, leaning close to hear his answer. "Do you mean your brother?"

Blood trickles out of the corner of his mouth as he murmurs, "Him, too."

"Oh!" Comprehension makes my tears flow even faster. I lean closer making certain he can hear me. "I will. I will. I promise."

My breath rushes in and out in desperate heaves. I don't know how the courts of heaven work. I only know how to beg. *Forgive him, God, please.*

In a foolish attempt to ward the demons off, I hold out my hands, hands dripping with Ghost's blood. "Go away!"

Still, they come.

Help me. I cry out silently for more strength.

What do I do, God?

Ghost groans with pain, and my heart nearly breaks. "Don't die." I stroke his cheek. The evil ones are chittering and getting ever closer. Too close!

I lift my head and stare into the face of the leader. Gritting my teeth, I tell them as forcefully as I know how. "You can't have him! Not this one. He's not yours."

I collapse then, sobbing, and lie across his body, spreading my arms out over the one man who truly understands me, the only person who truly knows the foul horrors I see and yet doesn't find me repulsive. "He's not yours! Not any more."

I cover him, as if my body will protect him and keep them away—ready to fight them if they come any nearer. Ghost murmurs against my cheek as if uttering a benediction, "Thank you."

Demons shriek and howl, chittering crazily.

I glance up. For some reason, the beasts of hell are drawing back. They're grimacing, cowering, snarling, as if an invisible whip has been snapped. Screeching in fury, muttering angrily, one by one they turn away and vanish into the void.

It confuses me until warmth washes over my back, and a brilliant golden light wraps around me and Ghost.

The *others* have come.

Their power radiates through the room like the sun. My shoulders slump in relief, and I can breathe again.

Thank you. Even though I know they are here, I don't dare turn to see. Instead, I whisper to them, "Please." Louder, I beg, "Please."

Ghost stares wide-eyed at those who stand just beyond my shoulders, his mouth gapes open, and he shivers.

I hold his face gently in my hands, feeling his scars against my palms, searching his eyes that always tell the truth no matter how harsh, silently imploring him to stay even though I know it is futile.

Those eyes, those beautiful eyes, flicker to me briefly and his mouth relaxes. "You are..." He coughs—choking on blood bubbling up his throat. "... love."

He doesn't look afraid. I blink at the tenderness in his expression. There's no more anger dimming his soul. In its place glows that brilliant blue I'd glimpsed once before, and it glitters with curiosity. This time though it doesn't just surround him, it fills his being.

Ghost looks on me one last time, his face luminous, as if he finds me as beautiful as the others he must be seeing. Then he fixes his gaze on them.

"Farewell—" I start to say, intending to say *farewell, my friend.* I want to say a hundred things—a thousand things more.

Thank you for saving me.

You saw my scars and weren't repulsed. I love you for that and for not thinking of me as an abomination. You asked for my help and that was the best gift anyone has ever given me.

I will miss you.

So many unsaid words, but now he's dying. Words have lost their meaning. Tears are the only language I can speak.

His chest expands as if he is trying to rise even though I'm holding him down. I close my eyes and feel him pass through me as his soul rises up.

೫ ೞ

The lantern gutters out. The *others* vanish. And Ghost is gone. It is dark again in the tower. Not as dark as night, more like the gray of a faded wool coat. I let go of Ghost's empty corpse and sit beside it. *Hollow. Weary. Alone.*

So alone.

I sit there, unmoving, beside his body for a long time. Or maybe it isn't a long time. What does it matter? Time is meaningless when measured in tears.

Cold is the first sensation that returns to me. I shiver against an overwhelming chill.

"Sera?"

Startled, I turn at the sound of my name. Not Ghost, but Mr. Chadwick stands in the doorway. "Sera."

He has seen too much. I can tell by the way he said my name, hushed and hesitant, as if he is nervous and knows he is intruding on my grief. "How long have you been there?" I ask dully.

"Awhile."

Too long. "How much did you see?"

He doesn't answer. So, I shrug and turn back to Ghost's corpse. "You should go after Lady Daneska. She ran away after she shot him."

"Yeah, I heard the gun blast. Afraid it was you who got shot." He relates this account in syncopated clips, as if full sentences would be too much for me. *He might be right.* "Dashed up the cliffs like a maniac. Saw her running away."

"Then you saw him die." It isn't a question.

"Lady Daneska won't get far in this storm." He says, ignoring what I'd said. "Rather than chase her down, I figured you might need me here."

"Go after her. I'll manage."

The dim light of early dawn inches through mist and rain in the outside world. I glance sideways and watch this man walk toward me, a man who said he wanted to marry me, but now will surely rethink his hasty decision. He walks over ever so quietly, the way one does at a funeral.

I don't expect him to sit. There is blood everywhere. It runs in rivulets between the stones on the floor, coagulating with years of dirt and grime. I am covered with it, my hands, my cloak, my face and hair. I'm bathed in it, and like spilt wine it pools in hideous puddles around Ghost's body. Even so, Quentin Chadwick takes off his coat, drapes it around my shoulders and sits down next to me.

The man says nothing. He simply sits quietly beside me.

I hug my knees and lean my forehead against them.

Resting.

Thinking.

And now wondering.

I turn my head, too tired to raise it and study him. He wears a serious expression, as if he is pondering the scene surrounding us, or perhaps he is grieving too. After all, he lost his father only a few days ago. It takes a minute or two before I realize I cannot see his aura today.

Perhaps, after today, I will never see anything of that realm again.

Too much grief.

Too much sadness.

Suddenly, from the murky marsh of my mind, another question arises. "Did they capture Napoleon and rescue Prince George?"

He doesn't look at me when he answers. "I don't know. Captain Grey let me run back to help you."

"What about your mother?"

His lips press tight before he answers. "Lord Ravencross promised to look after her."

"Oh." I squint at him considering what his words are not saying—that he abandoned his own mother for my sake. Yet I am still unable to see anything beyond the physical. There should be something, gray worry, shrouds of grief for his father, *something*. But no. I am as blind as the rest of the world.

Another concern enters my foggy mind. "Then we don't know if they survived or not."

"No."

This is a bleak morning, indeed.

It is too much. I hug my knees tighter. The world is crumbling apart piece by piece. For all I know I am alone again. Except for him. And maybe even he is lost to me now after what he witnessed here. I glance sideways at Ghost's ravaged corpse and mumble, "How much did you see?

Quinton takes a deep breath. "I saw..." He fidgets and doesn't look at me. "I saw you change a man's eternity in the last moments of his life."

I stiffen. "No. It wasn't me who did that."

"Wasn't it?" He stares at the growing light filtering through the doorway. The storm has abated, and a faint rose tints the horizon. "I think you certainly played an integral role in it."

"What makes you say that?" I lean over my knees fiddling with the now tattered and now dark red hem of my gown. "How much did you see?" I ask this for the third time, desperate to know his answer.

He turns to me, and there is that flash of confidence. The one I'd worried he might've lost forever. "There are more things in heaven and earth, Horatio, than are dreamt of in your philosophy."

I blink. "That's your answer? You're quoting Hamlet at me?"

"Seemed appropriate."

"I'd rather you told me what you actually saw?"

He tilts his head and considers me intently. "Saw or felt?"

"Is there a difference?" I ask.

"Ah! Now see, that's an interesting question." Quinton brightens considerably. His eyes almost smile, his mouth doesn't come along. But his eyes, they look... well... almost pleased.

Why?

He nods then, the way old men who've seen too much of the world nod, knowingly. And he doesn't look away this time. "I *saw* you protecting someone about whom you cared a great deal. I *watched* you order unseen entities to keep their distance. And I *heard* you calling for help from an invisible God."

He pauses but I am holding my breath waiting to hear the rest.

"I *saw* a man leave this life peacefully because you were there with him." He raises his finger as if pointing to a more important notion. "What I *felt* is a different matter entirely. Even though I stood way over there in that doorway." He gestures at the opening without looking away. Instead, he leans toward me as if his next words must be spoken in hushed tones. "I *felt* malevolence. Oppressive. Evil swarming in this room in such great numbers that it nearly choked me with despair." Quinton watches me closely for a reaction.

Is it denial or confirmation he's waiting for? Without offering him either, I rest my head on my knees, listening.

"Shoo!" He tosses a rock at an overeager rat skulking around the edge of the tower. Then he turns to me, bearing such a forthright sincere expression that a whisker of hope tiptoes across my shoulders, and I sit a little straighter.

"When you called for help, Sera." He bites his lip for a moment. "I felt another presence rush into the room. An overpowering presence, like nothing I've ever felt before. The instant it arrived I felt it drive away the evil simply by the sheer force of its goodness. Even as a bystander it pierced my soul with such... such joy, that I wanted to leap up and shout or fall down on my knees. I'm not sure which." He shakes his head as if this is all too much to believe.

I stare open-mouthed at him. This is not something I expected from Quinton Chadwick, not from a man who weighs facts and evidence in the balance as arduously as a shopkeeper measures flour.

He reaches for my hand though it is caked with drying blood. "You asked me if there is a difference between feeling and seeing. The answer is yes. There is a difference for most of us. But for you, I imagine that line is somewhat blurred."

Blurred.

That is almost laughable. Blurred. I lean my head on his shoulder.

Time passes quietly and peacefully. The sun offers a ribbon of orange to the spreading magenta. He is the first to break our lovely silence. "Sera, tell me, do you actually see these beings?"

Dangerous question.

I wince inwardly and pull away from him. There's no use in trying to lie now. We are past that. I shrug. "Sometimes I do. Although, I've come to question whether I'm seeing with my eyes or if it is some other part of me that sees that sort of thing."

He says nothing but rubs his chin, thinking.

I sniff. "I suppose you won't want to marry me now?"

"Hmm," he turns to me with a mournful sigh. "Not in those clothes."

I squint at him and look down at my dress soaked in another man's blood. Frowning, I say, "What do you mean... Oh, I see. You were making a joke."

"A poor one apparently."

"Yes. Given the circumstances, I suppose it is."

"Apologies."

"You were probably avoiding answering. But if you want to recant your proposal, I understand. Truly, I do."

He faces me then and grasps my shoulders. "Sera, I think it far more apropos to ask whether you still want to marry me. You appear to be in love with a dead man."

I catch my lip in my teeth and bite down. He is partially right. But...

"His blood is still smeared on your face." He pulls out a handkerchief and starts wiping my cheek.

I stop his hand and pull it away from my face. "He gave

his life to save me."

"Then he must have cared for you as well."

"He needed my help. That's all." I look away, knowing that isn't the whole of it, studying the bloodstained stones beneath my feet, hunting for the truth of what I felt for Ghost and what he felt for me. We knew each other for such a short time. And yet...

"Yes, all right. I confess, I did care about him—but not as you think. He understood me in ways no one else ever could. More like a brother. We'd both been severely beaten as children. I have scars, Quinton. Terrible ugly scars. You would find them hideous. But he didn't—he had scars of his own. Worse than mine. Deep wounds in his soul. And then there were the demons preying on his mind. He found out about my seeing things."

Quinton glances at the dead man beside me, his brow furrowed. "That's what he wanted from you, isn't it? To be free of them—that evil horde."

"Yes." Not wanting to watch Quinton wrestling with knowing these things, I rest my head against his shoulder.

He strokes my tangled hair. "You did that for him."

"Not me."

"Hmm."

Still leaning into his chest, I make one more confession. "Ghost told me that he never lies. But his last words to me were, *You are love.* Except I'm not. I'm like everyone else. I get irritated and selfish and fearful. That's not *love*. With his last breath he lied to me. Why?"

Remembering makes me weep again.

Quinton Chadwick pulls me closer. "He didn't lie, Sera. Ghost simply said aloud what is obvious to those of us who know you." He pats my shoulder with a slow comforting rhythm. "I don't have your ability to see beyond the physical. But a man would have to be blind not to sense the love inside you. I've only to stand near you to feel the warmth of it."

THE IRONY OF ROSES

THE NEXT DAY, we quietly bury Ghost in the graveyard at Ravencross Manor. There already stands a gray weather-worn headstone bearing his name. A twisted reminder of the first time he'd been thought dead. This time though, his remains will be interred beneath his name.

There is no priest here to mouth comforting words. No ceremony. No band of mourners. Only us. We six, a mere handful draped in black, gather around his grave. Lord Ravencross stands, head bowed, before the gaping hole and the mound of dirt that will soon swallow what is left of his brother.

Yesterday, when Gabriel came racing back to the old lookout tower and found us sitting beside his dead brother, I told him how Ghost had asked me to beg his brother to forgive him. All Gabriel could do was stare at me dumbfounded. They'd nearly killed each other once upon a time.

If only he could've been there sooner.

Now... there would never be anything else said between them. Not in this life. But at least there had been that—a last message.

Small comfort.

Tess tosses in her rose. She says nothing and goes back to stand next to Lord Ravencross, fitting in the hollow at his side as if she was born to fill that space.

Lord Wyatt steps closer to the grave and removes his hat. "You were a fearsome man, Lucien." He tosses in a rose. "And an unparalleled opponent."

"A terrifying opponent," Georgie mutters, and steps up beside her fiancé. "But I hope Sera is right, that you've found peace at last." Her rose tumbles in beside the other two.

And the silence falls to me.

I frown at the shadows in that open grave.

Ghost is not there.

He's not lying in that dirt.

I see no point in throwing in a rose. Or talking to an empty hole. The man I knew is somewhere else. I wish I really could speak to the dead as my mother accused me of doing. If I could, I would tell him what a difference he made in my life.

Instead, I stand there beside that meaningless pit, the thorns on the rose's stem biting through my glove, wind slapping my face, and these are the only words that climb out from my soul.

"I will never forget you."

"You—you changed me. Forever."

And this one rose is paltry thanks.

My friends glance awkwardly at me, all except for Mr. Chadwick. He reaches for my hand. And I let him hold it.

One by one, three more roses clutter the box in that dismal hole. And I stand here at this makeshift funeral, remembering those last moments of his life. Someday, I will not think of the blood or the smoke. Someday, Daneska's cruel words to him will no longer pain me. Someday, I will only think of the way his face looked when he saw the shining ones.

Georgie softly touches my arm, and whispers. "Come back to the house with us."

I shake my head.

"Leave her be." Tess pulls Georgie away, and they hurry back to Stranje House to see how Captain Grey fares.

I sigh. He is not well. Still unconscious. They roused the doctor as soon as they were able to transport him back to Stranje House. Maya assisted the doctor as he dug out the bullet. Even though they were able to recover the misshapen iron ball, it left a severe wound, and Captain Grey lost too much blood. Miss Stranje let us bind up the gash on her ribs, but she won't leave his side. Maya keeps checking our obstinate headmistress for fever and trying to convince her to rest, but Miss Stranje brushes her away, insisting she is fine.

Only she isn't.

I've never seen her this distraught. I kept vigil with her last night and heard her moaning as she drowsed in the chair. "If only I'd told you. *If only.*"

To me, those are the saddest words in the English language.

Yet here I am at this grave, wrestling with those same words.

Quentin and Sebastian take off their coats and give them to me to hold. They roll up their sleeves so they can shovel dirt. Sebastian tells Lord Ravencross he needn't watch, but Gabriel shakes his head and hands me his coat, too. "For better or worse, he is my brother. This is the least I can do."

The first shovelful lands with a dull thud, like a drum beginning a funeral march. And I stand there as the drum beats on and on in a final salute. All of us listening. Wordless. But not without thoughts.

If only I had helped him sooner.

If only...

At last, the drum stops.

The men rest, leaning against their shovels. Quentin breaks the silence and thanks Gabriel for helping rescue his mother last night. Gabriel nods. "I'm grateful as well that you were there when Lucien..." He glances sideways at me as if he's reluctant to discuss death in my presence.

Ironic.

Nevertheless, I pretend to study the clouds in the distance so that he will feel more comfortable.

Quentin takes Ravencross's shovel and stands next to him. "I've never witnessed anything like what happened at his passing. Not in church. Not anywhere."

Ravencross turns to him, his eyes narrowed with pain, wanting to believe.

Quentin claps him on the shoulder. "I've no doubt your brother finally found peace."

The wind gusts up, ruffling my hair, catching in my cloak, whipping it up like a sail, and I wonder which way it will blow our lives now. The King's legion took Napoleon into custody. Surely, the war will be over.

Will we, too, finally have peace?

CHAPTER 24

GATHERING FOR A WEDDING

A year later, on the Stranje House lawn

MAYA IS NEVER ONE to fret, but today she glances around our lawn with an air of consternation. The chairs are arranged and strewn with ribbons. Vases of flowers adorn the side tables. She nudges me with her elbow while looping a strand of trumpet flowers into the lattice work. "What can be delaying Lady Jane? She ought to be here by now."

We are decorating an arbor with roses and vines, but I stop and consult the timepiece Miss Stranje lent me for the occasion. "I should say so. Thank goodness Lord Castlereagh obtained a special license. We would never have been able to gather everyone at the parish church before noon."

"Don't worry. Lady Jane and Mr. Sinclair will be along in time." Georgie stoops beneath the arbor and straightens the white silk cloth where the bride and groom will kneel before the vicar. "They're traveling with Lady Jersey in her coach. And you know how that great lady likes to make an entrance."

"Not here, surely." I wave my hand at our homespun setting beneath the spreading oak. "It's only us. There's no one to impress."

Georgiana shrugs. "Most likely it's part of Jane's training. You have heard, haven't you, that Lady Jersey and Princess Lieven are grooming her to become one of the patronesses of Almack's?"

"Jane mentioned it in her last letter." I select another rose from the basket and weave it into the lattice work.

Georgie sighs. "She and Lady Jersey are inseparable these days. Even though I, too, live in London, they scarcely give me the time of day."

"I'm sure that's not true. Ouch!" I prick my finger on a thorn. "You know perfectly well why Lady Jane is taking on that role. Now that Lady Castlereagh plans to retire from covert work, if Jane didn't move in those circles, you would have to do so." I give her a stern look. "Especially considering Lord Wyatt's position in the foreign office.

How else would we continue our work behind the scenes."

"Exactly." Maya sprinkles more rose petals across the silk. "You have never liked all that high society fuss. Aside from that, *Lady Wyatt*," she grins at Georgiana's married title. "It is a well-known fact that you are far too busy with your dashing young husband, your musty books, and your infamous experiments."

"Ah! You have found me out." Georgie laughs. "At least I have not set anything afire lately. Oh, I nearly forgot to tell you, we sold the patent for my invisible ink to the foreign office."

We congratulate her and Georgie shrugs it off as if it is nothing. "You're right. I could never be a patroness. I'm not nearly stern enough. According to Lady Jane a patroness must remain dignified and aloof at all times. I could never be as intimidating as she is. It amazes me how Lady Jane, *our Jane*, strikes such fear in the hearts of society matrons. Just last week, I overheard ladies at a soiree whispering about the fierce wolf dog that always accompanies Lady Jane on her strolls through the park, and gasping about the fact that she carries a *fearfully dangerous* spiked parasol." Georgie grins.

"*Fearfully dangerous*." Maya laughs. "It's only a three-inch spike."

I smile, too. "Her parasol aside. Surely you don't mean they're afraid of Balthazar? He was always such a sweet playful puppy."

"Still is, except now he's as big and fierce looking as

Tromos. Think of it, those yellow eyes and that pitch black fur..." Georgie nods knowingly. "Suffice it to say, people in Town scatter like geese when she's coming down the path."

"It is only natural." Maya reaches up to twine more greenery through the arbor. "Our wolf dogs were bred to be frightening."

"For good reason." Georgie sprinkles another handful of rose petals. "Although I take Moonlight walking with me and no one scatters. Admittedly, she is much smaller, and her silver-white fur and blue eyes are quite pretty. Instead of running away, people stop to pet her and inquire about her mechanical leg." Georgie taps a finger against her cheek, surveying our handiwork on the arbor. "Do you think we've scattered enough rose petals?"

"Yes." I loop my arm through hers. "It looks beautiful. The bride will be quite pleased—I'm sure of it. And Cook has outdone herself." I sweep my hands wide, encompassing the entire tableau. "Did you see all the pies? There's beef, pigeon, and chicken. She even made pickled beets and artichokes."

Maya lifts the cover on a fragrant golden knot crusted with butter and herbs. "Fresh bread, of course." She points to one of the large platters. "These are something new, bacon wrapped asparagus. And those are apple tarts. Did you see the cake?"

Georgie shakes her head.

"Wait till you see it. It's a masterpiece." I lean close, as if confiding a secret. "She even made a marzipan topping."

"No!" Georgie laughs. "Not our Cook, surely." She inspects the buffet table. "I didn't realize Magda had it in her."

"It was the laudanum delirium." Maya glances pointedly at me and continues to explain. "Cook changed after Lady Daneska overdosed her."

This is an ongoing argument between us. I credit her burst of creativity to Magda's brush with death, but Maya insists it is the aftereffects of the opium. "No matter the cause, she has turned into a virtuoso in the kitchen." I gesture at the numerous platters and covers arranged on the table. "She's obsessed with attempting new recipes, and most of her creations are quite delectable."

"Speaking of that night..." Georgie clears her throat and asks in a hushed voice, "Has there been any sign of *her*."

Her.

The dreaded question.

We've all been wrestling with the mystery of Lady Daneska's disappearance for months.

"No." I sigh heavily. "Nothing. Lady Pinswary's estate seemed the most likely place she would go. It has been searched a number of times, and soldiers questioned everyone in the vicinity. I don't see how Lady Daneska could have survived. Not with that fever." I shiver as images of her soil my mind. "Not in the rain."

I don't mention that not only had she been wet to the

bone, but she was also spattered in blood.

Looking like that, like the murderer she is, who would've taken her in?

Maya takes a deep breath and squares her shoulders. "We must accept the hard truth. Lady Daneska is alive somewhere. You may be certain of it. Licking her wounds. Ruining more lives. Predators like her survive. They cling to life with tooth and claw."

Maya is right. I know she is. Even so, it stings. We all bear wounds from that night—wounds we do not care to reopen. I close my eyes and turn away, banishing those dark memories, refusing to let the pain of that night taint this day.

I open my eyes and witness the perfect distraction kicking her way toward us from Ravencross manor. Despite the cloud of agitation milling around her, Tess crosses the lawn looking more beautiful than ever in her finery.

"That man!" Tess exclaims with a stern glower and a stomp of her foot.

"What man?" Georgie turns to greet her with an embrace and must surely see the man in question off in the distance, starting across the heath in our direction. "Oh! You mean your husband?"

"Of course," Tess snaps. "He's spouting twaddle about not allowing me to spar with the new students." She crosses her arms indignantly, and it reveals her protruding belly. "*Not allowing.* Ha!"

Georgie's brow pinches up. "You *are* in a family way,

are you not?"

"Yes, but that makes no difference—not one whit. I am the dagger skills master. What good is it if I can't spar with our students? Aside from that, this baby is a boy."

"A boy?" Georgie steps back in surprise. "How can you be so certain? Did you have a dream?"

Tess rolls her eyes as if it is a foolish question. "It has to be a boy. I refuse to pass on these cursed dreams. And the males in my line seem to be immune to them."

I turn away, allowing her this brief illusion, afraid my expression will give me away. I can see and feel the giftedness of her unborn daughter. Tess will know soon enough. More importantly, she is capable of giving her daughter the guidance she will need. Guidance that Tess did not have until she came here to Miss Stranje.

Maya pats Tess's arm and glances at Gabriel striding across the field. "I am sure Lord Ravencross is merely worried about your baby."

"Fiddle-faddle! He has seen me fight. He knows perfectly well that I can protect myself *and* the little one." Tess sniffs with irritation. "Anyway, if this baby can't take a few bumps and bruises in here, how will he fare out in the world? There's another war coming, and I want my son to be prepared."

"What?" I jump to attention, and we all gape in alarm.

"Another war?" Maya cringes. "When?"

"Did you have a dream?" Georgie grasps her arm. "What did you see?"

Tess sighs and looks off in the distance toward the cliffs and the sea. "There will always be wars. You don't need dreams to know that."

"True. But let us not speak of unhappy things. Not today," I implore them. "Today is the wedding. A wedding we have all prayed for and eagerly awaited. Let there be no more talk of war."

"Very well," Tess bristles and smooths out her blue silk gown. "But I am *not* going to stop sparring."

"I heard that." Lord Ravencross strides up behind her. "You're in your seventh month. Bad enough you still ride your horse like an unruly Turk. Think of the child. I am simply asking you to switch for the time being to teaching archery and let Madame Cho teach knife-fighting."

"Archery. Fah! It's not nearly vigorous enough."

I edge back, tugging Georgie and Maya with me. "Come, help me with the flowers." We flee the warring couple and head back to the house. "I've gathered rosebuds and gardenias for a bridal wreath. You can help me finish."

We enter through the side door, passing the breakfast room where the vicar, Lord Wyatt, Mr. Chadwick, and Lord Kinsworth are still seated around the table, talking. I glance shyly in Quinton's direction. He has been pressing me for an answer all week.

"Did you tell them?" Lord Kinsworth jumps to his feet, calling to Maya.

With a furtive shake of her head, Maya glances guiltily

at Georgie and me.

Georgiana crosses her arms. "Tell us what?"

"It's not what you think." Maya reddens.

Lord Kinsworth rushes to her side. "Go ahead tell them."

She turns back and hesitancy tangles the air between us. She bows her head. "I—I did not want to distract from the joy of this day."

Distract from the joy?

Then this cannot be good news. I reach for her hand. "What is it? What's wrong."

"Not *wrong*. It is a... a *change*." She takes a deep breath. "I am going back to India to find my grandmother." She pauses, tilting her head toward me as if she hears the sudden thud of my heart.

She's leaving us.

Oh-no! I scream inside, struggling to breathe evenly. Somehow, I miraculously force a smile. "I know you miss your grandmother very much."

"Yes, I do. And I feel a strong need to see her again. It is as if she is tugging on me, calling out for me. Or perhaps I am simply feeling lonely for her. No matter which it is, I must go and find her."

My throat tightens, and I find it hard to swallow. "How long will you be gone?"

"A year, perhaps. Or less. It is difficult to know. My father has agreed to come and assist on the journey."

"And I am going with her." Lord Kinsworth beams. "I

have always wanted to visit the land of seven rivers." He leans toward us with a conspiratorial wink. "Wish me luck. Her father has already consented. And Maya has promised that if her grandmother gives us her blessing, she will finally marry me."

Georgie's hands fly up in a clap of celebration. "Huzzah!"

I hug Maya. "I am happy for you. I pray you will find your grandmother quickly and that she is well. But I shall miss you terribly. And you know Miss Stranje will, too. Promise to come back to us."

She nods, her dark eyes glistening as she tucks back a strand of my hair. "And you, my dear friend, will never be far from my heart." She is telling the truth. Threads of sisterhood run between us—between all of us—bonds that will last forever. And that bond makes it impossible to ignore how intensely she yearns to see her grandmother.

She lets go of me and steps back, taking her place beside Lord Kinsworth. When she glances up at him, plumes of joy and expectation shoot skyward.

Our lives are changing.

Mine as well.

I turn, looking for Quentin Chadwick, and discover his gaze resting intently on me, ever patient, and surprisingly warm.

I blush and look away.

I have been helping him care for his mother, mourning with her, and keeping her company. At first it was a struggle to get her to eat. She went about setting the house right, getting rid of any vestiges of Napoleon's men, as if that would purge the terror of those days when he and his men held them hostage. Later, she and I would walk in her gardens and talk. When my duties at Stranje House kept me from coming, she often begged Quentin to send for me, insisting that talking with me soothed her. He told her about the *things* I see. Rather than being appalled or frightened of me, she treats me with even more respect, and often plies me with questions about the *unseen world*. That is what she calls it, the unseen world. And she asks such intriguing questions—questions to which I often have no answer—which in turn makes me ponder this fascinating existence God created for us.

"The flower wreath!" Georgie recalls us to our task.

I turn, but just then, Greaves shuffles by and announces. "Lady Jersey's coach has arrived." He hurries into the foyer, flings open the door, and bows low. In a flurry of feathers and purple satin, Lady Jersey bustles into Stranje House. Lady Jane and Alexander Sinclair follow in her wake.

"Jane!" We all rush forward to greet them, everyone talking at once. Lady Jane hugs us and chatters on with her customary warmth, and I observe nothing of the aloofness Georgie mentioned.

"What?!" Lord Wyatt exclaims. "He's to be exiled?"

Our happy chatter comes to a sudden halt.

"Who? You can't mean Napoleon?" Georgiana pulls away from Lady Jane. "Not hanged? Not drawn and quartered?"

Lord Wyatt tugs her to his side, gritting his teeth, he grumbles, "They only draw and quarter someone who commits high treason against the Crown. Napoleon is a foreign leader. Immune to such punishments. But they could have shot him. Maybe if I'd been there—"

"There was nothing you could do, Wyatt." Alexander shakes his head grimly. "I would've sent word to you sooner, but the decision was only made late yesterday. The Austrians insisted it was best to avoid making him a martyr."

"It took all this time to decide his fate." Lord Kinsworth mutters, but then he looks up with a start. "They're not sending him back to Elba, are they? He'll only escape again."

Lady Jane leans over to Maya wearing a mischievous squint. "You ought to have poisoned him when you had the chance."

Lady Jersey overheard that remark and waggles a scolding finger at Jane. "Tch, tch. None of that. Bonaparte won't escape." She turns to all of us and smiles magnanimously. "Not this time, he won't. They're banishing him to St. Helena. A tiny little island in the middle of nowhere."

She pinches her fingers together as if they plan on

confining Napoleon to an ant-size speck in the sea. "Not even remotely close to France or Italy. It's in the south Atlantic somewhere." She sniffs. "Even if Napoleon manages to smuggle letters in or out. It will take more than a year for them to arrive in Europe. The nearest port is nearly two-thousand miles away in the south of Africa."

"I take it *you* had something to do with this location?" Georgiana quizzes the great lady.

"I?" Lady Jersey rests her gloved hand over her breast as if she's about to sing an opera. "Why, my dear girl, you flatter me. Oh, mind you, I may have offhandedly mentioned the island's existence in a ballroom or at a dinner here or there. But *I ask you*, who listens to that sort of thing while supping on mutton and wine?"

Who, indeed.

If not princes and kings, I imagine ambassadors and statesmen from Prussia, Austria, and the like, took note of her *offhand* suggestion. For it is a rare thing for our Lady Jersey to attend a dinner with any less notable company than heads of state.

Although he remained quiet until now, I noticed a few moments ago that Quentin came and stood beside me. I felt it long before I saw him. He still emits purple rays of confidence now and then, but ever since that day, his presence washes over me like sunlight through the trees, filling me with comfort and healing.

He leans down and whispers quietly. "*He* is on the stairs."

I whip around to see.

There he stands, the groom. He looks splendid today, composed as always, his sun-varnished hair swept to the side, his skin once again tanned from walking outdoors. His cravat is tied in an elegant waterfall, and his black coat brushed to perfection with the one sleeve, where his arm should be, pinned to the side. It was the price he paid to save Emma that dreadful night. Infection from his wound spread, but with that cruel measure the doctor was able to save Captain Grey's life.

He remains on the third step, quietly observing all of us, a half-smile on his lips, and I watch rays of contentment and pride radiate from him. He clears his throat, and a hush falls over us. With laughter in his eyes and a quick wink, he says, "I was told we were having a wedding today."

"Yes! Yes, we are." I smile broadly. It never fails to fill me with relief to see him standing among us again. With a quick curtsy to Lady Jersey, I excuse myself. "I must go attend to the bride."

When I enter her room, Miss Stranje is standing before the mirror, and it looks as if her eyes are watering.

Tears?

It can't be. She does not cry.

Ever.

And not today, surely.

"What's wrong?" I hurry to her side.

"I am old." She chokes and turns to me, releasing a flood of regret that nearly drowns me.

I catch my breath. "No! No, you're not. You look..."

But words fail me. How can she not see how radiant and vibrant she looks? Almost childlike. Her appearance stuns me. So much so that I question whether or not I am seeing her with my physical eyes. I touch her elbow. Yes. Yes, she is tangible and real. "You are beautiful. Breathtaking."

Now, I understand why we have never seen her in anything except harsh black bombazine or her dark blue fighting clothes. Today, she wears a pale butter-yellow gown, and Miss Emma Stranje does not look nearly old enough to be the headmistress of a school.

And I tell her so.

"Your hair is lovely." I gape. "You have natural curls. I had no idea. You always wear it tucked back so severely." I look down, embarrassed that I am behaving so dumbfoundedly.

She sighs and turns to the mirror, squinting as if straining to see what I see. Turning away, she shakes her head. "I remember looking younger... once upon a time."

I do not know what to say. She isn't old. Not really. Then again, she isn't in the first bloom of youth either. It doesn't matter. There is a beauty about her that does not bow its head to time.

"Flowers," I say, and hold them out to her, rosebuds, greenery, and gardenias.

"I started making a wreath. As it is, with your hair draped in the Grecian manner, they will look even prettier if I weave them in here and there. Come, sit in this chair. It will only take me a few minutes."

"I ought to have married him long ago when he first asked." She mourns and glances back at the mirror. "Years ago." She meanders to the chair and sits, allowing me to pin flowers in her thick curls. "I thought the work we were doing was infinitely more important than our happiness. He tried to convince me that we could work together. *Wait until the war is over*, I insisted. And because of my stubbornness I almost lost him."

She tenses, and I rest my hand on her shoulder. "He didn't die."

"Almost."

"Yes," I agree quietly.

It was a near thing.

I will never forget the long nights of his fever, the mixing of poultices and plasters, running to and from the kitchen for herbal concoctions and cool compresses. At times, I felt sure we would lose them both because she would not rest. Gray-eyed and determined, she spooned broth into his mouth around the clock. We tried to spell her, but she refused to leave his side.

"I should not have waited. I kept putting him off. Not yet. Not yet. *Not yet.*" She covers her face with her hands. "And I almost lost him forever."

"Except you didn't lose him. He is alive, and you're to be married."

"Yes, but we will never be young again. And now, his arm is gone, and... we are so..." she grimaces at the mirror again. "So, bruised. And damaged. And... *old.*"

I understand now. She doesn't mean old. This war has severely wounded them. And not just physically. *It scarred their minds.*

That's why she feels old.

It is a peculiar phenomenon—how coming close to death alters time. It is as if severe trauma causes us to see our life stretching into the vast eons, far beyond the mere years we've actually lived. When that happens, we do not simply become old, we become ancient.

It doesn't bring us closer to the end of life, becoming ancient begins an entirely new existence.

I pin a fragrant gardenia blossom in her hair. "I was *damaged* as a child. *Bruised. Scarred.* That is when *I* became *old.*"

She glances up at me, studiously. I watch those familiar sparks of hers flitter about her like curious fireflies.

Thinking.

Perhaps I should show her the scars on my back to prove my point. Although, I suspect she already knows. I quietly breathe in the fragrance of the gardenia. "If it is too late for you to be happy, then I never had a chance."

Neither did Ghost.

Her eyes widen, and she stares at me, until the fireflies settle into a calm halo and her lips rest in a peaceful curve. Those gentle white ribbons of hers come fluttering out and twirl around me in a motherly dance.

"You are right, little one." She stands and brushes out the sunshine yellow silk. "It is never too late for joy. Let us get on with this. There is a gentleman out there who has waited for me long enough."

CHAPTER 25

THE BRIDESMAIDS OF STRANJE HOUSE

"**WHAT** IN HEAVEN'S NAME are those vermin doing here?" Lady Jersey demands, wrinkling her nose at the two rats in Tess's arms. Punch and Judy have flower wreaths twined around their necks. At least they did, Judy is nibbling rather voraciously at one of his flower stems.

Despite Lady Jersey's glower, Tess smiles brazenly. "Why they're bridesmaids, of course."

"Bridesmaids. Ha!" Lord Ravencross snorts at the little troubadours squirming in his wife's lap. "They're both males."

PUNCH AND JUDY (JUDAS)

"It's time. Now." Georgie whispers to Tess and Maya. "They're coming!"

Arm in arm, Captain Grey and Miss Stranje walk from the house toward our gathering.

Maya plucks her lap harp, filling the air with soft music. Tess places Punch and Judy on the ground. Our two plump rats waddle down the aisle gobbling up the breadcrumbs that we'd sprinkled earlier. They run out of crumbs just shy of the white silk, where the Vicar stands frowning at them disapprovingly. "Shoo!"

Punch squeaks, and they scurry back to Tess's lap, just as we'd practiced.

Miss Stranje and Captain Grey walk toward the vicar wearing broad smiles. And we all stand. This is not the custom, yet all of us rise as if it were. It only seems right to honor the two people who have guided us through so many storms.

Madame Cho steps up and takes her place beside Miss Stranje as her witness, as does Lord Wyatt for Captain Grey. When they kneel, we sit, and I had not realized tears were falling on my cheeks until Mr. Chadwick hands me a handkerchief.

The ceremony flows like a river rippling over the stones of our lives, carrying all of us forward to a new life and new adventures.

Quinton reaches for my hand, "It will be our turn soon," he whispers.

And I suspect he is right.

AFTERWORD

MY DEAR READER,

As I write this, I am overwhelmed with gratitude for your unwavering support and encouragement throughout the Stranje House series.

Sanctuary for Seers is the most challenging book I have ever written. Seraphina is complex and she bears several traits that are drastically different from the other women at Stranje House. It often took days of contemplation to capture who Sera really is and how she would behave in a particular scene. Early on, I realized she is far too tender-hearted to participate in a physical battle. That presented a quandary. This final book in the series cried out for a culminating physical clash between Napoleon's forces and the heroines of Stranje House.

What was I to do?

The answer came from you!

An underlying theme in this series is that our decisions, as well as our gifts and talents change the world around us. YOU changed MY world. Many of you, my cherished readers, emailed me or contacted me on social media asking me to write more about Miss Stranje. You helped me realize that Emma needed to be an integral part of this last tale.

Not only that...

Time and time again, your emails or social media posts arrived at the exact moment when I needed inspiration. You are the reason I wrote this series, and I am honored to have you as my readers. I look forward to sharing more stories with you in the future.

♡ Thank you!

Kathleen Baldwin

PS: For those of you in reader groups and book clubs, I've put together a Discussion Guide and you'll find it on the next few pages of this book.

Stay in touch. Sign up for my newsletter on my website.
https://kathleenbaldwin.com/newsletter/

SANCTUARY FOR SEERS

ᴅɪꜱᴄᴜꜱꜱɪᴏɴ ɢᴜɪᴅᴇ

1. The Stranje House Novels illustrate each character accepting and developing her unique talents and gifts. In the books it is conflict that forces each of the girls to do this. Has conflict helped you develop your unique gifts and talents? If you are comfortable sharing, can you tell us how?

2. Seraphina seems to be the most secretive of all the young ladies at Stranje House. Are there other ways you think Seraphina differs from the other girls?

3. Many people report seeing auras. In order to write *Sanctuary for Seers* I interviewed several individuals who have this ability. What do you think about that? Were you able to visualize the emotional and spiritual auras that Sera sees?

4. Sera talks about how tangible emotions are. Do you agree? Do you feel or sense the emotions of others? If so what is it like for you? Do you get tactile sensations such as prickles, warmth, scent? Or like Maya, do you perceive audible impressions around others? Or yours a more empathic reaction?

5. During Sera's initial contact with Ghost, she touches him and sees invisible blood flowing from a wound that opens in his chest. What do you think this vision symbolizes in this scene?

6. Another theme throughout the Stranje House Novels is that our decisions change the world around us. Can you think of ways your decisions changed the world or the lives of people around you? This can be difficult or even painful to reflect on. Perhaps you would rather discuss ways you have observed someone else's decision altering your life or the lives of others in your community.

7. When the action in *Sanctuary for Seers* diverged into two separate story lines, did you enjoy getting to read Emma Stranje's point of view? Why?

8. Now that you have been privy to Miss Emma Stranje's interior musings, did you find Emma to be who you had expected? In what ways did she fulfill your expectations or differ from them?

9. Before the big fight with Napoleon, Miss Stranje warns Lady Jane not to let her fears undermine Alexander's

confidence before going into the battle. Do you think that without even realizing it we might sometimes undermine our loved ones when we communicate our fears for their safety?

10. Seraphina notes that trauma made Miss Stranje feel *old*. It can do that. Severe trauma is wearying, but it can also be enlightening. Sera said, "Trauma forces us to see our life stretching into the vast eons, far beyond the mere years we've actually lived. When that happens, we do not simply become old, we become ancient."
What did you think of her observation.

11. In reality, Napoleon's second exile was to St. Helena. After much research I have discovered that several Patronesses of Almack's wielded considerable political influence. Lady Jersey even held political discussion evenings in her home. What did you think about the method Lady Jersey is supposed to have used to influence the decision to send Napoleon to St. Helena?

12. Which of the Stranje House Novels did you like best? Why?

Thank you for discussing the **Stranje House Novels** with your friends. Kathleen is available via zoom or in person for local book clubs. Contact her at:
KATHLEEN@KATHLEENBALDWIN.COM

Other Novels by Kathleen Baldwin

———— ഇൻ ————

The Stranje House Novels:
Exciting Alternate History Spy series for Teens

A School for Unusual Girls
Exile for Dreamers
Refuge for Masterminds
Harbor for the Nightingale
Sanctuary for Seers

———— ഇൻ ————

The My Notorious Aunt series:
Humorous Regency Romps

Lady Fiasco
Mistaken Kiss
Cut from the Same Cloth
The Persuasion of Miss Kate

———— ഇൻ ————

A Regency Novella
The Highwayman Came Waltzing

For Reader Guides and Story Extras, visit:
KathleenBaldwin.com

CPSIA information can be obtained
at www.ICGtesting.com
Printed in the USA
LVHW041950150623
749927LV00004B/104